Z-LEVEL 10

A NOVEL BY MICHAEL COLE

SEVERED PRESS
HOBART TASMANIA

Z-LEVEL 10

ISBN: 978-1-925840-86-5

CHAPTER 1

Fluttering wings lifted its tiny body off of the fallen branch it was perched on. Carried in part by the wind, the beetle zipped between the trees. It often fed in the morning hours and food was plentiful in the wooded area it lived in. In fact, it was almost too plentiful. Its antennae were overwhelmed with the sense of smell. Odors usually travel in whiffs of scent, usually dissipating quickly like ghosts as the wind carried them away.

But even in the wind, the odors were plentiful. Food was abundant, so abundant that the insect's sensory systems felt overloaded. In the generations preceding its birth, pheromones would be picked up in pores of its antennae, bound with proteins, then carried through the nerve endings. Its brain could only handle so much. But now it was overloaded.

The many sources of smell were in motion, lumbering below it in dormant states. It had fed off many of them before, unknowingly infecting itself with a contagion its tiny brain would never understand. Lacking intelligence, it never noticed the connection with feeding off these organisms and the intense aggression and hunger it subsequently developed. Whenever it drew near to other species, it would viciously lash out. Hunger, thirst, and procreation didn't factor into its reasoning. There was just an overwhelming desire to devour the flesh of others.

With the sense of smell so abundant, the bug could not use its antennae to lock on to a specific source. It had to use its eyes to determine where to land. It dove several feet down, planting its six legs on the neck of a rotting human corpse.

It had been dead a while, its smell rising with the late summer heat. Maggots had grown and collected inside a gaping hole in its stomach, a wound that had likely ended its life. Its eyes were open, shriveled back into their gaping sockets. Slumped against the trunk of a tree, its skeletal face seemed to stare endlessly into oblivion. The bug scurried along the neck, moving up near the jawline. Using its mandibles, the bug peeled flakes off its skin. It moved upward, exploring the lower jaw and chin of the dead organism.

The lips were gone, exposing rows of jagged teeth rooted in rotting gums. The bug brushed the inside with its antennae, detecting the gooey remains of the tongue. It was softer than the rotting skin tissue. The jaw was slack, allowing the bug to crawl inside.

As it did, a loud whirring sound passed by above the trees. A heavy downdraft hammered everything below, causing the plant life to sway as though in protest. The combined sound and physical sensation clicked a surviving receptor in the dormant brain.

The bug was halfway inside when it felt its exoskeleton cracking. The jaws came down on it, severing it in two. Its abdomen fell away, spilling innards as it rolled into the grass. Its head and thorax slipped down into the black, slimy gullet of the very thing it fed off of.

Spurred by the vibration, the corpse looked to the sky. Whatever passed above, it was moving. Movement and sound were indicative of prey. It clicked its jaws together, biting the air, picking up any trace of scent. The sound increased, the strange object descending in the distance.

Driven by an infinite desire to feed, it pushed itself upright. It rocked back and forth on wobbly limbs. With its muscle mass heavily decomposed, it had to shift its weight to move forward. Slowed by this handicap, it was easily surpassed by the others that walked among it. The more freshly dead were able to manipulate their muscle tissue more efficiently, thus they could move with greater speed. It was all the corpse could do to keep up with them.

Soon, over a hundred of its brethren flocked ahead of it, their moans filling the air as they converged upon the possible source of food.

CHAPTER 2

Vertical draughts pounded the ground below as the Boeing CH-47 Chinook reached its destination. The pilots put the ninety-eight-foot long aircraft into a slow descent, stopping at one-hundred and fifty feet above the cement parking lot of a county hospital. Thirty thousand pounds of steel balanced as the rotors pushed a heavy downdraft on the crowd of the undead that lumbered along the hospital perimeter.

Inside its fuselage, seven marines stared down at their landing site.

"They said Level 5!" Private Dunn bickered. "This is not a Level 5!"

"Dunn, if you don't shut your mouth, I swear I will sew your lips with barbed wire!" Sergeant Keegan said. Private Dunn turned from the starboard shoulder window. The six-foot, broad shouldered marine's eyes were blazing with ferocity and alarm. The desire to protest was still there, and the will to suppress it was crumbling like a dam in a raging river.

"Sir, I'm not seeing any survivors," one of the pilots spoke through the headsets.

"Oh, you're seeing them alright!" Dunn said. "They're right there below us. You just can't recognize them because they're now walking piles of pus!"

Staff Sergeant Keegan prodded a finger in his face.

"That is the last time I'll tell you, Marine!"

Dunn tensed, quivering ever so slightly as he contained his rage. The anger was stronger than the fear. Despite his spiraling emotions, he was never insubordinate, though that was simply due to the fact that he respected the sergeant. Keegan was a man equal in height, though sporting a greater muscular frame. The Staff Sergeant was bordering on forty, twenty of those years being in the service. His hair had gone prematurely white, and his face was rife with the features of a man fifteen years older. War and chaos had a way of doing that to a person. The fall of mankind only perpetuated it.

"Staff Sergeant!"

Keegan turned around to face Corporal Reimer. With one hand pressed to his headset, he was listening hard to a transmission.

"What do you have, Corporal?" Keegan asked.

"Transmission's breaking up," Reimer said. "They're inside the hospital. Third floor. From what I could hear, the undead got here before we did and forced them into the building."

"How many?" Keegan asked.

"I can't say."

"Did you ask?"

"Yes, sir. I tried multiple attempts, but the transmission is too grainy, probably due to interference from multiple layers of brick and technology inside the building."

"I'm gung-ho for getting down there!" Binkowski said. She rocked her M4 Carbine and marched toward the loading ramp, where PFC Gordon stood near a mounted M240 machine gun.

"I guarantee that place is full of corpses!" Fisher said. Unlike Dunn, he expressed his concern in a calm and articulate manner. "The Corporal said it was third floor, right? We must consider the numbers and tight quarters. If we go in, we'll have to go through a swarm of those things."

"Hell, we can find the nearest stairwell and go up," Binkowski argued.

"Negative," Sergeant Keegan said. He was observing the building through the window. The pilots had circled the facility, bringing the main entrances into view. Crowds of the undead were moving in and out of the broken doorways, indicating that many more waited inside. Fisher was correct in his analysis, though Keegan wouldn't plainly say it, as Dunn would take it as ammunition in his argument to abandon the mission. "Corporal, make a call to Headquarters. Pronto! I will speak with them directly."

"Yes, sir!" Reimer said. Corporal Reimer moved up into the cockpit where he could access the radio. With a quivering hand, he twisted the knob to change the frequency, then pressed his headset to his ear to drown out the noise.

"Viking One-Seven to Border. Come in." He felt a hand on his shoulder. He shifted his elbow back. "Not now, dude!" The marine next to him knelt down.

"Hey!" he briefly yelled to get the Corporal's attention. Reimer tore his headset off and looked to his left, seeing PFC Kane standing near him. "You alright?"

"I'm fine," Reimer said. "What do you need?"

"Just letting you know you've got it on the wrong frequency," Kane answered. Reimer looked at the knob, realizing he was on channel 5.

"Shit," he muttered.

"You alright?" Kane asked again. He was aware that the Corporal had not slept in days, and his glazed eyes and sluggishness was evidence of this.

"I'm good. Do you mind?" He gestured toward the cabin. Kane stood up and joined Binkowski and Gordon near the ramp. Reimer readjusted the frequency then hit the transmitter. "Viking One-Seven calling Border. Come in."

"*This is Border Command responding to Viking One-Seven. Go ahead.*"

"Sergeant Keegan is requesting contact with General Spears," Reimer said.

"*Stand by.*" Reimer waited. With all of the rescue operations taking place around the western United States, or what used to be the United States, it would be a few minutes before the General could dedicate his attention to them.

"Sir!" Binkowski approached Keegan. "Are you considering actually leaving these people behind?"

"We are awaiting updated instructions from Command," Keegan said. His voice was lower, displaying mild sympathy. Fact of the matter was clear. They would ONLY conduct rescue operations in areas deemed Level 5 or lower. Anything higher, they were not permitted to risk. At least, that was the official policy, which was often overridden by the remaining government to rescue other officials or certain VIPs.

"Sir, we can't leave them. We're here to get these people out. We have to do something."

"Are you implying that I don't understand our orders?" Keegan barked. Binkowski took a step back, her discipline returning to her.

"No, sir!"

Keegan did an about-turn and followed Reimer into the forward cabin.

Binkowski paced by the window, keeping her eyes fixed on the third-floor windows. She could envision the poor souls trapped inside.

"Binkowski, I get what you're thinking, but this is beyond risky," Dunn said.

"I'm with her," Gordon said. "This is what we're trained to do, man! It was risky from the start!"

"There's a difference between risky and stupid," Dunn said. "We go down there, we're gonna lose more than what we'll save! I guarantee it!"

"What's got into you, man?" Kane asked.

"What's got into me?!" He kept his voice down enough to not be overheard. "We have improper intel. Improper equipment. Improper aide. We have lost Quill. Sanders. Harris. Coli! All in situations like this one, sir! This is not a Level 5. At best, it has escalated to Level 7."

"You don't think they'll turn us around?" Kane said.

"Oh, come on. They've pulled this shit before," Fisher interjected.

"Mark my words," Dunn said. "If they make us go in there, it means there's someone important down there."

Reimer's grogginess started taking over again. He felt a tremendous lack of energy. He felt his eyes closing automatically as he listened to the pilots speak on their radios. Feeling himself starting to slip away, Reimer forced his eyes open, immediately seeing the boot from someone standing next to him. Looking up over his shoulder, he noticed Keegan standing over him.

"Still waiting, sir," he said after clearing his throat.

The pilots continued circling the extraction zone. The co-pilot on the right was speaking on another frequency, his face appearing gradually troubled with each sentence.

"Copy that," he said. He looked back at the Staff Sergeant. "Sir?"

"What is it?" Keegan said.

"We've got another problem. Roosevelt Command says there's no HC-130 available for mid-air refuel."

"We're past the PSR," the other pilot said. Keegan looked down through the windshield at the landing zone. The National Guard in the area had arranged a fuel tank for refuel while the passengers were loaded up for transport. Nine-thousand pounds of fuel was waiting for them on the pavement, surrounded by a horde of the undead. Behind it, a large portion of the perimeter fence was down. From the looks of it, the six-foot barrier had succumbed to the combined weight and mass of hundreds of the undead pressing into it at once. As with many sanctuary sites, the fence barrier was rushed into production and not properly cemented.

"One way or another, we're making a landing," Keegan said.

"Sir!" Reimer said, extending the headset to him. Keegan put it on and listened to the General.

"This is Staff Sergeant Keegan...yes, sir. Sir, I have to advise you, there is increased activity in the area. Sanctuary is overrun. We have detected a radio transmission from inside the facility, but it is overrun with the infected...Infection level increased from 5. We will have to make a refueling attempt... Yes, sir... I understand, sir... Orders received and understood. Keegan out."

"I suppose those orders had nothing to do with picking up a pizza on our way back, did it?" Reimer quipped.

"Very funny," Keegan said. He observed the building, carefully watching the movements of the undead. "If they had to barricade themselves in the third floor, then that means they were forced up there. The first two floors are probably loaded with those things."

"You suggest we go in through the roof?" Reimer asked.

"It's the only way," Keegan said. "We're gonna need to refuel and get out of here fast, so we're gonna split into groups. First, we'll clear out the parking lot as best we can with the M240s. After we do that, we'll fly up to the roof. You will disembark with some of the men and work your way down. While you do that, I'll be refueling our ride. By the time we're both done, we should be picking you up on the roof. With some luck, the survivors will be working their way upstairs, which'll save some time. Unfortunately, you can't be sure what you'll be running into in there, so make you have rappel lines in case you can't make it back to the roof."

"Understood, sir," Reimer said. He followed the Sergeant into the cabin.

"Everybody listen up! And listen good!" Keegan yelled. The marines stopped all chatter and stood at attention. "We have received orders. We will be attempting rescue. Corporal Reimer will lead you down through the roof. From there you will work your way down. Get as many survivors out as you can. But first, we will conduct a sweep of the infected near the tanker." Keegan walked by each of them, staring into their souls with eyes that had seen Hell and then some.

"Remember! You are hardened marines! You are not fresh out of boot! You are an experienced force to be reckoned with. You have done this before, and you will do this again!"

"How many times?" Dunn muttered, seething at the sight of the hundreds of undead. His view was suddenly obstructed as Keegan got in his face

"What did you say?" he yelled point blank.

"Nothing, sir!"

"You lie to me, I will personally feed you to the uglies! Hell, if they get a taste of your smelly ass, that might just kill their appetite for us, I might say! Considering it might save what's left of humanity, I would suggest you not piss me off further, Private Dunn!" Keegan barked.

"Sir, yes sir!"

"Now. Repeat what you said!"

"How many times, sir?" Dunn spoke louder.

"How many times, what?!"

"How many times must we do this...sir?!"

"As many times as I fucking tell you!" Keegan pressed his forehead against Dunn's while continuing his lecture with increased intensity. "This is your life now! The Corps owns you! Mind, body, and soul! You WILL obey my instructions or you WILL suffer a wrath worse than what's in store down there! DO YOU UNDERSTAND ME?"

"Yes, sir!" Dunn answered. Keegan took a step back from him. Without taking his eyes off Dunn, he barked orders to the rest of the squad.

"Corporal Reimer, man the port M420!"

"Yes, sir!"

"Binkowski, take the starboard!"

"Yes sir!"

"Pick off those bastards as best you can and clear a landing zone! DO NOT hit that tanker. If they are too close to it, don't waste the ammo. Kane and I will take care of the stragglers once we set down!" Binkowski and Reimer raced to their assigned weapons, chambering a round and quickly inspecting the ammo feeds.

"Dunn! Fisher! Gear up! You will be going in with them! Kane! You're with me. Gordon, you will provide cover fire as we conduct refueling. Does everybody understand their jobs?!"

"Sir, yes sir!"

"I. CAN'T. HEAR YOU!"

"SIR! YES SIR!"

CHAPTER 3

The unrelenting downburst of wind spurred the undead into a crazed frenzy. Snarling their teeth, they gathered around near the chopper. Bits of rotted tissue peppered the concrete beneath their lumbering feet as they congregated. They reached up, trying to grab at its landing pads, not comprehending the fact that it was several yards out of reach.

Corporal Reimer extended his machine gun out of its port and aimed down at the army of the undead. He put the iron sights of his machine gun between him and their putrid faces. Through his helmet's visor, he gazed at the large congregation. Numerous reanimated corpses were lashing up at him in various states of decay. Some were fresh, others were barely able to stand upright. Some in fact couldn't stand upright, resorting to dragging their bellies along the ground. Black shards of diseased meat oozed into the concrete as their torsos scraped against it.

Their combined moans could be heard despite the rotation of the rotors. It was as though their souls had never been freed from their bodies. Corporal Reimer placed his hands onto the butterfly grips of the M240 machine gun. For a moment, he was lost in the empty eyes of the undead. He wasn't sure if it was the lack of sleep, the overall exhaustion, the struggle to maintain loyalty to his service, or all of the above.

The racket from Binkowski's machine gun knocked him back into reality. She fired in three-to-five round bursts, reciting "Die, motherfucker, die!" with each squeeze of the butterfly grips. Rounds ripped into the crowd of undead like individual lightning strikes. She kept her aim high, as she specifically needed to pull off headshots.

"What's the holdup, Corporal?" Keegan said.

"Nothing, sir," Reimer said. He yanked back on the cocking lever and started blasting the horde. The corpses absorbed the hits, jolting backward as 7.62mm rounds ripped through their upper torsos. Reimer gritted his teeth and focused his aim. Fixing his iron sights on one heavyset target in the center, he unleashed. The bullets grazed the top of its head, crushing the skull just enough to cave down on the functioning brain matter. The corpse, now truly dead, fell backward, the area above its eyes mangled into a mess of bone and coagulated blood.

Reimer tensed and sucked in a deep breath. It was exactly what he was trained not to do, but it was the only thing that seemed to allow him to focus. Another three-round burst exploded another head like a spoiled melon. On the other side of the chopper, Binkowski was cheering. Her three-round bursts were consistent, with hardly a full second's pause in-between them.

"Keep it up, ladies! We're not shopping at the mall here!" Keegan pressed them. "We don't have all day."

The pilots adjusted the Chinook's position, as the ghouls had begun to congregate beneath them. They rotated, giving the gunners a better view of their targets. Reimer and Binkowski kept up the assault, layering the parking lot with fallen corpses.

Reimer sucked in another breath, forcing his sluggish brain to cooperate. His shots were becoming more accurate, as he allowed the kick of the weapon to help him find his headshots. He fired in five-round bursts, the first of those rounds striking the bodies' torsos then working its way up to their skulls. Firing more consistently, he began putting more down in rapid succession. With the success came confidence. He reduced his bursts to three rounds.

Binkowski was on a roll, making a game of the situation. She wasn't just pulling off headshots but was finding new ways to immobilize the walkers. She deliberately aimed low on one target, putting several rounds into its abdomen. Pink and grey matter spilled from both the front and back. The ghoul rocked to-and-fro, its upper trunk sliding completely off its waist. Writhing on its back, it still tried to reach up at the chopper, as moldy intestines untangled from its gut.

"You're wasting bullets, Private!" Keegan scolded her.

"My bad, sir," she quipped. As the two gunners continued their assault, the crowd of over a hundred was reduced to a couple dozen. The targets spaced out from each other, stumbling over the bodies of the fallen.

Reimer sucked in another breath and unleashed another barrage onto another corpse. The bullets struck its shoulder, sending its left arm flying off as though jet propelled. He tilted the weapon, improving his accuracy into the target's brain. He watched the skull rip into massive shards, which opened from the center like flower petals. Behind the cloud of pink and charcoal colored goo was a speck of gold. The bullet had passed through the target and skidded on the rim of the tanker. Reimer looked up, alarmed. Luckily, it didn't appear to have breached the container.

"*Jesus, guys. Not too close!*" one of the pilots yelled.

"Alright, shut it down!" Keegan said.

"We still have uglies down there, Staff Sergeant!" Binkowski said.

"They are too close to the tanker," Keegan said. "*I* will take care of them. You, on the other hand, get ready to disembark!"

"Aye aye, sir!" Reimer said. Stepping away from the machine guns, he and Binkowski armed themselves with their suppressed M-4 Carbines. The chopper elevated as the pilots brought it to the hospital roof. Dunn and Fisher stood ready and waiting. Watching the windows, they could see the world seemingly spinning around them as the chopper rotated to position the ramp.

Reimer paid extra attention to be sure he had full magazines, including one in his rifle. The haze that was his wearied brain would not let up. The adrenaline did not help. In fact, it only seemed to perpetuate the shakes, which he tried to hide. In doing so, he was only exhausting himself further.

"We will be eight floors up. The civilians are five floors down," Reimer said to his squad. "Remember protocol. Ammo is limited, so use it sparingly."

The ramp door lowered, the edge of it scraping against the dead garden previously landscaped onto the roof.

"Go! Go! Go!" Keegan barked. Reimer was first to go, with Dunn jumping down right beside him. Fisher and Binkowski followed, the former carrying a supply bag. With their rifles lifted to eye level, the team moved toward a structure that resembled a security guard shark.

Dunn kicked the door inward and stepped in. A reanimated corpse, having slumped against the desk, rose to life at the sight of fresh prey. Dunn cracked the butt of his rifle into its nose, squishing the tissue as he drove it backward. The corpse fell on its back, immediately reaching back up, jaws snapping like a piranha.

Dunn stomped his foot on its jaw, pinning it to the ground, before plunging a knife through its temple. That was protocol. Bullets were not as high in commodity these days. Wind gusts swept the roof as the chopper pulled away behind them, lowering near the fuel tanker.

"Here we go," Reimer said. At the back of the building was an elevator and stairwell. "Binkowski, open that door and step back!" The marine did as ordered. The handle was unlocked. She yanked it open, stepping back for Reimer to observe the stairs beneath them. "Clear! Let's go!"

They took the stairs two floors down where it dead ended.

"Of course!" Fisher said. "Clearly, they have to make stairways that only go down partway."

"Must be staff use only. Since we came down from the roof, this would put us on the seventh," Reimer said. He positioned at the hallway entrance. "I'll go first."

The door opened to a hallway leading to the Oncology department. They passed a set of double doors on the right, where several dead patients lay motionless on their beds.

"Keep it down," Reimer whispered. They didn't know if they had reanimated or had their brains destroyed, nor did he care to find out. The team pressed on into the next hall, checking for signs along the way.

"Stairwell to the left, sir," Binkowski said.

"Everybody converge on it," Reimer said. "Fisher, watch our six. Dunn, open it."

Holding his Carbine by the grip, Dunn approached the door. It was a simple push-door with no latch. He pushed inward and stepped inside. A corpse wearing a hospital gown had been seated a few steps down. She turned, the white gown stained with foul residue from her flesh. Strands of hair fell from her scalp as the ghoul lunged at Dunn. Thrusting his rifle out, he pinned her to the wall, allowing for Binkowski to plunge a knife through her eye. Dunn let the corpse drop, its weight freeing the blade from the skull.

The sounds of moans rose from the bend in the stairwell. Fisher activated a flashlight attached to his rifle barrel and pointed down past the guardrail. Several corpses had been stirred into action.

"We got six, maybe seven coming up," he said.

"Go in hand-to-hand," Reimer said. "The stairwell will keep their paths narrow. Do not shoot, unless you want to bring more on us!"

Fisher and Binkowski fixed bayonets and hustled down to greet the enemy. Reimer fixed a flashlight down the dark stairway, illuminating the gaping mouth of a reanimated healthcare professional. Blood and skin dangled from the sleeves of the scrubs as it moved in to bite Fisher. He pulled the weapon back, looking for the best place for sticking the blade, as a thirty-inch M4 with a seven-inch bayonet was not as effective as a five-foot spear. The marine thrust his bayonet in an upward angle, ramming the blade under its jaw and into its brain. As he yanked it free, Binkowski plunged her blade into the next one, plowing it through the roof of its open mouth.

The remaining undead climbed the steps; the wall and guardrail keeping them narrow as though in an assembly line. Binkowski and Fisher stabbed with precision, silently and efficiently putting each one down as they drew near.

With a thrust of her knife, Binkowski killed the last one. Fisher stepped over their festering corpses and moved down the steps. He cleared the bend and continued ascending. Waving to the others, he signaled the all-clear.

"Good news. This leads to the third level," he said.

"So far, so good," Binkowski responded. Perhaps this would go quicker than expected. She knew well enough to keep that thought to herself.

****

The Chinook touched down, crunching several bodies into the pavement. Sergeant Keegan leapt from the fuselage entry, striking his rifle across the face of a surviving zombie. After it fell to the pavement, he stomped the heel of his boot on its face, caving the front of its skull into its brain.

He ran ten steps before dropping to a firing position. Three corpses walked from around the tanker toward him. They each hyperextended their jaws like a snake, reaching their arms as they lunged. With his M4A1 set to semi-automatic, Keegan tapped the trigger. The back of their skulls exploded into a thick black splurge as a round penetrated each of their foreheads.

Gordon and Kane exited the Chinook and covered the east side of the tanker. There were at least four stumbling out from behind it, and several more moving in over the fence. The nearest four were spaced out well enough to be handled individually.

Gordon took the nearest one, embedding a knife into its skull. Kane took the second and third, knocking one down with a kick to the chest and plunging a knife through the eye socket of the next. As he finished off the other by crushing its head with the butt of his rifle, Gordon took on the fourth. As it drew near, it lunged with a burst of speed. He stepped aside, dodging its grasp, before shoving his blade through the back of its head.

He sheathed the knife and joined Staff Sergeant Keegan in picking off several incoming zombies moving over the fence, while Kane completed a tour around the tanker.

"Tanker is clear, sir!" he said.

"Kane, you're with me! Gordon, keep those bastards off of us," Keegan ordered. Gordon dropped to a kneeling stance, carefully placing rounds in the heads of several approaching corpses.

Keegan pulled the heavy hose toward the refueling probe, while Kane waited near the lever. The Staff Sergeant hooked the hose in place then signaled Kane with a thumbs-up. Kane pulled the lever, pumping over a thousand pounds of fuel into its storage.

****

The stairwell door led Reimer and his team into a wide lobby. All four of them hesitated in a moment of stunned silence, seeing over a dozen walking corpses in a feeding frenzy. They were separated into three groups, each of them pulling the entrails out of freshly killed civilians.

One zombie turned its head, looking at the marines with white eyes. It stood up and snarled, red flesh dangling from its front teeth. As it started lumbering toward them, the others began standing up, spurred by the sight of living prey.

"Weapons free," Reimer said. He took the first shot. His aim was slightly low, plowing through the zombie's lower jaw. The force of the shot knocked it down on its back. He aimed to finish it off, but the others were quickly converging. The team stood side-by-side in a firing line, picking off the incoming corpses. Skull and brain matter splashed onto the ceiling, silencing the endless snarling.

Except one.

The first corpse leaned up, its lower jaw and tongue dangling by loose strands of meat. Reimer inhaled through his nose as he moved in. He stomped down hard on its face, driving it back down to the floor. It grabbed up at him with bony hands, pulling on his pantleg.

Lack of strength prevented the Corporal from crushing the skull. Now, with frustration added to his fatigue, he simply pressed the barrel of his gun to its face and squeezed the trigger.

"Let's go," he muttered.

"Hey man, you know you just wasted a…"

"I said, let's go!" Reimer nearly shouted. He pushed forward into the next hall. Binkowski hugged the right of the hall, shooting down two corpses that approached. Reimer held up a fist, signaling for the men to stop. Listening carefully, they could hear the numerous growling of several other walkers nearby. The sounds, though loud and numerous, sounded to be muffled by some sort of physical barrier. They approached a juncture, where they found a set of double doors leading into the Day Stay unit. Two zombies ambled near the back, oblivious to the marines' presence.

Reimer could still hear the intense moaning, but it wasn't coming from here.

"This way," he said, directing them past the door.

"What about these guys?" Dunn said.

"There's only two," Reimer said. "Not worth our time. Let's go."

The team pressed on, taking a left turn at the next juncture. The further they moved, the louder the groans were. Three zombies were on their hands and knees, digging deep into the flesh of a still-writhing victim.

"Fisher, Dunn, you're up," Reimer said. The two marines charged, their footsteps attracting the gaze of the three walkers. They each sprang to their feet, the motion tearing away the flesh their jaws had clenched while kneeling. Silver bayonets pierced their skulls like spears from the Roman era, ridding whatever spark of life that had spurred the corpses from their graves.

The two marines knelt down by the civilian.

"We got a live one!" Dunn said. The civilian was coughing uncontrollably, spewing blood between his gums. His stomach had been pulled apart, resulting in a huge fleshy crater. "Are there any other survivors?" Dunn asked him.

"He's not going to answer," Binkowski said. Dunn grabbed the civilian by his collar.

"Answer me now! Are there any others?"

Binkowski looked to Reimer, her eyes blazing. "Are you gonna allow this?" Blood and vomit shot from the civilian's mouth.

"There...there!" he said, pointing to a set of double doors. Dunn looked up, seeing a sign that read *Critical Care*. Through the windows they could see several figures moving about. He released his grip on the civilian. In extreme pain, he tried to form the words *help*, but couldn't get it out. There was nothing the marines could do for him. Even if he wasn't infected, the wound was too severe.

"Dunn, put him down," Reimer said. Dunn looked back at Reimer.

This is why we shouldn't have come here. It took everything to keep those thoughts subdued from reaching his lips. Binkowski helped roll the civilian over, whispering a gentle "shhh" to calm him down. Dunn pressed his rifle to the back of his head and fired, ending the agony.

"Let's finish this and get the hell out of here!" Dunn said. They gathered near the door, Reimer and Fisher on the left, Binkowski and Dunn on the right. All at once, they burst through, weapons blazing into their targets.

Several of the undead were in a feeding frenzy within the middle of the room, tearing internal organs from the bellies of freshly killed civilians. All at once, they sprang toward the fresh meat standing in the doorway. Their growls were suppressed by the blasts of multiple M4s. With their weapons set to full auto, the marines sent a wall of bullets into the horde, dropping their bodies at their feet.

After reloading, the group entered the Critical Care check-in lobby. In the center of the room was a large counter, where the supervising nurse would sit. To the left were the patient rooms, while the nurse's work station was off to the right. It was from there that they could hear the muffled yelling of someone yelling for help.

"Dunn, Fisher, maintain position here. Binkowski, you're with me," Reimer said. They rushed down to the end of the small hallway, seeing two zombies pushing hard to get through a closed door. Hearing the marines approaching, the two zombies turned to attack what they thought to be easier prey. Skin and nails dangled from claw-like fingers as they lashed out.

Reimer went in first, striking one with his rifle while Binkowski bayoneted the other through the eye. Reimer struck the fallen zombie repeatedly like a madman, gradually bashing its skull in. With its face completely folded inward, Reimer stumbled back. Binkowski stepped toward him to reach out, thinking the Corporal was about to lose his balance.

"I'm good," he said. He directed her to the door.

"United States Marine Corps! Open the door immediately!" she yelled. She had barely finished speaking when the door swung open, revealing two terrified men. They were both in their mid-forties, wearing windbreakers and suits underneath.

"Oh, thank God you're here!" one of them said.

"Where are the others?" Reimer asked.

"There are none," the terrified man said. "They came in through the fences. Everyone just panicked and ran everywhere! My escorts led me in here. We were trying to make it to the roof, but these things were on us at every turn!"

"Escorts?" Dunn said, marching into the hallway. "What do you mean, *escorts*?"

"Dunn, stow it," Reimer said. The survivors looked at him, flabbergasted.

"Don't you know who I am?" he asked.

"Never mind!" Reimer said, physically grabbing the man and pulling him through the hall. "Go! We're moving out. Back to the roof!" He adjusted the mic on his helmet. "Motherbird, we are en route back to the roof."

"*Copy that. How many civilians?*"

"Two."

A brief pause followed.

"*Ten-four. We are near complete on our refuel. Meet you in just a couple of minutes.*"

"Copy that, Motherbird." Reimer yelled to his marines. "Move! Move! Move! Sir, you're gonna have to pick up the pace!"

"Don't have to tell me twice," one of the men said. Reimer felt a hard tap on his shoulder. Dunn was almost in his face, keeping pace with them as they ran out into the hallway. Fisher and Binkowski led the way, with the contacts right behind them. Moving back the way they came in, they ran to the end of the hall and took a right at the juncture.

"Who the fuck are they, Reimer?" Dunn pressed the Corporal. Reimer shot him a tense expression.

"NOT NOW!" He looked back, seeing Binkowski stop suddenly. The Day Stay doors were open to the left side. Sunlight was streaming in through the windows of the back of the check in, casting two limbering shadows into the hallway. The two corpses they had spotted were now much closer to the door. Binkowski stood just outside the doors, ready to ambush them. By now, Reimer was growing increasingly frustrated and impatient. "Binkowski, just let them be."

He spoke too loudly, drawing the two zombies out into the hall. They scampered out, walking like giant birds with their arms tucked close to their chests. Toes snapped off their bare feet as they locked soggy eyes onto their prey. The nearest one gaped its mouth, spitting saliva and teeth. Toes broke off its bare feet as it lunged.

Its own momentum drove it right into Binkowski's rifle stock as she thrust it out, cracking the forehead. She continued pummeling it, while Fisher bayonetted the other through the roof of the mouth. In seconds, both corpses were motionless.

Yet the shadows kept coming. Fisher's eyes grew wide as he looked into the Day Stay lobby.

Spilling into the Day Stay lobby were several dozen of the undead, previously hidden from sight as they were feasting in the nurse's station. By the time Fisher saw them, they had swarmed at the entrance like an army of bugs. In the following moment, they spilled into the hallway. Grasping hands were reaching in every direction, while teeth clicked together in biting motions. These ones had been freshly killed; the very people the team was trying to save. Their muscles not yet rotted away, allowing them to move with greater speed and mobility.

Fisher and Binkowski fired wildly, while Dunn and Reimer pushed the contacts past the door. In seconds, the group of corpses were wall to wall. The marines were forced apart from each other, like helpless victims caught in a raging river.

With the horde between her and the team, Binkowski was driven backward toward the juncture. She fired wildly into the horde. They overwhelmed her, driving her into the back wall with the force of a tidal wave. Her vision was obscured by the sight of a dozen pairs of teeth, already bloodstained from their previous encounter. She screamed as skin throughout her body was ripped away in large chunks.

Fisher swung his rifle outward, clobbering two corpses that bit at his body armor. They fell away, loosening their grasps on his Kevlar.

Backpedaling swiftly, he fired his M4 at full automatic, plastering the walls with brownish red blood from numerous heads. Binkowski's screams were deafening, unnerving Fisher as he tried to get to her.

Through the bodies, he could see his fellow marine pinned to the wall. Her arms were subdued by multiple corpses, which gnawed on her wrists and fingers. The others were tearing the Kevlar from her uniform and reaching their hands deep into her open wounds. Blood gushed from her mouth as they pulled her ribcage apart, yanking intestines and balls of flesh.

The screams seemed to stretch on forever. Dunn felt himself tensing as the sound of pain pierced his soul. He refused to look back. It would do no good at this point. But the mental image was almost worse. His whole body shook from both fright and anger, as well as the instinctive urge to go back and help as he listened to Binkowski being eaten alive. The sight of it would only make it worse. He continued forward with the civilians, while Reimer shot into the crowd to allow Fisher to gain distance.

With several undead right behind him, Fisher ran after the group into the lobby. Dunn goaded the civilians up the stairwell.

"MOVE IT!" he yelled. His voice wasn't just firm, but it showed disdain. Disdain for them. Disdain for the mission. Disdain for the dead. Reimer and Fisher were right behind them, loading fresh mags into their Carbines. The door hadn't even swung entirely shut before it was pushed open again by the flood of undead. Loud shrieks left their deflating lungs as they surged into the stairway.

Reimer and Fisher fired short controlled bursts into the crowd, dropping at least two corpses. There was no time to count. The bodies had soon disappeared as the others scampered over them. Fighting was no use. Their weapons would run dry before they slowed down the crowd. The two marines turned and ran as fast as they could, following the others up the winding staircase. They reached the fourth floor, then the fifth.

Dunn was half a floor ahead of them, already clearing the sixth.

"Hold it!" he yelled. Looking up through the vertical space between the stairs, Reimer could see the others already moving back down. They met at the sixth-floor entrance, the civilians hyperventilating with terror. Behind them were over a dozen walking corpses, which had followed the sounds of chaos into the stairway.

"Out this way!" Reimer ordered. He opened the sixth-floor entrance, letting his team run inside ahead of him. As he followed them inside, the two groups of undead were converging. The air was filled with their hungry moans as they began crowding the doorway.

Dunn fired a few shots at some straying walkers in the corridor, putting them out of their misery.

"Where do we go?!" he said to Reimer.

"Keep going this way," Reimer said.

"This way?!" Dunn said. "This leads to nowhere!"

"You see that window at the end?! We're going through that! We'll use our harnesses and cables and climb down the outside!"

Dunn looked back, seeing the undead spilling in from the stairway.

"Hell, he's got my vote!" Fisher said. The group took off running, the non-combatants looking more and more terrified as they approached the large window.

One of them started to babble. "I don't know if I can…"

"YOU CAN! 'Less you want to stay here," Dunn interjected, shutting down any protest.

****

"Okay, shut it off!" Keegan yelled to Kane. The marine pulled the lever, shutting down the flow of fuel. Keegan tossed the hose aside before gripping his rifle. "Gordon, Kane, get on board!" They followed his orders as he lay down some cover fire.

Heads exploded into a brown splatter surrounded by a grey mist. He fired off two more rounds before lowering his aim. His teeth grinded together as he looked past the fence. A huge horde of the undead were moving in through the trees, drawn by the Chinook's engines and gunfire. The crowd stretched on as far as the eye could see.

"Holy Jesus," he muttered. He ran into the Chinook. "Pilots! Get this bird off the ground!" The rotors increased their momentum and changed their angle, lifting the thirty-eight-million-dollar aircraft into the air. It elevated high above the pavement and rotated to place the ramp onto the roof.

****

They passed several junctures before reaching the end of the small hallway. It was a corner juncture, leading into another hall. Numerous undead were packed several meters down, oblivious to their presence. That changed as they heard the loud bursting of glass as the marines busted the window.

Fisher used the bolt gun to secure the cables. Reimer pulled two harnesses from the bag and clipped them onto the civilians.

"Dunn, you go with him. I'll take the other," he said. Dunn, who was laying suppressing fire into the incoming herd strapped his weapon over his back and clipped on a harness. Fisher, having already harnessed himself, took a firing stance as they prepared for descent.

Dunn grabbed the civilian and clipped their harnesses together. The man gasped as they leaned out the window, six stories high. Clipped to a ring on the cable, he gradually lowered them down. Reimer did the same with the other civilian. After Dunn was six feet down, he went out the window. With his hands on the metal grip, he lowered himself and the package down to the pavement.

"Get down here, Fisher!"

Fisher fired several more shots in the hope of slowing down the horde. For every corpse he put down, it seemed two more would show up. Not only were they not slowing, they were speeding up! Dropping his Carbine, he rushed over the side of the window. With no time to clip the belay device to his harness, he clasped his fingers over the cable and started walking himself down.

The undead flooded the corner juncture. Several arms reached at him through the open window. With two long steps, Fisher put himself out of reach. He held tight on the cord, his arms growing tense from holding his weight.

The crowd pushed harder against the window. Bodies bulged through the opening as they were pushed over the ledge. Fisher yelled as one of them spilled over and fell to the pavement. Another one quickly followed, landing face-first, its body reduced to a fleshy goo upon impact. He turned his eyes back up to the window, as two more corpses fell. They landed right on top of him. With no sense of gravity or self-preservation, they dug their fingers into his fatigues.

Reimer looked up, seeing Fisher squirming two floors above him. Blood trickled down, landing on his arm. It was fresh: Fisher's.

The marine was screaming, still desperately holding onto the cord. Teeth sank into his neck. The biter pulled back, ripping strands of tissue from its place. It didn't even swallow. It simply dropped the mouthful and went in for another bite. Fisher twisted and struggled, trying to get it off of him.

Finally, the cable loosened from his grip. His screams contained a sense of velocity as he freefell past Reimer and Dunn. He landed hard on his side, landing on the biting zombie. Its soft body broke his fall enough to prevent major head injury, but not enough to spare him two broken arms, several busted ribs, and a leg that was bent backward at the knee. Blood spilled from his body as the other corpse, which had landed on him, pulled itself to its hands and knees.

"NO!" Dunn yelled, watching the corpse from above as it bit down on the defenseless marine's throat. He could see Fisher's legs shaking as he attempted to kick. Streams of red shot out in small fountains, smothering the biter's face.

Dunn extracted his M9 and extended it downward. It quivered briefly as one bullet pierced its shoulder. It felt no discomfort, as it felt no pain. It continued digging into Fisher's throat. It ripped its face back, curious by further sounds of gunshots and the simultaneous jolt from bullets striking its back. It turned to look at the other marines. It watched them, holding Fisher's trachea between its teeth as they came down to the ground level.

Dunn unclipped the harnesses and pushed the civilian away. He charged the corpse, planting several rounds between its eyes. With its brain turned to mush from multiple penetrations, it collapsed in a pool of Fisher's blood. Dunn stood over his fellow marine, then turned to look away.

It had bitten into his face as well, resulting in one of Fisher's eyes being completely exposed. His throat was nonexistent at this point. The marine was dead. Dunn turned violently as Reimer tapped him on the shoulder. The Corporal had called him at least twice, but he never heard it.

"Come on," Reimer said. Dunn gave his friend one last glance and then ran with the others around the corner of the building. Shooting down multiple targets in their path, they made their way to the fuel tanker.

Except the chopper wasn't there.

Reimer looked up to the sound of its rotors overhead. The Chinook was waiting at their planned rally point. In the midst of the confusion, adrenaline, and extreme brain fog resulting from fatigue, Reimer had forgotten to notify the Sergeant of their plan.

"Oh, GOD!" one of the civilians said. A wall of the undead were stumbling over the gate. Hundreds of corpses were bearing down on them in various states of decay.

In that same moment, Staff Sergeant Keegan's voice blared through the radio.

"*Motherbird to Bravo Team. What's the holdup?!*"

"Motherbird, this is Corporal Reimer. We are down on the pavement. Three hundred feet north of the tanker. We have many boogies moving in on us!" He could picture Keegan's anger, wondering why he wasn't notified. However, he wasn't going to waste time and breath asking questions.

Dunn was already firing. He aimed behind them, where many other corpses approached from the north. Unable to retreat, they had no choice but to wait for the Chinook.

The chopper lifted away from the roof and swung around. The undead had swarmed past the tanker, now less than a hundred feet from the marines. Like the ones from the hospital, many of these were freshly dead, and capable of speed near to that of a jog.

The Chinook set down, smashing three of the leads into the cement. Sergeant Keegan waved from the ramp while Gordon and Kane laid down suppressive fire. Reimer and Dunn pushed the civilians over the ramp.

"We've got corpses climbing the nose!" the pilots called out.

"We've got the package!" Keegan said. "Ascend! Now!"

As he finished speaking, several sets of hands reached from the edge of the ramp opening. Kane tried to scamper away, only to fall backward as one of the undead grabbed his pantleg. Immediately, two other sets of hands grabbed onto him.

The chopper lifted off in that same moment. Kane felt the metal floor sliding under his back like a conveyor belt as the undead held him back. Suddenly, he was on the cement floor. His view of the sky vanished, replaced by the sight of teeth. Fingers and teeth pressed into his skin, ripping it like fabric.

Kane's blood curdling screams were muffled by the immense crowd as the feeding frenzy commenced. Two of them pulled on his right arm with undying strength, ripping it out by the roots. Kane gagged as several others pulled away at his uniform, exposing his chest and stomach. All at once, they set upon the meat, each digging their teeth and fingers into the flesh and pulling in different directions. His skin came apart like tissue paper, exposing a mix of blood and organs that fell apart as his legs were pulled away from his trunk.

"GODDAMNIT!" Keegan yelled, seeing his marine disappear under the horde several feet below. The ramp closed, sealing his view behind a metal barrier. He composed himself then walked to the forward cabin. The two civilians were seated up front, both in a state of shock.

Reimer was walking back away from them. He was sluggish, his eyes heavy as though he had seen a ghost.

"Binkowski? Fisher?" Keegan asked. Reimer shook his head.

"KOA."

Dunn was pacing back and forth, his face looking like a man possessed.

"Are you injured, marine?" he said. He knew better than to word it as "are you okay" as he was clearly not.

"I'm fine, Staff Sergeant," Dunn said. Before Keegan could continue, Dunn stepped in front of him. "I need to know. *Who* are those men?"

"Dunn, what difference does it make?" Reimer said.

"It makes ALL the difference!" Dunn shouted.

"Keep it down," Keegan said. He took a breath. "One's a U.S. Senator. The other is a vaccine developer. They were ordered to depart with the civilians here."

"Oh, lovely," Dunn said. "I guess outbreak levels don't matter when you're a couple of VIPs in a..."

"Don't say another word, marine," Keegan said. "Those were our orders. We followed them. We're going back Stateside. Reimer, come with me. I'm gonna need your statement for my report."

"Yes, sir," Reimer said. As they walked away, Dunn slumped in one of the seats. He glared at the two men they had rescued. Gordon was tending to them, checking for any bites as well as any other injuries.

Dunn's eyes were locked on the men. Two men, the last of a group of fifty. A group he knew was gone before they even went in, trapped inside an area above a Level 5 outbreak. Dunn's eyes went across the cabin, unable to not notice the absence of three fellow marines.

Two VIPs. Three marines.

CHAPTER 4

A heavy fog lingered over the air, giving the forest a wetness that matched that of a heavy rain. Soggy leaves dangled from thick branches, seeping a thin secretion into the soil below. Charcoal in color, it mixed in with the rain water before being sucked into the grass.

Sandra Hill had huddled to her knees, compacted into a small foxhole with her two escorts. Joe, a college basketball player, was peeking through the thin, grass covered tarp. He looked at the never-ending fog, watching for any lumbering shapes that moved through the forest. He pulled the tarp back over his head and kneeled next to Sandra and their third companion, Kevin.

"I think it's safe," he said.

"No such thing as *safe* around here," Kevin whispered. As far as he was concerned, he wouldn't believe it until he saw it for himself. He stood up and peeked through the edge of the tarp. The moisture immediately hit his face, compelling him to run his hand over his eyes.

"Careful. Don't get any in your mouth," Sandra said.

"I remember," Kevin said. "Can't trust any water around here." He continued gazing out into the surrounding forest. Despite only being ten-in-the-morning, the heavy fog and overhead canopy gave the appearance of dusk. Whatever streams of sunlight that made it through were heavily obscured in the area's constant cloud cover. But so far, there didn't appear to be any sign of the undead. "Okay, I think Joe's right for once."

"How far is it?" Joe asked Stacy.

"We're almost there. Maybe about three hundred yards," she said. "Like I mentioned before, we can't miss it. The trees had been thinned out around it."

"I suggest we move," Joe said. "Sooner we get there, the sooner we can go back."

"Hell, I say we bunk down once we're there," Kevin said. He took another peek, covering all three-hundred-sixty degrees around them. After feeling confident that nothing was around, he pulled the tarp back completely. Pressing his palms up onto the muddy rim, he pulled himself out of the four-foot foxhole, before reaching to help the others. Joe, with a height over six-feet, easily lifted himself out without help. Stacy, however, was more than gracious to accept the offer.

Joe pulled the tarp back in place after she emerged. Brushing his muddy hands against his cargo shorts, he gazed into the forest.

"Shit, which way again?" He kept his voice low. Any noise would certainly attract the wrong kind of attention.

"There," Stacy whispered, pointing her finger over to the left. She pulled her revolver from her belt and double-checked the cylinder. Joe held a bolt action Remington to his shoulder, while Kevin, a County Sheriff recruit, kept his Glock holstered, opting to hold a baseball bat until being forced to spend any rounds.

He moved first, hustling up a small hill, bat poised over his right shoulder. He waited a few seconds for the others to catch up, all the while looking everywhere for walking corpses. But the fog seemed to thicken as they neared their destination. At best, he could only see thirty feet ahead. A small breeze brushed the branches above, causing the fog to drift like one enormous ghost. The leaves rustled overhead, spilling some of their secretion down in large streams.

Kevin was suddenly frozen in place. He could hear rustling along the ground throughout the forest.

Joe and Stacy could see the terror building up in his eyes.

"Come on. We're almost there," Stacy said.

"Shit, Doc, we should've stayed in the foxhole," he said.

"Dude, get a grip," Joe said. "You're wasting time." Kevin drew a deep breath, then shook some of the watery residue from his beard. Taking another step, he tensed at the sensation of his shoes sinking into the mud. The ground squished with each step, making it impossible to keep their movements silent.

Just two hundred yards, he reminded himself. The mud squished even louder with the next step. His foot sank over one centimeter, then hit something rigid. Before he took the next step, he felt pressure under his foot. He froze. Whatever it was, it was moving. He looked down, seeing the dirt and mud swooshing beneath him. Long thin formations squirmed like giant worms. One reached up, extending five bony fingers that grabbed at his leg.

Kevin shrieked and jumped back. The arm continued reaching, while the mud continued to unfold, exposing the eyeless face of a shriveled corpse. Its lips and cheeks were gone, leaving a large overstretched jawbone. Despite having no eyes, it still turned to face Kevin, reaching with one of its arms. Covered with skin and worms, it grabbed at the air between them.

"Jesus!" Kevin squealed. With terror consuming him, he wildly bashed the baseball bat into its head. He smashed down repeatedly, squirting brain matter through the broken skull.

The rustling around them intensified. Mud squished from behind the blanket of fog. The wind carried the groans of hungry corpses, now drawn to the sounds of the living. Joe and Stacy looked around, unable to determine the source of the moans.

"We can't stay here," Joe said. "Come on, Kev. We gotta get the doc to the bunker."

"Fuck. This," Kevin said. Finally, he had pulled his Glock. He held it in his right hand, keeping it pointed outward. In his other hand, he held the bat high over his head. The snarls increased in volume. He moved down a small hill, increasing as he came into a region where the ground was drier. Looking ahead, he saw a shape forming through the fog. He stopped, ready to fire. It was about a man's height, almost twenty inches in width. He inched forward, seeing there were no arms or legs. Reaching out with the bat, he scraped off loose chunks of bark. It was the trunk of a fallen tree.

Christ, is this a fucking joke?

Arms sprang out from around the tree as two corpses emerged from the fog. Kevin shrieked, firing wildly into the duo. Bullets punched through their breastbone and traveled out into the forest. He could feel their hot breath as they closed in. He tried backing away, only to slip on the mud behind him. He looked up, seeing their scrawny figures falling down over him.

Stacy and Joe rushed in to help, only to be stopped by the sight of numerous other figures that appeared through the mist. Kevin was screaming by now, his Glock discharging as one of them bit into his bicep.

"This way! Let's go!" Joe shouted. They ran down the small slope, while several of the undead converged on Kevin. One of them was right on top of him, pressing its head toward his face. Kevin gritted his teeth as he pushed back against its forehead. He called out in agony, feeling its fingers press between his ribcage. The other undead joined in, seeing the sight of fresh blood.

Huddling around him, they pried their hands into the same area and pulled outward, opening his ribcage like a book. Bones snapped and blood spat. The ghoul pulled its head from Kevin's, opting instead to bury its entire head inside his open ribcage. Arms left the shoulders as the others tore away at him. The last thing he would see were several fleshy fingers grabbing around his head. Looking for a place to grasp, those fingers pierced his eye sockets, turning his eyes to jelly as they reached deeply. The corpse pulled away, its brain not having the capacity to sense a limit in its strength. Blood spurted and tendons snapped, leaving a red trail as the head detached from the neck.

Joe and Stacy ran at a full sprint. Kevin's screams had ceased, now making way for the dozens of moaning bodies that surrounded them. Joe raised his rifle at three figures that emerged ahead of them. He blasted the first two, while Stacy shot down the third. Joe paused and looked around, having lost his sense of direction in the chaos.

"This way!" Stacy said. She ran through a small clearing in the woods, stopping once to shoot another ghoul before continuing in a full sprint. Winding between several trees, they came to a thinning in the fog. The ground dipped and flattened after several yards.

They had found it; the abandoned bunker. With it being underground, there wasn't much to see aside from a small concrete structure. The structure resembled a small house, with a huge mechanical door in the front. On the door was a small keypad for Stacy to punch in a special code.

The mud squished behind them, provoking Joe to glance over his shoulder. In a sudden reaction, he jumped forward out of the reach of several hands. Several ghouls stumbled into the clearing, many of them dragging wet strips of torn clothing behind them, revealing mushy looking flesh.

Joe and Stacy sprinted for the door. Stacy holstered her revolver and activated the keypad, while Joe fired several rounds into the advancing crowd. Heads split down the center as bullets carved their path, dropping the corpse into the earth. Stacy punched in her code. The computer, sluggish from the exposure to moisture, read the code.

Joe fired his last shot.

"Open the damn door!" he yelled.

"I did!" Stacy yelled back. The keypad flashed, then finally a loud metallic *thomp* echoed from inside. Gears grinded inside as the door opened electronically. "Come on!"

She heard the crunch of the rifle collide with one of the ghouls. Next came a horrific scream as the corpses ganged up. Joe tried to go for the entrance, only to be held back by several hands. Stacy emptied her revolver into the crowd, doing little to stop the pile-up over Joe. There was nothing she could do, except slip through the slow-opening door. She grabbed a handle on the inside and pulled it shut, stopping once to thrust a kick into an advancing corpse to drive it back.

Joe yelled for her help as his body registered pain from head-to-toe. Several bony faces pressed into his body. Chunks of flesh were torn from him, some simply being tossed aside like slabs of meat at a butcher shop. Before long, Joe's identity had been degraded to various mangled pieces of meat and organs, many of which would reside forever in the gullets of walking corpses that would never digest them.

Stacy dry heaved as she stumbled into the radio room. The overhead lights came on, as did the various computers in the room. The code she had entered had likely initiated a motion tracking system.

She drew in a deep breath and remembered what she was instructed to do. She looked to the left, seeing a doorway that led to a concrete stairway. She descended the fifty-step flight, which led into another open doorway. The lights in the radio room came to life, bringing several computers into view.

In the back corner was the com unit. Stacy dashed to the large computer. She pushed the seat aside and tapped her initials into the login, along with her prescribed password. The communication system came to life. Several buttons emerged on the touchscreen. She tapped her finger on the one that read *SOS Transmission.*

A mechanical drum sounded from above as the facility protruded its antenna array. The automated message had begun its transmission.

****

FORT STROSHINE

West Coast United States, Inhabitable Zone. Previously known as Washington.

Bill Rico thought he'd seen enough chaos at the dawn of the plague. It was just two years ago when he was a simple air traffic controller. The job was busy, requiring constant attention to detail. It was that same skill that prompted him to move his family to the coast, well before his home state of Nevada increased to a Z-Level 6.

They arrived only days before the outbreaks went rampant. The world governments were too fixated on trying to find a cure. There was debate on whether the carriers were even dead. Not to mention the outcry about insensitivity. People referred to the resurrected as *zombies*, a term deemed derogatory by many commenters on social media. Before the world understood how to deal with the carriers, it was too late. Of course, the government, still more concerned with votes for the next election, caved to the vocal minority. In turn, they opted for treatment procedures for the undead rather than euthanasia. Yet, despite this, the feds were setting up various settlements to the west, condensing all major political figures into the coastal states. Such a move was not kept secret for long. It was then that Rico packed his family and moved to the coast.

In the following year, the world fell under the weight of an ever-increasing number of infected. The United States, what was left of it, was now condensed into the states of Washington, Oregon, and northern

California. The rest was deemed uninhabitable. To prevent the undead from getting in, this area was separated from the rest of the continent by the use of a large concrete barrier. Stretching from Port Angeles and curving down to San Rafeal, what remained of the U.S., and North America, resided.

Everyone was recruited into some kind of service. For Rico, his air traffic control resume placed him into military dispatch service. To this day, the military was conducting what seemed to be an endless amount of rescue missions into areas deemed Z-Level 5 or lower, bringing civilians back behind the Border. In addition, he would have to intercept radio calls for aid, and pass the information over to the Station Commander.

In doing so, he was required to reference the caller's location in the satellite map in his computer. The computer displayed the area's outbreak level, which would ultimately determine whether resources would be spent for rescue.

A physical, laminated copy of the rescue program was tapped to his desk. It was the same text as the brochures that were handed out in the early days of National Emergency being declared, listing the various outbreak levels. Except the difference with this brochure was that somebody had taken a pen to it, labeling a 'Z' next to all the outbreak levels.

Z-Level 1 – Undead Population minimal. Infection Risk minimal. Area considered suitable for inhabitance.

Z-Level 2 – Low Undead Population. Infection Risk low. Inhabitants are warned to monitor surroundings.

Z-Level 3 – Undead Population increased. Threat Level low but has potential risk of elevating. Approximately 10 undead per every 100 inhabitants. Citizens encouraged to remain indoors. Pack precautionary items in case of evacuation.

Z-Level 4 – Undead Population at 20 percent. Martial Law declared. Citizens remain indoors pending further details.

Z-Level 5 – Undead Population deemed too uncontrollable. Infection Risk High. Area residents ordered to sanctuary areas to await military pickup for evacuation.

Z-Level 6-7 – Escalated Undead Population. Considered highly contaminated and highly dangerous. Military intervention deemed improbable.

Z-Level 8-9 – Undead Population Overwhelming. Rescue operation considered impossible. Any residents left behind forced to fend for themselves.

"I copy. Border Command, out," he said. He got on the computer to type in the log for a successful rescue in Utah, and another in Idaho. It seemed that the operations would never end. Rico often wondered if they could even spare the fuel and resources. Sure, the government had built a manufacturing facility for armaments, but that was slow moving and would surely not keep up with the demand.

He was too busy to think too hard on it. In minutes, he would have to take the next call, and he really needed to get the log completed. He typed in the time, location, and name of the officer in charge. Then it came to the event description. He was a few words into the first sentence when the computer froze.

"What the hell—"

A green bar flashed at the top of the screen. A new tab opened, displaying a beacon on the map, located somewhere in Montana. He read the glaring red text, then shot up out of his chair.

"COMMANDER! You'll want to see this!"

From across the room, the officer in charge hustled in his direction, winding between several moving bodies in the busy dispatch center.

"What have you got?" he called out to Rico. The dispatcher sat back down in his chair and zoomed in on the beacon. As the Commander arrived, he enlarged the text. The Commander studied the screen, then grabbed the landline next to Rico's computer.

"Get me the President!"

CHAPTER 5

General Spears inhaled the salty air as he waited at the Fort Anese landing pad. He had been informed of the successful extraction of Senator Baker and had been instructed to personally escort him to Headquarters.

Fort Anese was only five-hundred yards away from the concrete barrier. As the General waited, his eyes were busy looking over the top of the twelve-foot wall. Soldiers marched with assault rifles along the guardrails, constantly looking down at the group of the undead that congregated on the other side. Like a miniature Great Wall of China, the barrier was consistently patrolled by soldiers. They walked over the top and the sides, checking for any weakness in the structure. Luckily, the weather was good, providing excellent sunshine and a blue cloudless sky for the aircraft to glide across.

Soldiers moved about all around him. All around, he saw camouflaged uniforms stained with dirt and sand, if not the blood of victims. There was hardly a recruit in the battalion that had not been face-to-face at least once with a member of the infected. The sky was filled with medevac choppers both leaving and returning. By now, he'd be hard pressed to even find a civilian who hadn't had to fight for survival at some point.

His promotion came with his arrival to Portland Air National Guard Base in Oregon, when he was a Colonel. With it came the responsibility of overseeing the continent-wide rescue operations. In addition, he was given jurisdiction of maintaining defense procedures near Fort Anese, Washington. His responsibilities meant he never left the base. Rarely had he seen the residential areas, old and new. After a year, he was detached from anything that wasn't his job. The pay rate meant nothing to him anymore. He was owned by the government. And his men were owned by him.

The Chinook passed over the Border and began to descend onto the landing pad. General Spears stood unfazed as the downdraft swept around him. The ninety-eight-foot aircraft set down, and the ramp opened up.

Private Dunn was the first to step out. The General could hear Sergeant Keegan yelling after him.

"Private Dunn, get your ass back here!"

Dunn had already reached the General and shoved the crumpled flyer into his hands.

"You might want to have that revised, seeing we're not going by it anyway," Dunn said.

"Private!" Sergeant Keegan marched from the Chinook. After giving the General one final glare, Dunn stood at the position of attention and waited for Keegan's chastisement.

"Yes, sir," he said. Keegan looked as though he was about to burst into flames.

"Report to the barracks! Now!"

"Aye aye, Staff Sergeant," Dunn said. With one final grimace directed at General Spears, he turned and marched away. Corporal Reimer walked alongside Gordon down the ramp, escorting the two VIPs to General Spears.

"Sir, I will enact disciplinary measures against the Private," Keegan said.

"Negative, Staff Sergeant," Spears said. "You're gonna need him. After I'm through with these folks here, I have to report to an emergency meeting with the President. I'm not yet informed of the specific situation, but I suspect your team's services will be required."

"Sir..." Keegan paused, holding back on his desire to inform the General of the team's low morale and exhausted state. But he knew his words would land on deaf ears. Even he couldn't help but notice the General's full figure, slightly rounded belly, and the cleanliness of his uniform. It contrasted vastly with the ragged appearances of the marines and other soldiers he commanded, particularly those being sent into the hot zones. Keegan feared a sense of disconnect. Unfortunately, he didn't have the rank to address it. He would just have to hope that the next mission would be a fast and simple one. "Aye aye, sir."

Dunn arrived at the group of buildings that made up the barracks. He walked past several of the structures before arriving at Building D, where his assigned bunk was.

"Hey man, wait up!" Dunn glanced over his shoulder, seeing Reimer and Gordon following him.

"What?"

"What? What do you mean *what*? How about, WHAT the hell was that back there!" Gordon said. "That's General *Spears*!"

"You're kidding, right?" Dunn remarked. He shot an icy stare at his fellow marine, knowing full well it was obvious why he did what he did.

"No, I'm not kidding," Gordon said. "Is it your intention to get yourself put in the brig?"

"Hell, now that you mentioned it, I should've socked the bastard in the jaw. Maybe get myself discharged."

"It'd be the brig first," Reimer corrected him. "And that's a best-case scenario."

"Whatever gets the job done," Dunn said.

"What the hell are you talking about?" Gordon said.

"Marine, are you blind? Have you seen what's been going on?"

"It was a rough day. Rougher than usual. But it comes with the job, Dunn," Gordon said.

"Job? What job? Being thrown into the fire for the sake of two useless guys who the government couldn't manage to extract before the area was overrun? Maybe you like being cannon fodder for the big wigs in government. I don't. Just because we're marines doesn't mean we're useless bullet sponges that can be thrown to the fire whenever they need a little favor. They see us as tools, man! Wake up."

"Dude, I think you're getting a bit paranoid," Gordon said.

"Either I'm paranoid, or you're blind," Dunn retorted. "They never intended us to pick up a large crowd. We were there for the Senator, and whoever that other guy was. They KNEW that area was overrun. And they sent us down anyway." He looked to Reimer, his expression demonstrating a search for validation.

"We don't know that, Dunn," Reimer said.

"I've been on plenty of missions I wasn't sure of, but it turned out to be worth it in the end. One time, we thought we lost the civilian group. Like today, the undead had overrun their barriers. We thought they were gone, but before calling it quits, we infiltrated the school and found them hiding in the gym. They thought we left, but we didn't. There were some doctors and nurses in that crowd, as well as some old vets. They would be dead if not for me and my unit. It's what we do. You act like we've never been in rough zones before."

"Being in a rough spot is one thing," Dunn said. "It's when we lose more than what we save, in a mission where such a result was obvious, is when I have a problem. I don't like having my ass put on the line to rescue," he formed air quotes with his fingers, "important people."

"You don't think we should be out there?" Gordon said. Dunn snickered. The question felt more like an accusation than anything else.

"In my case, no," Dunn said. "My contract was supposed to end months ago. Yet, here I am. "It has been so ordered you extend your time of service in the United States Marine Corps. Your nation, her citizens, and government are forever grateful for your service and sacrifice." Yet, I'm risking my life saving the President's special buddies."

"You're an E-2," Reimer said. "Perhaps if you would stop getting busted for conduct, you'd probably be a lieutenant by now. Probably wouldn't have to go over the wall anymore."

"Bullshit," Dunn said. "Why do you think you're only a Corporal? They're constantly sending people over that wall, and they're running out of people to send. The rescue missions are not the same. They've become personal favors now. We're running errands. Like that time when we had to report to that University in Idaho. There were no survivors, so instead they had us ransack the medical department."

"Well, hell!" Gordon remarked. "Not like we don't need stuff like that these days."

"Except the area was a Level 6, not a 5," Dunn said. "And wasn't it convenient that Senator Ruiz's nephew happened to be holed-up in there? Of course, I figured out who he was by accident. Saw the bastard give his uncle a big hug by the convoy. You see? They don't see us as marines. They see us as personal errand boys, who can also be cannon fodder. We're their personal slaves, doing work that nobody else will volunteer for. Hence everyone's being forced to remain in service after their term has expired."

Gordon wasn't ready to give up on his argument. Whether it was a desire to know his job meant something, or just a patriotic sense of duty, the twenty-five-year old marine always clung to faith in people. Dunn simply thought of him as naïve.

Both men turned their eyes on Reimer, as though looking for him to settle the debate. The Corporal wasn't sure what to think in this instance. Like Gordon, he had taken great pride in his responsibilities. But now, all he felt was worn down. He lacked Gordon's enthusiasm, though he wasn't sure he was as skeptical as Dunn. The military was growing too thin for soldiers to be uselessly hurled into senseless missions. Even the military officials would question it. In fact, they had. Even Spears had declined authorizing special operations into dangerous locations, where the objective was just to save a handful of civilians.

His head felt too foggy to think it over. He could still hear Binkowski's screams in his ears. He could still see Fisher falling to the pavement. And his brain kept replaying a certain false memory of him radioing the chopper on their way out. Undoubtedly, it was his subconscious beating into him what he should have done but failed to do. Had it played out that way, Kane would be partaking in this debate.

Reimer couldn't even think of anything to say. Nor did he desire to contribute in another debate between these two. Instead, he passed between them and entered the barracks. He walked down the long row of bunks, before finding unit D-38. He crashed down and stared up at the ceiling. Veils of glassy imagery curtained his vision and he dozed off.

CHAPTER 6

General Spears sat near the middle of a long rectangular table. The room was brightly lit, the interior completely clean. The conference building was only fifty miles from the new capital, which was still undergoing construction. During which time, the President and staff were sheltered in a large bunker. Just like in past presidencies, he still had a secret service following his every move. Currency still moved in the functioning area of the country. Only now, taxes were much higher. New laws were being enforced, including the outlawing of prolonged unemployment for anyone without a disability.

Spears was surprised how few government officials were attending this meeting. It was just the President, Vice President, and the Border station Commander, all sitting across from him. Often, such meeting would include the Chief of Staff, Secretary of Defense, and numerous Senators.

The President was a man in his mid-fifties. Three years ago, at the time of his election, he could've passed for a decade older. But inheriting the worst time in a nation's history had visibly aged the man. He still wore his suit without any unwanted speck or wrinkle. His tie was straight and his demeanor calm, as though he had total control of the situation.

Part of that was due to having greater control. It was already determined that there would be no election cycle come next year. Emergency powers had been granted during the time of the outbreak, giving him the authority to evacuate to the west coast. But Spears never questioned his actions or authority. In times like this, it was best to be a good soldier and get in line.

The Commander stood at the front of the desk, addressing the radio call his team had intercepted thirty minutes prior. He pointed to the satellite imaging on the map, with a red pin on the approximate location. It was in Montana, roughly 500 miles from the border.

"And that's it," the Border Commander concluded. The President rotated in his chair and looked at General Spears. He clasped his hands and leaned forward slightly, his facial expression as cold as ice.

"General, it is IMPERITIVE that this subject be extracted," he said. He carefully enunciated each word as he spoke in an effort to get the point across. "I know what the rules of engagement are. But this is Top Priority."

"How soon can you make it happen?" the Vice President said. The question also served as a statement. These leaders were applying pressure to the General. He had felt it a hundred times before.

"Sirs," he began. "We are running short on manpower. I can, and will, make this operation happen, but you will have to give me some time. My best team has just arrived over the border. Staff Sergeant Keegan's unit. I'm sure you remember his name." The President nodded. After all, he was the one to implore Spears to order that team into the hospital after it was declared above Level 5. "I want him leading the charge."

"Good. I want the best going out there," the President said.

"Why would this present a delay?" the Vice President asked.

"They just lost three more marines on a rescue op in Idaho," Spears explained. "Frankly, to conduct an operation such as this, there will undoubtedly be casualties...."

"I'm sorry, General, but it's peanuts compared to the cost of not completing the mission," the Vice President said.

"I'm aware, sir. But to maximize the possibility of success, we need to have a larger team sent in of at least ten personnel. To do this, I'm gonna have to reassign men from other units, and with most of my units being unavailable, I'm left with few options other than to wait for some of those units to return."

"I have a simple solution," the Vice President said. "There are men available in Naval Base Kitsap and there are Army personnel in our newly constructed facility in northern California. We will send some of their manpower up here."

"Good idea," the President said. "It flows into our discussed ideas of condensing the military branches into a unified armed force, with three environmental commands."

"What else would you need, General?" asked the Vice President.

"The team is going to need special equipment for them. Considering the terrain and outbreak level, there won't likely be a good place for the chopper to set down in that area. It won't be the same kind of simple pick-up operation like most of the others. They will be on foot for a good part of the journey, meaning stealth is the key. That being said, I'm going to have to arrange chopper flights and refueling. Because of travel time on foot, the chopper will not be able to wait. It will have to return, or risk being overrun while the team is out on mission."

"So, when then?" the President asked. "Tonight?"

"Having this op at night is almost a guaranteed fail," Spears said. "At best, it'll be early dawn. If you can, I would suggest continuing to regain contact with the VIP. If you do, tell her to remain in the bunker until we arrive." The President inhaled slowly. His stern face expressed dissatisfaction with the delay. However, he did understand the situation. The military was spread thin with multiple missions at once, and their numbers were dwindling by the day.

"Okay. Thank you, General. That's what we will do," he said. "Keep me updated. As I've said before, it is IMPERITIVE that Dr. Stacy Hill be brought back in one piece. The future of humanity might be resting on it. You understand me?"

"Yes, Mr. President," General Spears answered. "I understand."

CHAPTER 7

Reimer could not stay asleep for longer than an hour at a time. He hoped that being on his own bunk would remedy the situation but being away from the action somehow made it worse. Every time he managed to doze off, images of his fellow marines flashed in his unconscious mind. It was something he repeated on a daily basis, only now it felt worse. The only way he could think to describe it was being really far away. The fifth time was the worst. Binkowski's screams seemed to echo through the sky as he was watching a marine be eaten alive on concrete pavement several yards away. The dreams triggered stress in his brain, causing a wave of adrenaline that snapped him back into reality. Each time, he woke up as exhausted as he was when he had laid down.

It was sometime in the middle of the night when he decided to get out of the bunk. Dunn was sound asleep a few rows down, snoring loud enough to bring the building down. By now there were only a few other marines sleeping in the barracks, as many of them were still out on duty.

Reimer went to the sink and splashed water over his face. The sensation of grime was constant. No matter what he did, it always felt as though he had his face buried in grit. After hitting his eyes with a third handful of water, he stared at himself in the mirror. His face was unshaven for two days, which was something he would have to correct. But in this moment, he didn't care. He needed to get his mind off the constant nightmare that replayed in his brain.

****

Ceiling lights beamed down over the training facility. He stood at the start line, reloading the issued Cold 9mm SMG. In front of him was a large plywood setup of a building structure, with a few concrete obstacles for him to maneuver around. Rectangular holes had been carved out to mimic windows in the two-story structure. The Corporal finished loading and waited for the timer to go off. This was his second go at the raid course. Even at night, there was a training officer always manning the station. Marines were allowed to come in on their own endeavor, provided they use no more than two magazine's worth of ammunition. The trainer, a stone-faced Sergeant who stood a foot taller than Reimer, walked out from the setup after rearranging the targets. He always had a different scenario to challenge trainees. After all, running the same setup over and over would create a sense of rehearsed action, which was counter intuitive for trying to hone spur-of-the-moment marksmanship.

The buzzer went off. Reimer burst through the plywood entrance. There was the first target of an illustrated ghoul lunging with outstretched jaws. He aimed for the bullseye on its head. A three round burst hit around it. Good enough in his eyes, as long as he hit the damn head.

Reimer weaved through a bend in the pathway before coming to an open entry to the left. He hugged the corner for a moment then whipped inside. The room was clear. Reimer proceeded back into the hallway, finding another room on the right. In the back was a large corpse. He put two bullets in it and began to exit the room.

"Ah! Ah!" the arms trainer said. "Still alive, marine!" Reimer looked back. His bullets went low, one through the neck, the other through the mouth. The trainer did not let up. "Get it! It's on you now! It's got its arms around your neck! It's gonna rip your damn guts out!"

Reimer sprayed bullets, destroying the illustration that was the ghoul's face. He whipped back into the hallway, the trainer following at his heels. He took a right turn and entered a lobby. He managed to shoot around the 'human' targets, striking the ghouls in the head. The opposite door led him upstairs, where the final target awaited.

A thin cardboard slide sprang up, propped by a mechanical prop. As instructed, he plunged his bayonet into its head, sending thin shards of carboard into the air as he ripped it free. He aimed the rifle as another prop held dual targets. The first one was that of a fallen marine, the other was a ghoul that was drawn to seem as though it was about to devour him.

Flash imagery of his teammates pounded the Corporal's mind, causing a complete freeze-up.

"What are you doing! You're getting your teammate killed, you dumb shit! You fucking coward!" the trainer yelled. The Corporal tensed, then ran forward as the trainer continued to shout. "You waited too long! He's dead now! Good going!"

Reimer ignored him, proceeding to kick the target with his boot. He aimed down and emptied his mag into the shoulders, neck, and torso. The enraged action even caught the trainer by surprise.

"Whoa! Knock it off, cowboy. You're wasting precious bullets!" he said. He clicked on the timer. "Three minutes, seventeen seconds. You blew it at the end there, Corporal. Don't know what your issue was today. Whatever happened to the badass that duel-wielded Berettas like he was in a video game?"

"I thought you hated that," Reimer muttered.

"I do. It's dumb practice you only see in the movies. But at least you had your confidence and kept your temper under control. Better keep yourself in check, boy, because you fail like that out there, you'll end up like one of those drooling freaks. Now, unload your weapon and set it on the table. Your two freebies are up."

Reimer was already halfway done. He set the weapon down and yanked his pistol free. After ejecting the mag and clearing the slide, he placed everything down next to the submachine gun. Without saying a word, he walked out of the training station.

The cool air felt refreshing as he walked back to the barracks. It was a quarter mile walk from the training station, but something about it was therapeutic. Perhaps it was the quiet. Looking around, the area was void of activity except for a few night patrols. Looking to the east, he could see the lights lining the top of the Border.

At that moment, the brief peace he felt slipped away. He knew that behind that wall were hordes of the undead, all clamoring to get into the safe zone. In the silence he could hear their combined moans echoing in the night. He wasn't sure whether he was literally hearing them or if it was just his imagination. It didn't matter, as either one would be enough to bring back the images of death to the forefront of his mind.

He quickened the pace of his walk until he reached the barracks. He reached to open the front door, only to step back as it opened before he could touch it. There stood Gordon, all dressed up in tactical gear. He looked to Reimer with equal surprise.

"Corporal? I thought you had already gone," he said.

"No, I'm just getting back from the range," Reimer said. He could see Dunn approaching the entrance behind Gordon. He too, was geared up and ready to go. "What's going on?"

"We've got new orders. We're supposed to report to the hangar bay for briefing. Keegan's already there," Gordon said. "Where did you go?"

"Just getting my ass kicked by paper drawings," Reimer said.

"Surprised any of us had time to do that," Dunn bickered. "Or anything for that matter. Hell, I thought they'd at least let us get a full night's sleep before shipping us off on another wild goose chase."

"Have they said anything about where we're going?" Reimer asked.

"They said they'll tell us at the briefing," Dunn answered. "Now, if you would excuse me." Reimer stood out of the way as Dunn proceeded to march for the hangar bay. Reimer could sense the suspicion in his voice. Even before hearing the details, he was already questioning Command's purpose for sending them. Usually, when notified, the team was at least given a location and outbreak level right away, then given the rest of the details at briefing. Sometimes, it would even be while en route to the site. Something about this seemed more on the DL. Already dressed and ready to go, Reimer followed his fellow marines to the hangar bay.

In the hangar, Keegan stood alongside a Sikorsky Seahawk helicopter. The rotors were already turning, generating gusts of wind that kicked up sand and gravel.

"Come on, ladies, we don't have all damn day! Get aboard," he said to them. The three marines picked up the pace and boarded the chopper. Keegan slammed the fuselage door shut. "Hope ya'll got a good nap, because you've been chosen for a special mission."

"Yeah?" Dunn remarked. "We going on a grocery run? President need some ding dongs?"

"Knock it off," Reimer said.

"Why would he need ding dongs when he has you?" Gordon quipped. "So, seriously, what is it Sarge? Another rescue op?"

"That's correct," Keegan said. "Special VIP. Top Priority."

"Oh, really?" Dunn said, his voice complete with sarcasm. "Who is it this time? Somebody's niece?"

"A doctor," Keegan said.

"A doctor?!" Dunn remarked. "Haven't we rescued a hundred of them by now?"

"Not like this one."

"Why? Is she hot?" Gordon quipped.

"Maybe," Keegan said. "More importantly, she might know how to save the human race." The marines sat silently. Even Dunn's interest was piqued. Keegan smiled. He knew that'd get their attention.

CHAPTER 8

The marines disembarked in a base just west of what used to be Baker City. There, they entered another hangar, which was located less than a hundred yards away from the Border. Like Fort Anese, the area seemed empty, as many of the personnel were out on missions.

They passed through the enormous closed building structure. It was like a vast cave made from steel, void of almost any aircraft. For them, it was odd to see it so empty. Only one helicopter, a Sikorsky CH-53E Super Stallion, rested in place. Seeing Navy mechanics testing the rotors and giving it its checkup, Reimer knew it was a safe bet that he was looking at their ride.

They passed into a corridor on the left and entered what appeared to be a classroom-style setting. There, six other soldiers were seated and waiting. General Spears stood at the front. He held a remote for an overhead projection device on the ceiling.

"Marines, meet the rest of your squad. These men will be going in with you."

"Going where?" Dunn asked.

"About to find that out, son," a deep voice called out from across the room. The marines gazed across the room, unsure which of the soldiers spoke out.

"Let me help you out," Spears said. "Marines, meet Lance Corporal Bolden." The soldier stood up, his six-and-a-half-foot stature towering over the others.

"Should we just call him *Goliath*?" Reimer joked.

"And I'll call you *John Wayne*," Bolden said. He was eyeballing the two Berettas strapped to the marine's thighs.

Spears grinned. "I suggest you get to know each other. We're gonna be starting in a moment." The General turned and accompanied Keegan in the next room.

The nearest soldier stood up and extended his hand. "Howdy. Name's Carlson." Reimer shook his hand. Then Gordon. Carlson reached over to shake Dunn's, who simply stared at his hand. The cuff of the sleeve had peeled back a bit, revealing a tattoo of an Air Force Cross.

"You're not marines," he said. "Who the hell are all you?"

"Due to lack of available personnel, they had to *branch* out a bit," Carlson joked.

"I know the marines are short of personnel, but are we really THAT short?" Reimer asked.

"Yes, actually. They were gonna pair you up with another marine unit, but their last rescue resulted in a bad crash. All members KIA. Another unit was overrun while attempting a rescue mission near L.A. They set their chopper down, and just couldn't keep the freaks off of them."

"Jesus!"

"Not to mention the issues down by Gold Beach," Bolden said.

"What's going on at Gold Beach?" Gordon asked.

"People are flocking here from the Pacific," Carlson said. "We're like the only functioning entity in the world right now. Europe is in shambles. China's got a few settlements as far as we can tell. I think Russia's government is still functioning, sort of. Hate to sound political, but one big reason we held out the best is our good ol' right to bear arms!"

"Now we know," said one of the men sitting beside him. "Washington, Jefferson, and Adams KNEW we were gonna have a zombie epidemic! They totally knew!"

Carlson pointed down at the two men dressed in Navy camouflage. "Meet Cable and Dallas, both Navy. Believe it or not, Dallas is a heavy gunner. Doesn't look it, though."

The Navy gunner shifted in his seat. The only thing shorter than his height was his temper. He spat on the floor.

"You talk too much, Carlson," Dallas said in a cold tone.

"I concur," Dunn said. "What about you?" The other Navy sailor, Cable, looked up.

"Communications and navigation," he said. "Wherever we're going, radio signals are sporadic. That's where I come in. I'll be the guy with the SAT phone and map."

"You've already met Bolden back there," the talkative Carlson continued. "He's an Army Ranger, previously with the 75th Battalion."

"Gotta love his voice! We call him James Earl Jones," a muscular bearded soldier joked from the middle of the room. He munched on chewing tobacco while offering a casual wave to the team's new additions. "Lance Corporal Bell!"

"*Bell*? I hope you gave your parents hell for that," Reimer joked.

"Part of the All-Lady-Tank-Crew," Bell proudly announced. Reimer looked to Carlson for clarification.

"See, all four dudes in his armored unit had names that could be passed for a lady," the Air Force Paratrooper said. "There was Francis, Casey…I forget the third…you get the idea."

"I see you all want to be marines now," Dunn quipped. "Now you'll know what it's like to do some real work."

"Actually, you got one more. Private Lowry! He's a marine, fresh out of boot!" Carlson said. The marines looked to the back of the room, seeing an eighteen-year old kid sitting quietly in his seat. He stood and gave a proper salute to his new teammates.

"You okay kid?" Reimer asked. "You look like you don't want to be here."

"He's smart," Bell said.

"I'm okay, sir," Lowry said. "Life has taken a sudden turn in the past few months is all."

"Hasn't it for all of us?" Dunn said as he pulled a chair from behind the back table.

"Not what he means," Bolden's booming voice called out. "You DO know they've reinstated the draft...right?" All three marines perked up.

"No," Reimer said.

"Good lord, have you three been living under a rock?" Dallas, the cranky Navy gunner griped.

"No," Dunn said, hostility in his voice. "Like I said, we've actually been working for a living."

"Don't mind Dallas," Carlson said. "He's always in a bad mood. Hence, we've nicknamed him *Callous*."

"I know the type," Reimer said, glancing to Dunn. He turned his eyes back to the young marine. He understood now. Here he was, having received his draft notice, now fresh out of boot, about to be sent on his first mission. And now, he was listening to talks of marines dying in the line of combat. He didn't ask for this. As far as Reimer was concerned, he had the most right to be unhappy with this situation. "Don't worry, Lowry. These men and I will have your back."

"And not the way they do it in the Navy," Gordon quipped.

"Oh, ha-ha," Cable said. General Spears and Staff Sergeant Keegan stepped out of the office and stood off to the side.

"Okay! Sounds like you're all acquainted. Let's get started!" He dimmed the lights, while Keegan tapped various notes into the computer. Its monitor was linked to the projector, which brought up an image of a woman in her early-to-mid thirties.

Wolf whistles streaked from the team as they looked at the image. Gordon's earlier question had been answered. With blond hair that hung an inch beneath her shoulders, innocent looking eyes, and spotless tan skin, she was VERY attractive to look at.

"This is our contact," Spears explained. "You've already heard this, but I'll say it again: this subject is TOP PRIORITY!"

"You don't say," Cable said.

"Knock it off," Keegan said. "Don't forget, sailor, you're under MY command now."

"Her name is Dr. Stacy Hill," Spears explained. "She's a genetic researcher, specializing in virus mutation. She's worked for the CDC, and now is directly overseen by staff who report directly to the President. She's been studying the contagion from day one in the hopes of developing a cure. We received her transmission yesterday afternoon. It was an SOS signal from a government bunker located in the cliffs of Montana. Your orders are to extract this woman and bring her back. Alive."

"A researcher," Dunn said with a smirk. "There's been hundreds of them studying this thing since it began, most of them federal. What's so important about her?"

"What's important is that you shut up and follow your orders," Keegan snapped at him.

"To answer your question," Spears said, "this person actually did it." The room went silent.

"Hold on," Bolden's voice boomed. "Sir, you mean to say that this person actually has the *cure* for this virus?"

"That is correct."

"Like...does it make the undead...not-dead?" Carlson asked, unsure how to word the question.

"No, son," Spears answered. "From what I understand, whatever formula she's created will prevent the rest of us from being infected. So, whenever someone dies, regardless of the cause, we won't have to worry about them getting back up again. Another thing, if you were to be bitten by one of the ghouls, theoretically you shouldn't turn."

"Like I said, men: you will be saving the world."

"Shit, aren't we a little late for that?" Dallas asked.

"It's never too late for that," Spears said, his voice stern. "Keep in mind, marines, soldiers, and sailors..."

"Damn, I feel left out," Carlson muttered.

"...Mankind's been battling plagues from the start. Perhaps we were overdue. Maybe. Maybe Mother Nature had it in for us. Maybe she planned to wipe us out entirely. But the U.S. Military does not adhere to that. That's where you men come into play. YOU are gonna go toe-to-toe with Mother Nature, and bitch-slap her across the fucking face."

"And where is it that we're gonna bitch-slap her?" Bell asked, his teeth yellow from the chewing tobacco. Spears fought against a solemn feeling that started to boil within. He hit a button on the remote to bring up the map. It was a satellite image of a forest region. In the center was a red square marked several inches south of a large lake.

"It's in the Gallatin National Forest, Bordering Yellowstone National Park," Spears said.

"Shouldn't this be an easy pickup?" Reimer asked. "If we know where the bunker is located, can't we just chopper down, send someone with a harness, and haul the Doc aboard?"

"I wish it could be that simple," Spears said. "The problem is the canopy. It's too high for us to put you down right there. The forest is thick in that region, with trees standing as high as a hundred and eighty feet. Unfortunately, we're gonna have to put you down around this region here near the town." He pointed at a cement-colored spot on the map. "You're gonna disembark around this area here, in this nearby town. Satellite imaging shows that the number of infected should be low enough for a successful incursion. We're instructing the pilots to keep far enough away from the town, due to the large gathering of hostiles."

"Sir, that's like three or four miles away from the target zone!" Cable said.

"I'm aware," Spears said. "That's why you have to move silently. The area is going to be crawling with the infected, so you won't want to attract attention."

"Oh, I KNEW it," Dunn said. "What is the outbreak level?"

"Listen, men," Spears said. "I would never send you into such a dangerous area if the mission wasn't of ABSOLUTE importance."

"Sir?" Dunn said.

"Bear in mind, this was one of the earliest locations to fall. It's where the first documentation took place. It's part of the reason why we established a foothold on the west coast in an attempt to prevent..."

"SIR?!" Dunn was standing up now.

General Spears stopped and turned to look at him. "Yes, Marine."

"What is it? What is the outbreak level?"

Spears took a breath. "Outbreak is at...Level..." he took another breath, "Ten."

The room came alive with loud exclamations. In the blink of an eye, the disciplined military personnel's calm disappeared into unruly clamoring. Even Keegan was astounded by the information. He stood silently, taking several seconds to process what they were going into, before remembering to take control of the team.

"Okay, knock it off!" The soldiers quieted down, with the exception of Dunn and Dallas. "Get your act together. Quit acting like a bunch of virgins."

"There's always a catch," Dunn said. "Good ol' Uncle Sam's gonna have us prodding around a Zombie Outbreak Level 10...a Z-Level 10!"

"Hope that cure works, cause nobody's coming out of that place untouched," Bell said.

"Sir?" Cable stood up. "If that's a Z-Level 10, and this Dr. Hill is such a high-value scientist, what the hell is she doing in such a hot zone? Why wasn't she extracted at the start?"

"And how the hell does an area like that become a level-fucking-ten?!" Dunn said. "It's not New York City!"

"Like I mentioned before, this location was one of the earliest to fall," Spears said. "Several CDC and military personnel were sent to the region to help contain it, which only resulted with more and more being infected. We weren't sure exactly what the disease was at that time, so the proper quarantine procedures weren't being followed."

"Was Dr. Hill there for that?" Reimer asked.

"Initially, yes," Spears said. "She was sent there as part of a team. Despite the team being overrun and most killed, she decided to stay and continue studying the cause of the outbreak and develop an anti-virus. During which time, she was given coordinates to a bunker, as well as the necessary codes. During the last several months, we hadn't heard anything from her, which forced us to assume she was KIA until receiving the SOS."

"Listen up, fellas. There's no choice in the matter," Keegan said. "We're low on manpower, and unfortunately the world doesn't care about our staffing problems. The longer we wait, the more likely Dr. Hill will be dead, and her data lost forever. Meaning all of this will be for nothing."

"What the Staff Sergeant means is that you all don't have a say in this," General Spears said. "You can complain all you want, but it won't change a damn thing. You'll still be getting on that chopper. Give me a problem and before I'm through with you, you'll be begging to be eaten alive by the infected." He turned to face Keegan. "Sergeant, why don't you show them to the armory."

"Yes, sir. Men, follow me!" The group stood up from their seats and assembled out in the hangar. On their way out, Dunn tapped Reimer on the shoulder.

"What did I tell you?" he barked.

"This is different," Reimer said. "At least the objective makes sense. Calm down."

"*Calm down*? Corporal, we're going into territory that'll make Idaho look like a picnic."

"Quit losing your head," Gordon said. "Look, I'm scared too. But with everything that's going on, they wouldn't waste our men and resources if this individual wasn't of great importance."

"Right, sure! You keep telling yourself that, Gordon. I'm not buying it. I'm sick of having my ass put on the line for petty shit!"

"Then stay behind," Reimer said as he followed the rest of the unit out.

"Believe me...if I could..." Dunn shook his head in anger, then reluctantly followed the others. After they assembled, Keegan led then across the hangar to the armory.

CHAPTER 9

"We will NOT be using our standard armaments," Keegan explained to the unit as they assembled into the armory. Several tables were lined up with tactical gear, grenades, weapons, and ammo. "As you well know, the ghouls are highly attracted to sound. Considering their high numbers in the region, it is of utmost importance that we remain silent as we journey to our destination."

"What about suppressors, sir?" the rookie asked.

"It depends on the weapon, but suppressors aren't like how they are in the movies," Keegan explained. "They tone down the volume, but typically, the gunshots are still loud enough to attract the undead. So, General Spears took the time to gather some actual silent weapons for us." Keegan grabbed an army-colored bolt action rifle and pulled back on the bolt. "This is an Accuracy International .308. It's designed by our lost friends in the United Kingdom. It's a manually actuated bolt action system. Holds five rounds at a time. Effective at 800 meters."

"Sir, we're gonna need more than five rounds at a time if we're going into a Level 10," Cable said.

"Sailor, I'm aware of that," Keegan said. "Problem is, you fire a single shot from your M4 or H&K, suppressed or not, you'll bring every ghoul in Montana down on us." He shoved the rifle into Cable's hands then moved to the next table. He held up the next weapon, which was a submachine gun. "This is an Izhmash AK-9. This is a shortened format, AK-105 variety. Nine-by-thirty-nine caliber and adjustable iron sights. It's got a removeable suppressor. Its magazine capacity is twenty rounds. It's capable of firing subsonic and standard ammunition. This gun is VERY quiet. Check this out."

Keegan moved to the other side of the large room, where an indoor shooting range was set up. Without putting on ear protection, he inserted the magazine and aimed the AK-9 down range. With it set on semi-automatic, he fired off three rounds. All the team could hear was a light *puff* with each shot, barely breaking the sound barrier. The puffs were rapid as he fired off the rest of the magazine in full auto, tearing up the paper target twenty meters at the end of the range.

"Damn Russians making us look bad," Carlson quipped.

"We're still here. They're not," Keegan said. He held the gun out for Carlson to take, then grabbed another example. "Also, we have the Suppressed M3A1 Grease Gun. Here, Dunn, this looks like your style."

"Thanks a lot, Sarge," Dunn responded, taking the submachine gun from Keegan.

"Listen up. We will be packing explosives, MP5s and Carbines along with us as backup, but we will primarily be using the weapons I've shown you here. Now get your asses geared up. I encourage you all to take a few practice rounds at the range there. Especially you, Carlson. We know you Air Force guys can't shoot for shit. Army's not much better. Meet in the hangar in ten."

"My feelings are hurt, Sarge," Carlson quipped.

"Feelings? Only pussies have feelings," Keegan said. He picked up his AK-9 and walked toward the hangar. As he walked past Carlson, he allowed a brief smile. "That why you joined the Air Force?"

"This is gonna be a long trip," Carlson said. He joined the others at the range and fired off several rounds. The target at the end disappeared into a series of paper shards that sprinkled down, leaving several holes in the center. After emptying the magazine, he gazed at the weapon. The AK-9 was very quiet indeed.

Reimer took several shots with the Accuracy International. Like the AK-9, it barely broke the sound barrier. Using the scope, he punched several rounds into the red of the paper.

"I'll be using this," he said.

"I'd take one of these as well," Dunn said, handing him an AK-9. "The freaks aren't gonna allow you time to get set up like that. Plus, I doubt there'll be a nice fencepost for you to rest it on."

"In that country? I wouldn't doubt it," Bell said. The Army Ranger grabbed an AK-9 and familiarized himself. The weapon seemed to disappear in his enormous hands. The burly soldier emptied his mag. The weapon wasn't too different from weapons he had fired in the past. In fact, he really liked it. He turned to look at his Army buddy, Bolden. "Maybe they'll finally promote us when we get back."

"If we get back," Dallas remarked.

"Hell, I better make it back," Bell said. "I was supposed to be out in March. That includes Reserve Duty."

"Wait," Dunn said. He lowered his voice to not be heard by anyone outside. "You're supposed to be out by now?"

"Yeah. Wait? You too?" he asked.

"Yes!" Dunn said. "I'm assuming you've been in for eight years. And you're a Lance Corporal?"

"Yeah."

"Fuck, you should be a freaking Sergeant by now. Hell, maybe even an E-8 by now."

"What are you?"

"E-fucking-2," Dunn said. "They keep docking me. It's almost like they're trying to keep as many grunts as possible."

"There's a lot of weird shit going on, man," Dallas said. "I'm telling you, we're not just doing typical rescue missions."

"Thank you!" Dunn said. "I'm telling you, these politicians are working around the system. The rules are simple. If it's a Z-Level 6 or up, we don't go in. Plain and simple. But yet, they keep sending us into these areas where the threat level "happens" to increase while we're en-route. Every single time, we're picking up somebody or something that has some sort of connection to the big wigs. Seems like if they owe a favor to a major contributor, boom! Just send the military to the rescue. No problem. We'll only lose three more people than we'll save. But hey, the special interest can still contribute to the presidency when he's in behind the border."

"Fuck, man," Dallas said. "There's all kinds of shit going on. I heard one unit had to be diverted to the southeast bend of the wall to keep migrants from getting in. Another guy let it slip to me that he and his fellas had to burn a bunch of documents in a federal building."

"What the hell's all that about?" Dunn said.

"I don't know, but it sounds like they're erasing physical profiles of certain people. That, or there's something else they don't want anyone to know. Hell, maybe they're the ones who started the apocalypse."

"Wouldn't put it past them," Dunn said.

"Good God, you guys are paranoid," Gordon said. He burst out in laughter as he strolled out the door.

"He's the patriotic type," Dunn muttered.

"I miss being that," Dallas said.

"I still am," Bell said. "But it doesn't mean I trust everyone calling the shots."

"HEY LADIES!" Keegan called. "The hell's going on in there? Having an orgy or something?"

"Hell, no, sir," Dunn said. He went to the table and loaded up with grenades and Beretta magazines. "Shit!" he yelled as one grenade nearly slipped from his fingers. As he secured it, he could hear Carlson laughing at him. "What's so funny, dweeb?"

"You know what they say," Carlson said. "Leave a marine in a round room with a steel ball, he'll either loose it, break it, or get it pregnant."

"You know, you remind me of someone I knew at the enlistment office. He was standing by the Air Force desk, saw three pairs of marines standing in the booth and two sets of pull up bars. He wanted to go but realized he was too short to reach the bars. So, he stuck with the Air Force booth."

"Dude, stand straight. I'm an inch taller than you!" Carlson bantered.

"Your ten minutes is up! Get your asses out here, ladies! On the double! Move it!"

Even Dunn hustled at the sound of Keegan's voice. He followed the rest of his squad outside, where the Sikorsky Super Stallion had been rolled out of the hangar. The ramp door yawned open under the ninety-nine-foot long aircraft's tail. Standing outside the cockpit were the two pilots. The one with a Lieutenant insignia had a smile on his face as he prepared to board the craft. The other pilot noticed Dunn and Reimer's odd expression as they noticed the jolly-looking pilot.

"Don't mind Lieutenant Heard, he's an adrenaline junkie," the other pilot said. "Don't worry. Ensign Zucco," he raised his hand, "is here to keep him from getting you into too much trouble."

"If he wants trouble, he's going to the right place," Reimer said.

"Hell, if he's looking for a rush, he can fast-rope down and I'll fly the bird," Dunn said.

"He's more of a 'rollercoaster ride' kind of a guy," Zucco said.

"Hell yeah," Heard said. "Let's get this rollercoaster ride on the way. Once more into the breach, dear mates!"

"Your wife's already been to my bunk," Bolden called out.

"Get aboard," Keegan scolded them.

"You *can* fly this thing, right?" Gordon said to Heard.

"Is that a question?" Heard said.

"Well, you know. I've seen plenty of montages of Navy aircraft splashing down. You guys are like ducks. Just can't stay out of the water. And there's a lake where we're going."

"That why you couldn't join the marines?" Dunn added.

"Actually, I originally enlisted in the marines," Heard said. "But then they said I wasn't a good fit since my parents were married!"

"Hey man," Gordon joked. "Thank the marines for your existence! We invented sex!"

"Yeah, but the Army introduced it to women!" Bell called out. Laughter echoed through the hangar as the men boarded the chopper. Heard and Zucco sat into the cockpit and activated the flight systems. The seven-blade rotor began to rotate as the hangar doors opened. Sunlight streamed across the early morning horizon, reflecting off Heard's aviator glasses.

"Let's get this show on the road," he said. The rotors increased speed, elevating the Super Stallion into a low hovering flight. With a change in angle, he accelerated the aircraft over the Border.

Inside the cabin, the team continued exchanging their banter as they endured the mild turbulence from takeoff. Reimer sat quietly, grinning as he listened to the men exchange shots at the other military branches. This was a unique crew indeed, but it helped ease the stress of what was to come.

Private Lowry was seated next to him. Unlike the others, he was not in the moment. He was constantly looking out the window. Every twitch in his face was reminiscent of someone on their first mission. It was something Reimer could relate to, even now.

"You'll be fine, kid," he said.

"I'm not sure I will. This is a fucking Z-Level 10," Lowry whispered. "I'm not made for this, sir."

"Yes, you are," Reimer said. "You're a Marine, whether you want to be or not. Time to grow up and act the part. It's the only way you'll make it out alive." Reimer wondered if he was only talking to the rookie, or himself as well. Suddenly, he found himself looking out the window. The chopper was only about three-hundred feet high. The Border was still in view. In front of it was a large moving mass comprised of hundreds of the undead. From high above they looked like ants trying to besiege an enemy anthill. Flamethrower units seared the corpses, driving them back and preventing them from forming mounds of bodies. From afar, the flames looked like tiny sparks as the chopper gained altitude and distance.

"How long till we get there?" the nervous Lowry asked.

"About five-hundred miles. The pilots are pushing our speed to one-ninety. About two-and-a-half hours."

Lowry laid his head back, nervously tapping his foot on the floor. The wait seemed to worsen his anxiety. Reimer could feel his heart fluttering as well. Each time he shut his eyes, he saw another flash of memories, many of them of teeth and curling fingers from outstretched hands. His nostrils were filled, not only with the rotting smell of corpses, but of fresh blood. Each time he lost a teammate, that smell was further ingrained in his senses. The very sight of his teammates, combined with his fear of what lay ahead, triggered that dreaded scent.

Reimer stared at the window, trying to conceal the very same anxiety the rookie displayed.

CHAPTER 10

The landscape changed from coastal, to urban, to rural, as the chopper passed over miles of country. Gordon stared out the window, watching the scenery pass underneath as though on a film reel. As the pilots counted up their miles, the vegetation changed from pastoral to large groupings of trees including various firs, pines and broadleaf species. At the moment, the ground was still visible, displaying vacant communities and empty roads that stretched through the landscape like veins. But as he looked east, he saw nothing but green fill the upcoming countryside.

All at once, it was beautiful and horrifying. From high above, the area seemed untouched, leaving a serene environment. But it was serene only to the naked eye. It was when his conscious mind remembered the death which lurked in that supposedly peaceful environment that the dreaded feeling took over. Looking closer, he could see cars and trucks overturned. Bridges had been collapsed either from explosives or under the excessive weight of vehicle pileups. In the ditches they crossed over were various smashed vehicles, some blackened by fire.

A flashing streak of red suddenly passed high over the green landscape. Gordon's eyes opened wide, now alert. A small trail of smoke twirled behind the streaking light.

"Staff Sergeant!" Gordon called out. Keegan stepped out from his seat and hurried over. "We've got a flare! Someone's trying to hail us."

Intrigued by the information, the team grouped to the starboard side. Pushing their faces into the windows, they watched the flare angle downward. It was nearly a quarter-mile off to starboard and was beginning to dissipate.

"Looks like someone saw our chopper and are hoping for pickup," Reimer said.

"That's a shame," Dunn barked. Reimer and Gordon looked at him with disgust.

"Seriously, dude?" Gordon said.

"Yeah, seriously," Dunn said. "That is not the mission. There's a reason we're not constantly setting down for pickups in this region."

"Lieutenant, how's our fuel situation?" Keegan spoke into the headset's microphone.

"We have enough for a brief diversion," Heard responded. "As long as you don't spend too much time. This mission is under your jurisdiction, so it's up to you."

Another flare ripped into the sky, launched from the same location.

"Damn it, Sarge," Gordon said. "We have plenty of room."

"True, but we don't know how many fellas are hoping to fetch a ride," Bell said.

"The General didn't specifically say anything against picking up stragglers along the way," Carlson said.

"No, he only repeated 'Top Priority' a hundred times," Dunn said. "He'd be pissed if we risked our mission to check on someone..." he stood up, "who may be attempting to set up an AMBUSH and steal our supplies!"

Keegan knew he had to make a decision fast. Doing so seemed to be getting harder and harder. Occasionally, he found himself being the judge between duty and morality. He always thought it would get easier with age and experience. Turns out he was wrong.

"Damn it," he muttered. "Pilots, take us in closer. Let's have a look. If it's too dangerous, we'll move along."

"You got it," Heard said. The chopper turned to starboard and zipped toward the flare.

"You've got to be kidding, sir," Dunn said.

"Get a grip, Dunn," Keegan said.

"Not sure I disagree with him," Dallas said.

"I'm not sure I care," Keegan responded.

The chopper descended, barely clearing the fifty-foot trees as it passed over them.

"It was over here somewhere," Heard said. Suddenly, a voice started yelling over the radio receiver.

"Looks like they've found our frequency," Zucco said. "This is Echo-two-nine-Charlie, responding to emergency transmission."

"*Oh, yes! Thank God! We're less than a click to your right. We're in a two-story house in a small clearing. You'll see a big pond surrounded by a line of trees. We're right to the northeast of it.*"

"Standby," Zucco said. He looked over his shoulder at Keegan, who was now standing between them. "Your call, sir."

"How many are in their party?"

Zucco relayed. "Sir, how many are in your party?"

"*Three. Myself, one female, and another male. We're stuck on the roof. Those things, they're in the attic!*"

Heard and Zucco glanced at each other, the former mouthing, "In the attic?"

"Didn't know ghouls were known for climbing," Zucco remarked. He looked back up to the Sarge. "We're not going to be able to land.

You might be able to pull off a fast-rope incursion and haul them out with a harness."

"Coast Guard style," Heard joked. He steered the Super Stallion ten degrees to starboard until he located the clearing in the woods. He brought its nose over the edge, immediately spotting the lake. "There!" He pointed to the right, where the large house resided over a large hill. The beach and shallow waters were crawling with the undead. The front door was busted inwards. From what he could gather, these people had been holding out for months, until finally the undead managed to force their way in. Whatever the case was, they were stuck on the roof. Three people waved at them near the chimney stack.

"Fuck," Keegan groaned. "How low can you get me?"

"If you were just doing an incursion, you could do it as high as here," Heard said. "But we're talking about hauling up three persons. Which means, we're gonna want a lower altitude to save time. But we don't want the downdraft to knock them right off the roof, so we can't get too low. Best case, probably thirty-feet."

"Do it," Keegan ordered. He hustled toward the back. "Reimer, you're up!"

Shit. The Corporal silently grabbed a harness from the rack. The shakes, which were absent through most of the trip, were making a surprise return. He did his best to suppress them as he clipped the harness over his torso.

Dunn went up to him and helped him with attaching the spare harness to his. "Dude, you need to say something," he said.

"What?"

"I'm telling you, your ass is being put on the line for nothing," Dunn said.

"Dunn!" Keegan called out. Dunn's face tensed as he realized he'd been overheard.

"Sergeant, you sure about this idea?"

"Yes. And guess what? You just volunteered! Thank you for your contribution. Now get your harness on, because you're going down there with him!"

"Thanks a lot, Sarge," Dunn said. Reimer tossed him another harness. As he clipped it on, the pilots lowered the chopped into a descent. Keegan opened the bottom hatch. The wind swirled into the fuselage like an invisible tornado. Directly beneath them was the roof and the three civilians. They were waving their arms wildly, as if somehow the chopper would take off if they stopped. The look on their faces was made of pure terror, and their screams rivaled the drone of the rotors.

Reimer couldn't help but notice various holes in the roof. From what he could tell, it wasn't damage from wear and tear. Rather, they appeared fragmented as though something the size of a fist had burst its way up through from the attic.

"What's the holdup, PFC Dunn?" Keegan said.

"No holdup, sir," Dunn replied, his voice full of resentment. He clipped the secondary harness to his, then stood with Reimer at the hatch. Bell and Cable secured the ropes and handed one to the marines.

"Have fun with that," Cable said.

"I see why you Navy guys aren't going," Dunn said. "No frogman down there to save your ass when you fall!"

"Yeah, speaking of falling...don't!" Cable said.

"God, I've never heard such good advice," Dunn said.

"Done flirting, or are you gonna get down there?" Heard called from the cockpit.

Reimer went first. Gripping it with heat-resistant gloves, he gradually slid down his rope, using his feet to help control the pull of gravity. Dunn went directly after, descending just five feet behind the Corporal. The swirling air was warm and dusty, causing ripples across the pond's surface.

An ear-piercing scream pierced the air, followed by the screams of the other two. Behind those screams was the sound of splintering wood. Reimer looked down at the roof.

Only two people were atop of it, moving away from the chimney. Jagged sections of wood and roof tiles marked the edges of a large gaping hole where they had previously stood. Through the space, Reimer could see movement in the attic. With the shade cast from the trees, he couldn't get a clear look at the walking corpses inside. But the blood that splattered the edges was enough to know the civilian was gone. He could hear his screams resounding over the groans of living corpses as they tore him apart limb-from-limb.

The two remaining survivors huddled at the edge of the roof, standing twelve feet above the reaches of the undead that gathered below. The woman screamed and fought against the man's grip in a futile attempt to save her husband who had been dragged through the roof. The man kept his arms wrapped around her while yelling at her to stop.

Reimer swung forward and landed beside the large hole. Hands reached up from the attic, the skin peeling from the fingers as they tried grasping his boot. What little light made it through the hole landed on broken teeth that clunked together in gaping jaws. He pointed his submachine gun and fired, spraying bullets into the faces of several corpses. Reimer reloaded as Dunn set down beside him.

"What in the name of hell? Those things couldn't have pulled this down!"

"I'm not waiting to find out what did," Reimer said. The two marines ran toward the remaining civilians. The woman was now in a state of shock, her eyes gaped wide and her teeth clenched. The man kept his arms around her waist, unsure if she'd attempt another hopeless rescue.

Reimer slung his weapon and unclipped the spare harness. The man released the woman and reached out for the marine to secure the harness around his waist. Dunn took the woman, who made one last struggle to get to her dead husband.

"Ma'am!" Dunn yelled to be heard over the wind. "He's gone! I'm sorry, there's nothing we can do!"

"We need to get you up!" the man said to her. Reimer stepped around him to fasten it tighter. He clipped it around his torso, then reached for the metal clip that hung from his own harness.

An explosive tremor burst under his feet, shooting fragments of roof up around his face. Two jagged arms extended from the newly formed breach. The hands were large, twice as large as a normal person's. The fingers were elongated, extending nearly twelve inches from the knuckle. They grasped the man by the ankles, sinking curved nails through the battered jeans. The man yelled and grabbed at Reimer, who failed to hold him back as it pulled him below.

The woman screamed and staggered back from Dunn's reach.

"NO!" Dunn yelled as he lunged for her. It was too late. The woman's screams came to a sudden halt as she fell over the edge of the roof. She plummeted into the horde, breaking several bones as she hit the ground. Before her brain registered what had happened, she was looking at the countless hands that tore chunks from her body. One last scream escaped her lungs before her throat was torn from her neck. Rotting jaws munched on her flesh, separating the meat from the bone with their teeth.

"Damn it!" Reimer yelled.

Through the rupture, he could see the undead feasting on the man's limbs, all detached from the body. One walked while holding his head close to its chest like a basketball. Through their snarling, the marines could hear a tense growling sound, resembling that of a grizzly.

"Take us up!" Reimer said. "Take us up, now!"

The marines held tight to their ropes as the chopper ascended. As they lifted, another heavy impact rocked the roof. The claws reached out, falling millimeters short from hooking their boots. Dunn gazed down.

The ghoul, or whatever it was, had already dipped out of sight. All around the house, the undead were converging where the woman had fallen. Bodies crushed together as each one tried to squeeze in for a chunk of flesh.

The rope reeled up, bringing the two marines back into the fuselage. Dunn blew a sigh of relief upon feeling solid metal under his feet.

"Holy FUCK!" he yelled.

"What the hell was that?" Keegan said. "What happened down there?! Talk, Marine!"

"Don't know if it was a zombie on steroids, but it wasn't an ordinary corpse, I'll tell you that much!" Dunn said.

"It tore the roof out right under us," Reimer said. He fought to catch his breath. "We couldn't move fast enough. One target was already gone before we even touched down."

"We saw it," Carlson said. "What the hell was it? An animal?"

"Shit, probably a bear," Cable said.

"It was no fucking bear!" Dunn said. "Bears don't have claws like that."

"Claws? What claws?" Lowry asked.

"I don't know, we only saw them for like a second," Reimer said. "They were human, but…not."

"Probably just an over-rotted dead guy," Bolden said in his loud booming voice.

"Hey, Army, you do remember what happened to Darth Vader in Episode 6, right?" Dunn gripped his knife handle and grimaced at the Ranger.

"Keep in mind, Luke got his first," Bolden threatened back.

"Alright, you all knock it off. NOW! Everybody shut it!" Keegan ordered. The cabin quickly became dead silent. The soldiers spaced out, some taking their seats. Keegan turned to the pilots. "Proceed to the objective!"

"You got it, Staff Sergeant," Heard said.

"That was a supreme waste of time," Dunn muttered to himself. He inhaled a deep breath through his nose, then approached the Sergeant. "Sir, I must urge you to abandon this mission."

Keegan glared at him with pity and astonishment.

"Have you lost your nerve, Marine?"

"Sir, I'm telling you, this person is dead! And if she isn't, I guarantee she's nobody actually worth risking our lives for."

"We're soldiers," Gordon called from the back. "That's what we do! It comes with the job."

"Dunn, I recommend you stow it," Reimer said.

"Why don't you stow *this*," Dunn snapped, holding the middle finger to his teammates. "Sergeant! I'm telling you, there's no cure. The General already admitted we lost contact. All we need to do is go to the site, hang around a bit, then turn around, head back, and report that Dr. Hill is deceased."

"Son, you've lost your nerve," Keegan said, his voice full of disgust.

"I'm six months extended from my contract!" Dunn said. "Not by my choice, either! I signed up for eight years of service. I'm on nine, now. I didn't sign up to be killed needlessly chasing some woman who's been playing with cadavers in the woods!"

"You don't think getting the notes for the cure is worth bringing back?" Lowry asked.

"Give me a break," Dunn said. "There's no cure! Why haven't we've heard of this until now? It's pure nonsense, if you ask me."

"Nobody did ask you," Keegan said. "But I'll tell you what, PFC Dunn. You are right. In my eyes, you have served your country. I'll even attest that you've been a good marine overall. Despite your attitude, you have gone above and beyond, and have been through the shit. So, I'll offer you a deal: Pull yourself together, get through this mission. Help us bring Dr. Hill back alive...and keep your damn conspiracy theories to yourself...then, when we get back, I'll file an official request for your discharge."

Dunn stood quiet, surprised and grateful at once.

"Seriously, sir?"

"Seriously," Keegan answered. "But, for chrissake, quit your damn complaining. You ARE going into this region whether you like it or not."

Dunn exhaled sharply, his brain flooding with dopamine.

"Yes, sir," he said. "You have my word."

"Good." Keegan stepped away from him and looked to the rest of the team. "Everyone! We're thirty minutes out! Get your shit together. You think that was bad, you're in for a real surprise!"

CHAPTER 11

Lieutenant Heard's relaxed grin disappeared as he stared ahead. The horizon had disappeared behind a giant veil of fog. The fogbank was extremely vast, covering the entire stretch of forest. It was as though the atmosphere had fallen from the sky onto the trees. Twisting masses of vapor swirled around the rotors as the chopper punched through the outer wall.

"What in the hell is this?" he said to himself. The fogbank was a light grey, looking as deathly as the undead that lurked beneath it. It was thick, though not so thick that he couldn't see ahead. The tops of the trees were still easily visible. From Heard and Zucco's perspective, they almost resembled shark dorsal fins cutting through water beneath them.

"How far from the drop zone?" Keegan asked.

"A thousand meters, roughly," Heard answered.

"Where's the town?" Keegan said.

"Half a click to the east."

"Take us over the town. I want to get a look at how bad it is," Keegan said.

"You got it," Heard said. "Ensign, you've got map duty. I'm gonna be a little busy."

"Rotate seven degrees to starboard," Ensign Zucco said.

In the cabin behind them, the mixed-branch team stuffed their vests with spare magazines, grenades, med-kit equipment, and knives. A microphone protruded from the side of their helmets over their mouths. An M4 Carbine was strapped tightly along their back, while in their hands they held their silenced AK-9 or M3A1.

In addition to his AK-9, Reimer held his Accuracy International rifle. He slammed the five-round mag in place and adjusted the scope. Beside him, Private Lowry loaded his M3A1. He pressed his helmet over his head, his appearance now lacking fear. Fresh from boot camp, the training was fresh. "Do not show fear!" The young rookie was now in combat mode. But behind that composure was a very nervous kid, and Reimer could see it. For him, it was easy to detect. After all, he was masking the same fearfulness in the same way.

"Remember your training and you'll be fine," Reimer said to him.

"Yes, sir," Lowry said.

"What was your marksman score?"

"Three-one-nine, sir," Lowry answered.

"Jesus! Are you serious?!" Gordon called out, overhearing the conversation. "Freaking expert!"

"I moved a lot between Oklahoma and Texas. What can I say?" Lowry said, smiling.

"So, you mean to say there's actually a marine that knows how to shoot?" Bell joked.

"We can shoot AND we know the difference between East and West," Gordon bantered.

"Hey, at least we're not Navy sailors, who only go south if you know what I mean!" Bell kicked his foot out, tapping his boot on Dallas' rear.

"Hey, cut it out, fag!"

"Someone's embarrassed," Carlson joked.

"Alright, fun's over," Keegan called out. "Assemble at the ramp. We're gonna disembark in three!"

Keegan leaned in between the pilots as he watched the fog swirling over the windshield. The trees were more spaced out as they neared the town, eventually opening into an enormous clearing near the base of a mountain.

The downdraft from the rotors sent swirls of fog rippling out like shockwaves from an explosive detonation. Beneath that fog was the town of Atkinson, Montana. Once a lively area, now a ghost town. Grocery stores lay collapsed, with many bodies rotting in the pavement. The chopper passed over churches and residential communities, seeing several homes and buildings either abandoned or in shambles. When the plague hit this area, it didn't come quietly. There were clear signs of riot and looting, and much of the damage was due to shell fire from the National Guard. Cars, many overturned and others blackened by fire, lay in pileups along the streets. SOS signs were scribbled on several roofs, a last reminder of those who attempted to hold out when the plague grew beyond control.

Atkinson was once a busy town, home to at least a thousand people. In addition, thousands of tourists visited the area every month, during all four seasons. And Keegan was looking at them all, lumbering between the buildings and streets. There was hardly a square-inch of ground visible between the enormous crowds.

"Christ," Zucco said. "If it's this bad here, how bad will it be at the drop zone?"

"Only one way to find out," Keegan said.

"Before we go there, let me do a roundabout and take us out of sight," Heard said. "Otherwise, these things will attempt to follow us.

Unless I'm mistaken, I'm under the impression you won't want a thousand of these things converging on you while you disembark."

"No. I do not," Keegan said.

The pilots accelerated speed, taking the chopper through a thick wall of fog. They turned to port, following a winding path to their drop point. The trees towered around fifty-feet in this region, which would allow the team to fast-rope.

Heard squinted and removed his aviators as he looked down at the trees. The grey fog had suddenly turned black as smoke. The blackness rose in one large mass, which fragmented into individual bodies as it engulfed the Super Stallion.

"Birds!" Zucco yelled.

They were birds of all species, many the size of ravens. All at once, they bombarded the aircraft. They battered the windshield like stones, smashing their bodies in kamikaze flight. Audible alarms blared overhead, while streaks of red flashed through the cockpit. The Centralized Warning Panel came alive, notifying the pilots of fuel pressure droppage, rotor speed slowing, and engine trouble.

"Damn fucking featherbrains!" Heard yelled. "They're getting into the engines!" Showers of red rained down all around the Super Stallion as birds found themselves sheared in the rotors.

Heavy turbulence rocked the chopper, forcing the pilots to adjust the trajectory and speed. Hundreds of bodies bombarded the fuselage, the hull reverberating as though in a hail storm.

The team couldn't see anything but black as the birds had completely covered the aircraft like an enormous python.

"What the hell is this?!" Dallas yelled. He pressed his face to the window. "They're attacking the Stallion!"

He jumped back as a black crow smacked into the window. Its body hugged the glass for a moment, showing a red bulging, veiny eye. The feathers were ragged, many having fallen from its body, exposing diseased skin. It pushed itself away and flew off as another bird smashed head-on in its place, splattering its head against the glass.

"Get us out of this!" Keegan yelled to the pilots.

"Working on it!" Heard said. He pulled up on the controls in an attempt to elevate. Gears crackled from outside as the rotors began to seize from the jampacking of birds along the shaft.

"Sir, we're gonna have to set down now!" Zucco said.

"How much distance can you make?" Keegan said.

"Not much," Heard said. He accelerated the Super Stallion in a downward angle, brushing the belly along the tops of numerous trees. He watched the terrain through the fog and the birds, seeing nothing but thick forest. "You're gonna have to fast-rope out of here."

Keegan marched to the cabin. "Men! Get your gear together right now. Get your rifles and silent weapons and get ready to bail out! Bell, you better have those explosives."

The team slung M4 Carbines over their shoulders and prepared the fast ropes around the center hatch. Reimer and Lowry worked together to fasten the ropes. As they did, an unending assault of pine branches scraped against the hull. Heard descended another five feet, keeping the top rotor just above the tree-line. The birds kept the assault, many of them getting caught either in the trees or torn apart in the blades. Before long, their numbers thinned out. Finally, like a swarm of bees moving in unison, they backed off until disappearing behind the fog.

But they could still see black. The port engine was sparking. In the cockpit, the alarms were screaming at Heard and Zucco. They reached up, diverting power to the third engine to keep the rotors going.

"What's the status?" Keegan asked.

"Fucking birds got caught up in the engines," Heard said. "Hate to tell you this, Sarge, but one way or another, we're going down."

"Open the hatch!" Keegan yelled back. The soldiers stepped out from the middle of the cabin. In its center, two doors opened up, showing the edges of several pine branches swaying in the draft.

"We got freaks on the ground!" Dunn said.

"We'll just have to deal," Reimer said. He lowered the ropes fifty feet until they touched the ground.

"I'll go first!" Carlson said. "Let the Air Force show the rest of you pussies how it's done!" He grabbed the rope and slid down. "YEAH BABY!"

Reimer went down after him. The chill in the air hit hard with the swirling downdraft. Pines scraped against his uniform as he descended between branches. He looked down, seeing Carlson below him. As he passed through another wall of pine green, he saw the ground.

And the dozens of ghouls that awaited him.

Carlson yelled, unable to stop his descent. Drooling jaws gaped wide, filling the air with gurgling growls. Two heavyset corpses reached at him from the center, their lumberjack overalls and flannel shirts tearing as they stretched.

"PULL UP! PULL UP!" Reimer yelled.

It was too late. Deathly grips tore into Carlson's fatigues. The Airman yelled as he tried holding onto the rope while grabbing his weapon. As he fumbled, the strap of his M1A3 slid off his shoulder and disappeared under the crowd. Six or seven sets of hands were ahold of his legs, pulling him further down the rope.

The rope slid through his gloved fingers. Then, gravity did the rest. His grip was gone. He landed on two corpses, their moldy flesh squishing under his weight. Laying atop of their twisting bodies, Carlson pulled his Beretta and fired into the crowd as they converged on him. Like an avalanche of rot, they buried him under the stink of hot breath and clanking teeth.

Holding tight to the rope, Reimer couldn't see him. But his screams were evident, as was the splattering of blood. One of the ghouls stood up over the others, holding a string of red intestines like a lasso.

"*Having a hard time here!*" he heard the pilots saying through the headset. Looking up, he saw the black smoke billowing from the engines. Several feet above his head, Bolden, Bell and Gordon dangled from the rope, while Dunn, Cable, and Dallas hung from the other.

The chopper rocked back and forth, as though caught in an invisible raging river. Finally, the shaft was able to tilt, allowing the pilots to shift the gears from hovering flight. The soldiers held tight, hitting several pine branches as the chopper soared several hundred feet ahead.

Reimer spat as branches slashed his face, pricking the skin around his jaw.

"SHIT! GODDAMN!" Dunn yelled from the other rope as he endured the same punishment.

Reimer felt the rope slipping from his hands. With each blow he sank six or seven inches. Then, he noticed his feet were pressing into each other with nothing in-between. As the leg support vanished, gravity took full hold. His weight sank him down twice as fast. He barely completed a full breath when the rope went from his hands. He fell six feet, landing hard on his back. Hearing the footsteps of approaching ghouls, he fought against the haziness and pushed himself to his feet.

Bony fingers tugged down on his shoulders, and the open jaws closed in on his neck. Reimer yelled, throwing his elbow back. He clocked the ghoul hard on the nose, flattening it into its face. The ghoul staggered back from the force, only to lunge again. By now, Reimer turned. He put his iron sights on its wrinkly face, watching the skin peeling around the eyes in the split-second before he fired. Two bullets reshaped its skull into spade-shaped shards that folded out like flower petals.

A large group of the undead were moving in from his right. Reimer turned, spraying his mag across the front line. The wave of bullets spilled into a group of eight. Several bullets went low, striking numerous targets along the chest and shoulders. They jolted and spun as though struck by lightning, only to continue their march.

"Fuck." Reimer aimed high and fired off the rest of his mag in semi-auto. Bullets crunched jawbone, spilling teeth and flesh into the dirt below them. Some shots hit their mark, piercing heads and their brain matter. Reimer backed away, only to find himself in the grasp of a towering ghoul. Yelling, he pulled away, throwing several punches and kicks at it. The corpse was large, fresh, and muscular, the skin still retaining much of its color. Its fingers squeezed around Reimer's vest and pulled him in. Unable to free himself from its tight grip, he pushed his palms against its face to keep its teeth from reaching his neck.

The ghoul snarled, leaning its head back, then rolling its neck to angle its jaw. Its mouth gaped open, the teeth slamming shut on the ridge of Reimer's right hand.

The Corporal yelled and pushed away with the might of a racehorse. The ghoul, fixated on what was in its jaws, had loosened its grip, allowing Reimer to pull away. His hand slipped away, leaving the glove in the corpse's teeth. The ghoul shook its 'meal' wildly like a dog with a toy.

Reimer quickly examined his hand. Luckily for him, the glove prevented the teeth from breaking the skin. Unlucky for him, the ghoul was already pressing forward, as were the several dozen around it. Reimer let the submachine gun sling at his shoulder as he grabbed his Beretta. Gripping it with both hands, he fired a shot. The ghoul's head jolted back, throwing its body into such a tight backward arch that Reimer could only see its chin.

It straightened its posture and gazed at him with white, blood-soaked eyes. The bullet had cut through the top of its head, splitting the skull literally down the center. The two halves leaned apart, stretching the skin across the face, and exposing the pink brain inside.

The ghoul yelled as it prepared to lunge, only for its head to disappear in a puff of pink. Several suppressed gunshots rattled off, reducing several corpse heads to puddles of brown and pink.

Dunn led the charge, followed by Keegan, Gordon, Bell, and Cable. They formed a firing line and blasted the incoming horde. Decaying faces indented back into their skull cavities as the bullets made their marks.

The chopper teetered back and forth over the trees as the pilots attempted to stabilize. The minor damage to the starboard engine was worsening as the effort strained the mechanics. Now, smoke was swelling from both sides of the aircraft. Bolden and Dallas had made their descent, with Lowry now halfway down the rope.

The group huddled, keeping their backs together in a tight circle as they fired off into a forest full of corpses. Their numbers seemed infinite, constantly moving between the trees.

"Come on, kid!" Bell called.

"I'm hurrying," Lowry called back. He was still thirty feet in the air. A fall from that height was more than enough to break bones.

"Pilots!" Keegan yelled into his mic. "Once Lowry's complete, get the hell out of here and find a place to set down. Then radio for pickup!"

"Working on it, Staff Sergeant!" Heard said.

The group moved back under the chopper, blasting the corpses that bunched under the rope. Lowry was almost there, only about fifteen feet from the ground. Reimer and Gordon reached up to help him set down.

"Almost there," Heard said. His eyes went back to the fog that whipped over the tops of the trees. He looked dead ahead, seeing the fog stirring nearly two-hundred yards out. The draft wouldn't have that far of a range.

"The fuck?"

The mass of black burst through the fogbank. With the force of one enormous titan, the vehement flock of birds torpedoed into the nose of the chopper. Hundreds of bodies collided at once, bursting the windshield into the cockpit.

Birds swarmed the interior, driving their beaks into the fresh meat inside. Heard and Zucco screamed for dear life as they felt their skin being shredded. Twisting back and forth, Heard jolted the joystick, banking the chopper hard to starboard, towing Lowry underneath him.

The marine screamed as he was lifted away at forty miles an hour. A thick branch in his path cut that scream short. Lowry felt his ribs cave inward as his body folded over it. The ropes tore from his hand and he fell thirty feet down onto the forest floor.

Blood streaked from his mouth as he hit down.

"KID!" Reimer yelled. He and the team dashed toward him, striking down any corpses that stood in their way.

Heard and Zucco threw their arms wildly, unable to keep the birds off. Their beaks pecked through their glasses and pressed deep into the soft tissue below. Heard screamed, feeling the sharp rigid beak of a raven twisting within his eye socket.

The raven yanked its head back, holding Heard's eye impaled on its beak. It darted off, as several others dove in at the scent of blood. In seconds, the bones in their fingers were splintered, their faces left unrecognizable. The birds continued lashing with beaks and claws, tearing sheets of skin from the pilots' faces, exposing muscle and bone.

The chopper went into a wild tail spin, whipping up fog and smoke above the trees.

Reimer pulled his knife and plunged the blade between the eyes of another walker that intercepted his path. His fellow soldiers raced alongside him, smashing heads along the way, bringing their snapping jaws to a permanent halt. Reimer quickened his pace, trying to find the location where the rookie fell. He had promised Lowry he'd watch his back, and he wasn't going to back down from that.

A deep yell from Lowry swept through the forest. Reimer stopped, seeing a large group of corpses thirty yards out. They were amassing near the trunk of a huge tree. Laying along the ground was the kid, his spine and stomach distorted from the fall. He was squirming in place, clearly in agonizing pain, attempting to fend off the horde that assembled around him.

"HELP! HELP!"

Every muscle in Reimer's body tensed as terror struck him. Yelling, he started to run to Lowry's aide, only to be stopped by Keegan.

"We can't help him," the Staff Sergeant said. Reimer looked at him, his eyes bloodshot, his teeth clenched. Lowry's screams intensified as bony undead fingers prodded through his flesh and slipped between the ribs. Like pulling a tent stake from the ground, they yanked the loose bones free, tearing blood and muscle tissue along with them. As they munched on the bones, others dug into the gaping cavities, tearing the organs from place. The grey fog suddenly turned a shade of red as Lowry's blood sprinkled the surrounding forest.

The drone of rotors above the forest overtook the dying screams. All eyes went up to see the Super Stallion spiraling in the air like a car on an icy highway. Sparks zipped from the engines as they ceased to function, slowing the rotors to a stop.

"Take cover!" Keegan yelled. Forty-five thousand pounds of aircraft and equipment plummeted between the trees, landing into the horde. Flesh, debris, and fire tore through the forest in one enormous ball of destruction. Corpses flailed as the shockwave tossed several of them through the forest like confetti. Now the fog was a fiery orange. The air smelled of fuel and charred meat.

The team emerged from behind a wall of pine trees. Several of the undead moseyed toward the crash, having been drawn by the sound, while many others converged on the feeding frenzy several meters to the northeast.

"Shit! Where do we go, Staff Sergeant?" Bell said.

"Cable!" Keegan yelled out.

"Here, sir!"

"You got that map?"

"Aye aye, sir!"

"Get it out! We're walking from here." Keegan pointed east. "The crowd of undead has thinned this way. Let's go while most of them are distracted by the crash. Everyone on me!"

Keegan took point and ran through the forest. The men followed, weaving between ghouls as they disappeared into the forest.

As he ran, Reimer took one look back where Lowry's body was being consumed. Looking back was a bad habit and he knew it. But the guilt of failure was overpowering. And he knew he had failed Lowry.

He turned his eyes away and pressed east, following his team down a steep hill while the undead gathered behind him.

CHAPTER 12

With the fog and canopy blocking out the sun, it felt as though they were moving in the dead of night. The mist carried a vile smell as it lingered in thick clumps of fog. Secondary explosions crackled in the distance, drawing the attention of stray zombies in the area.

Discolored skin stretched along yawning jowls as they stumbled toward the orange flow. Distant moans from hundreds of their herd members resonated through the trees. They were the sounds of feasting and hunger. Recognizing these sounds was the only problem-solving intelligence the ghouls contained in their decaying brains. Whenever it was heard, it was a call to arms, alerting others, whether intentionally or unintentionally.

A dull whistle zipped through the air, ending with the splattering of brain tissue. Reimer watched as the headless ghoul dropped, spilling blackened tissue into the mud below. He aimed his crosshairs beyond its corpse, seeing numerous others moving his way in unison. There were maybe a dozen, and they were spaced out well enough from each other, meaning the team wouldn't worry about being overwhelmed. By the looks of it, they couldn't see him in the thick fog. That's the way he would keep it.

Down on one knee, he carefully placed the next ghoul in his crosshairs. It wore a ballcap with a badge, possibly having been a park ranger in life. The hat, and the head it covered, erupted into bits as the .308 round cut through it.

Keegan flanked the group along the left. Armed with his AK-9, he fired individual rounds into a faction of three. Each round landed perfectly through the nose, spraying blackened matter out the back of each head.

Dallas, armed with an Accuracy International, picked off two that lingered in the back. Their corpses hit the ground, generating splashes of mud that attracted the gazes of the remaining walkers. Bell and Bolden advanced, quietly shooting three that stumbled in from the right. As they did, Reimer and Dallas sniped the remaining two. Dallas' round cut through temple-to-temple, taking the whole top of the ghoul's head off above the ears.

Reimer saw a spatter of decaying matter ripping from his target's head. It stumbled to the left, dropping down to one knee as though sucker punched. Yet, it still moved. It stood up, thick blood dangling from its face like black saliva. He had fired low, taking off its entire jaw. Its tongue dangled freely as it began to march toward them.

Finally, it fell backward, its forehead opened up by a shot from Dunn. The PFC stepped alongside Reimer and waved a hand in front of his face.

"You still with us, buddy?"

"I'm fine," Reimer said, brushing his hand away. He stood up and hustled down the small hill. The team branched out, confirming that they had eliminated the presence of undead in the immediate area.

"Cable, get your map out," Keegan said.

"Aye aye, Sir," Cable said.

"Sir, should we attempt to make a SAT call out to Headquarters?" Dallas asked.

"Already tried," Cable said. "Canopy's too thick. We'll need to move to higher ground."

"Just get that map out," Keegan said. "And for chrissake, keep it down!"

"Sir, if I may…"

"What is it, Bell?" Keegan said.

"Sir, I just want to point out that it might not be safe to travel in these woods. If those birds attack, we're screwed."

"Not much we can do about that," Keegan said. "We will proceed with the objective."

"What the hell was that back there?" Gordon said. "There's been no reports of zombie birds anywhere else."

"I'm not even sure they were zombies," Reimer said. "You'd think, waiting here all this time, their wings would've decayed to the point they wouldn't fly."

"All I can say is that birds don't go around attacking helicopters in swarms," Gordon said.

"What did I say about keeping it down?" Keegan said, his voice low, but forceful.

"Yes, sir," the marines said. Cable unfolded the map and held it to the Staff Sergeant.

"Sir, we're about three clicks northwest of our objective," Cable said. "When the pilot tried avoiding the birds, he ended up almost taking a mile off our travel time. Not trying to put a light spin on it, just saying instead of four—"

"I get it, Sailor," Keegan said.

"We're gonna have to cut through this way," Cable said, pointing his hand toward a dark patch of forest. All eyes turned toward their new route. The trees looked black, and it wasn't a distortion from the fog either. The pines and branches were sickly in appearance, with strange veiny vines growing along the trunks.

"We sure we want to go in there?" Dallas said.

"We don't have a choice," Keegan said. "We're in Level 10 territory. If we wait here, we'll die."

"Something tells me that Level 10 doesn't only account for the population of corpses," Dunn said.

"What do you mean?" Gordon asked.

"Just pointing out what I'm observing. The birds, the trees... if this is one of the first places to be hit hard by the plague, I'm wondering if there's more than just reanimated tourists we have to worry about."

"Staff Sergeant," Reimer said. "May I offer a suggestion?"

"What is it, Corporal?"

"Our plan is to get to the bunker, retrieve the VIP, and bring her to the extraction point. I would suggest we try to find an alternate location close to the bunker for extraction."

"If they'll even have a bird that'll make the trip," Dallas said.

"I'm just saying..." Reimer looked back to the burning glow in the distance, his face twitching at the thought of Lowry being eaten alive. His eyes then went to the black forest. "I'm not sure we can endure two trips through this place. Hell, we might even lose the Doctor on the way back."

"Understood, Corporal," Keegan said. "I was already thinking the same thing. Alright, men. Reach down and reattach your balls. All of you. We're going. Cable, put that map away and hang tight to that SAT phone. Bell, you still have those C4 explosives?"

"In my pack, Sarge."

"Good. We might need to use them if we come across a herd too big. Bolden, you take point. Put that deep voice to use. Let us know if you see anything."

"Aye aye, sir," Bolden said.

"Alright, let's move."

The team pushed off into the black section of forest, keeping their movements quiet as they entered a landscape filled with rot and stench.

CHAPTER 13

Mud squelched under their boots as the team moved in deeper. The air was almost black as night, with thin streaks of sunlight making it down to the ground. The fog and canopy gave each visible sunray an essence of twilight. The darkness forced the soldiers to turn on their flashlights, keeping them dim to avoid attracting attention. They had only encountered a few wandering ghouls so far but knew that could change any second. Their lights beamed over the discolored bark along the trunks of pine trees. Their branches hung low, the pines taking on an ash-colored shade.

Even the Staff Sergeant couldn't help but occasionally stare at the strange mass that accumulated on each tree like vines. They seemed organic, like octopus arms, twisting up from the roots and wrapping around the tree. The outer layer looked leathery in texture. He wasn't even sure if it was a plant, or something else. But whatever it was, it was a functioning organism. A strange secretion dripped from pores in its "stem" down into the mud where it was absorbed into the ground.

The team had ventured a mile in by now. With each step the mud seemed to be getting deeper. It was becoming more of an effort to simply walk, much less walk silently.

"Christ," Gordon said, looking at the tight wrapping of vines along one of the trees. It was wrapped around its trunk like an anaconda. In the space between two of its curls were the gaping jaws of a rotting corpse. Its eyes were gone, as was the majority of its skin. It was still alive--in the way zombies were considered alive, its mouth moving ever so slightly. Its entire body was pinned under the vine, its meatless arms protruding in impossible postures.

He stopped and gazed ahead, watching Bolden wander ahead through the mist. He watched as masses of fog drifted in and out of the lights, consuming the trees as it went. His stomach knotted up, forcing him to fight to keep its contents intact. The smell wasn't helping matters and was only made worse by the fact that the mud was shallowest near the trees. He was looking at a real haunted forest.

"The fuck is all of this?" Dallas whispered.

"Keep it down," Keegan said. The team continued in, keeping close to the trees to keep from getting stuck in the mud. They moved in a single-file line, with Dunn watching the rear. Reimer scanned the distance area with the scope of his Accuracy International for any signs of hostile activity. To his surprise, there was nothing that he could see.

Of course, walking corpses could easily be concealed by the fog and darkness, but then again, if any were around, they'd likely hear them.

Keegan walked near the front of the group, with only Bolden and Dunn ahead of him. He took the next step, feeling his boot sinking nearly twelve inches deep.

Shit! He held a fist up, signaling for everyone behind him to stop.

"Hold it," Reimer whispered into his mic, alerting Dunn and Bolden. They looked back, seeing Keegan struggling to free his foot.

"You okay, Sarge?" Dunn whispered.

"Working on it," the Staff Sergeant muttered under his breath. Letting his weapon hang over his shoulder, he grabbed his knee with both hands and pulled back. With a loud squish, his foot came free. He stepped back to the nearest tree and waved Cable over.

"Get that map back out. See if there's any record of a bog in this area."

"In this forest? I can tell you right now, sir, this swamp, whatever it is, wasn't here before." Cable got the map out anyway and displayed their location to the Staff Sergeant. "Looks like we've gone a bit too far to the south. We should be finding higher elevation by now."

"It's this damn mud. We're constantly trying to avoid ending up in a sinkhole," Keegan said. He shined his light out at the trees. "Not only that but can't see where the hell we're going."

"Give me a sec, sir," Cable said. He pulled a compass out and started examining their distance and direction. As he did the math, the team fanned out to defend their position.

Dallas took long strides as he marched toward a tree to the left. He looked out into the forest behind it, seeing no movement other than the drifting fog. He chose to hold position there. As he stared, he couldn't help but stare at the strange vines. Each tree was entangled in them. Their secretion gleamed in the light, looking like saliva from a dog's mouth.

Further out, he noticed another tree. Its trunk had been draped almost entirely, the tentacle-like vines extending out into the ground. Some of them curved upward like thorn bushes. This organism, whatever it was, seemed to have progressed further than the others. It had grown little bulbs along the stem, each the size of baseballs. They were leathery in texture, appearing like a flower that had yet to bloom.

Reimer and Gordon noticed their teammate moving out.

"What are you doing?" Gordon whispered.

"I'm not getting too close," Dallas said. He took a few steps closer then stopped, keeping at least ten feet between him and the nearest vine.

He gazed at the strange formations, wondering what its function was. Then again, part of him didn't want to know, either.

Meanwhile, Keegan and Cable continued to look over the map.

"We're gonna have to keep sticking to the trees if we want to go that way," Cable said, pointing out where they needed to go.

"Any idea how far this bog extends?" Keegan asked. "Because I'm not too keen on getting too close to these vines."

"It's not on the map, sir," Cable said. "Your guess is as good as mine."

"Damn it. Looks like we don't have much choice," Keegan said. He gripped his rifle and motioned for Cable to put the map away. "Alright, ladies. Let's carry on. Dallas, get back over here."

"Aye, sir," Dallas said. He turned to walk away, only to wince in pain. He nearly twisted his knee, as his foot had sunken into the mud. "Fuck, hold on," he whispered into his mic. He pulled on his leg, generating another loud squishing sound as his boot came free. Blowing a sigh of relief, he started to walk away, only to stop at a prolonged sound of gurgling mud. He turned back, seeing one of the large vines had protruded toward him. The bulb on its end appeared to stare directly at him like a snake eyeing a mouse.

The top of it peeled back like flower petals, exposing a red interior. Just as he thought to step away, a thick syrupy liquid launched from the bulb, splattering over his face.

Dallas stumbled back, dropping his gun and covering his face with his hands.

"The hell?" Keegan muttered. Reimer and Gordon rushed to help him.

"Dude, you alright?" Reimer said. Dallas didn't answer. He kept his face covered, muttering pained squeals. Reimer lifted up on him to straighten his posture. Gordon pulled back on one of his hands to examine him.

Strands of skin peeled back with Dallas' hand, exposing teeth and red muscle tissue. The syrup ate at his face like an acid, dissolving one eye into the socket. Now, Dallas was screaming.

"Good God!" Reimer muttered. "Medic!"

"Corporal, what the hell's going on?" Keegan said. Reimer couldn't answer, as he was busy trying to control the sailor. Dallas staggered back, flesh pulling outward with his other hand. The smell hit the entire group like a freight train, even causing Keegan to briefly stop on his way toward them. Dunn aimed his gun at the bulb, exploding it with a single round.

"Stay the hell away from those things," he warned.

"Everyone, maintain a perimeter," Keegan ordered. "Dallas, son, I need you to calm down and let us help you—"

His words landed on literal deaf ears, as they were gone. The acid ate through the skin and cartilage, now going deep into the channels, turning his eardrums to foam. His cheeks were entirely gone at this point, his face dissolving in red-and-white suds.

"Sir, what the hell do we do?" Gordon panicked.

"Open your canteen and get some fucking water on him!" Keegan ordered. Dallas again staggered back in agony, unwittingly wading into deep mud. In seconds, he was stuck up to his knees, his face dripping around him.

"Damn it! Pull him out!" Keegan was yelling now. He and Reimer grouped around it, while Gordon fought to keep from retching. He wasn't the only one, as the muscular and seemingly fearless Bell was undergoing the same struggle. The broad-shouldered Ranger sucked in several breaths to maintain control, which only added to the inner peril, as the air was so foul from the bizarre solution.

He leaned forward, putting his hands on his knees as he retched. He spat, clearing out what little he got out. As he recovered, his eyes gazed up at the lake of mud ahead of him. The ground was moving, bits of mud swaying back and forth. It reminded him of fishing trips as a kid, when he dug for worms to use as bait. Whenever he found dirt full of them, the loose soil often moved in the same way.

"Staff Sergeant!" he called out.

"What is it?" Keegan yelled. He looked up and saw what Bell was seeing. Ripples of mud moved toward the group. Then, like miniature tidal waves, they swelled as bodies stood up from the bog. Rotting corpses marched through the mud, their clothes hanging from their skeletal figures.

Bell looked all around. Everywhere he turned, he saw undead converging on their location. What was seemingly a barren swamp was now teeming with ghouls.

He and Dunn started firing off rounds, popping skulls and dropping their bodies back into their muddy graves. Keegan and Reimer pulled on Dallas. He was stuck too far into the mud. With his other eye melted away, he seemed to have no understanding of what was happening. His movements were completely panicked, spurred further by the pain.

Keegan staggered as he tried to fasten a better grip, nearly getting himself stuck. He looked up, seeing several ghouls closing in.

"Fuck!" He and Reimer let go of Dallas and resumed the gunfire. It was like an ambling army which stretched far out across the bog. It was clear to the Staff Sergeant that there was more undead here than they had bullets. There were only two choices; move or die. "Withdraw!"

The men pushed back away from the deep mud, making sure to keep their distance from the vines. Keegan remained, making sure his men all got away safe before moving back himself. He aimed his submachine-gun at Dallas, intent on putting him out of his misery.

As he squeezed the trigger, one of the ghouls lunged at him. The Sergeant turned, putting the bullet meant for Dallas through the eye socket of his attacker, blasting the back of its head outward. He tried again for Dallas, but now it was too late. The corpses were all over him, ripping the clothes from his arms and shoulders as they bit into his flesh. Keegan gritted his teeth, feeling every bit of pain that the sailor was going through. The horde converged from the enormous mud puddle toward him, forcing the Sergeant to push back.

The team was forced to scatter, fighting off numerous undead that rose from around them.

Dunn and Gordon ran side-by-side, picking off ghouls that stood in their path. Mud splashed under their boots, sinking them down six-inches per step. Gordon pitched forward as one of his feet was caught. Dunn turned just in time to keep him from falling. He held his fellow marine up and tried to straighten his posture.

Splashes of mud crunched behind him. He felt the hot breath of another ghoul bearing down on him. Dunn tensed, believing this to be it. A wet texture sprayed over his shoulder, followed by a thump as its body fell against him before hitting the ground. Dunn glanced down, seeing its headless body laying at his feet. Looking back up, he saw Reimer, his AK-9 held at eye level, his face expressing relief for pulling off the shot.

Dunn pulled hard against Gordon, helping him to get free of the mud. With a hard yank, they both stumbled back, successfully freeing Gordon, and sinking Dunn waist deep into another sinkhole.

"Shit!" he yelled. He struggled and grabbed for anything to pull him loose. He looked back toward the sound of growling ghouls wading effortlessly through the mud. Their eyeless faces were fixed on him, clanging splintered teeth together. He aimed his gun and fired, cursing as he and Gordon repelled the advancing group.

"Could use a little help here!" Gordon yelled out. Reimer and Keegan were already there, while Bell and Bolden fought off the several walkers that moved in from the south.

Reimer reached for Dunn, only to nearly sink in himself.

"Get anything to pull him out with!" Keegan yelled.

Cable ran ahead, reshaping a scrawny ghoul's face at point blank range. He aimed carefully, firing sounds at semi-auto into a gathering near a tree. The four targets slumped to the ground, buried chest deep in mud. As dozens of others moved in, Cable hurried toward the tree. He grabbed a large branch, which had nearly broken from the trunk, and pulled. The branch swayed but didn't give, as the fraction still attached was still firm.

"Here!" Bell yelled, running to the sailor. The muscular soldier grabbed the branch and pulled down with all his might. Wood crackled and snapped as it gave way. It released, coming down on the head of another ghoul. "Let's go!"

Cable followed Bell back to the others. He and Bolden stood several feet out from the group, providing cover fire while they extended the branch to Dunn. The marine wrapped his fingers along its rough surface and held tight. Bell, Reimer, and Keegan pulled at once, hauling Dunn free of the pit.

"Oh, finally!" Dunn muttered.

"Don't think you have to thank us, or anything," Gordon said.

"Actually, don't! Instead, let's get the hell out of here," Keegan said. The team moved left around the bend of the sinkhole. Bell took the lead, pummeling ghouls as he pushed through. Looking to the north and west, the herd was thickening, appearing like an unbreachable wall of bodies. The only way was eastward.

Bell and Cable stopped on their heels as they found themselves nearly submerged into another deep mud pit. The team bunched behind them, trying to keep from getting too close to the trees. Behind them, the undead closed in, forcing the team to spread out.

Dozens of bullets tore through the air as the soldiers dispersed. Seeing a tight gathering moving in from the northwest, Keegan yanked a grenade from his vest, tore the pin away, and tossed it. The metal ball landed in the center of the group. Mud and bodies tore several feet off the ground from the ensuing blast, its echo surging through the trees.

The wall of ghouls snarled, writhing in the mud in various stages of decay. The fresher ones quickened their pace, spurred on by the blast.

Bolden tried to maneuver around a tree, only to find another huge vine armed with bulbs. He spun on his heels and dashed from it, nearly embedding himself in another lake of mud.

"Sir, there's no way out!"

"Don't you even think about panicking!" Keegan yelled at him. They continued popping off rounds, adding several small mists of brown as skull and brain matter were breached. Yet, despite the number they put down, the gathering only seemed to grow larger.

Cable moved along the lake of mud, sticking his foot along the edge to find any shallow region. Every few feet, he found nothing but depth.

Cursing, he moved further back. He stopped to fire his AK-9 at a group of ghouls that lashed at him from the mud.

He stuck his foot out one more time. To his surprise, beneath an inch of mud was solid ground. He leaned more weight onto it. Whatever it was, it held.

"HEY!" he yelled to the others. "THIS WAY!"

He stayed in place, marking the location for the team to move. The team assembled, moving in a single-file line over the shallow region. Bell was first to cross. After about six feet, he started to sink about eight inches, but by then the mud was diluted enough for him to wade through. The rest of the team moved one-by-one, with Keegan being the last to go.

"Good work," he said to Cable. He ran past him, then stopped to wait for the bunched-up team to wade to more solid ground ahead.

Cable reloaded his weapon as he waited for more space to clear up. Suddenly, the earth beneath his feet started to shift. At first, he thought he was standing on a submerged ghoul. After stepping back, he realized that wasn't the case. The shifting area took up the entire ground under his feet. Stricken with anxiety, he started to shift back, only to see the ghouls beginning to gather on his location.

Keegan turned back to provide cover fire. He paused, seeing the miniature earthquake rocking under the sailor's feet. He stepped in to grab Cable, only to be driven backwards as enormous vines lashed up from the mud like kraken tentacles. He staggered back, joining the others near a shallow region.

Cable shifted his weight as the ground elevated.

"Holy shit!" Dunn called out, seeing the huge, bulb-shaped mass rising from the mud.

Cable looked to the ground, seeing rows of jagged teeth clamped together under his boots. The "solid ground" he stood on was the closed mouth of a seven-foot Venus Flytrap. The jaws gaped wide and gravity did the rest of the work.

"CHRIST!" Bolden yelled. He and Reimer yanked out machetes and lashed out at the vines to make a path to Cable. The sailor screamed and clawed at the walls of the mouth. The jaws sealed tight around him like an airlock, and the plant's enormous head sunk back beneath the earth.

Vines fell away as the soldiers cut through them. All at once, they threw themselves at the ground where the plant had sunk.

Cable screamed in horror. He was trapped in absolute darkness, his head at least two feet under the ground. The walls illuminated in a dark red pigment, exposing veins that traveled along the plant's mouth. Pain and terror struck together as digestive acid showered down from pores near the roof.

"Get him out!" Dunn yelled as he and the others clawed at the roof of the plant. They could hear the muffled screams from below, along with shouts of Cable begging for help. The jaws would not pry apart, nor could they cut through.

The ghouls were now stepping foot on the other edge of the submerged plant, while others waded chest deep in the mud.

"Come on!" Keegan reluctantly said. "There's no time! We gotta move!"

"But sir!" Dunn yelled.

"Marine, move, or die!"

Dunn looked down, his eyes enraged. But behind that rage was a rational mind. The Staff Sergeant was right. There was no helping Cable at this point. He stood up and followed the rest of the team out onto solid ground, while the herd of undead jampacked themselves into the deep mud.

CHAPTER 14

The team had run for over a mile, zigzagging between trees and the corpses that lurked between them. There was no opportunity for the men to rest and gather their wits, as they were in the heart of hostile territory. At the end of the bog, the team slowed their retreat, using stealth to carefully move around other hordes of undead undetected.

This tactic took over a couple of hours, requiring patience and calm, something some of the soldiers were rapidly starting to lose. It was almost afternoon when they finally cleared the herd and found a place to take a breather.

The trees were spaced out on a hill they found, allowing brighter streams of sunshine to seep through. It was still dimmed by the heavy fog that lurked, but compared to the bog, it might as well have been a clear day.

Gordon and Dunn took a few moments to shake the mud from their gear. It had dried while they waited to get past the herd. Mud had completely crusted their boots and pants. In Dunn's case, it was all the way up to his waist.

Reimer leaned against a boulder that stuck like a shelf from the ground. He found himself staring back into the woods, watching for any movement. Yet, all he could see was the image of a melting face, a burning rookie, an airman disappearing between a horde, and a sailor disappearing into the ground. The screams of all four were pounding the inside of his head. Behind those screams was the debate between Gordon and Dunn.

"They're not concerned with our lives. I'm telling you, dude, we're cannon fodder," Dunn whispered to Gordon. The twenty-five-year old marine was shaking his head.

"I don't think it's as simple as that, Dunn," he said. "We're the freaking military. Risking our lives is part of the job description."

"Risking our lives is, yes. Wasting our lives is not! We lost three people last time...to save two people. We've lost SIX people this time...for one person. Not to mention what the others were talking about. Remember? Fighting off civilians from rescue convoys to secure space for whatever valuable person or equipment the government ordered."

"Come on, Dunn. I know we've been in fucked up situations before. Anyone with a brain knows the government has been involved with fucked up shit before and probably now. But *this* mission? I just don't think they'd send us through this hell if this lady wasn't as important as they say."

"Kid, you've placed your faith too easily in your leadership," Dunn said. "Shit like that will be your downfall. I'm telling you, Gordon, we're gonna have to start looking out for ourselves."

Gordon sighed, frustrated by what he believed were incoherent rantings. Dunn was a good marine and Gordon trusted him to have his back in any situation. But these paranoid ramblings about the government were becoming a little much for him.

"Corporal," Gordon whispered. "Why don't you talk some sense into him?"

"Talk sense into me?" Dunn was starting to raise his voice. "Talk sense into Mr. Positivity here."

Once again, he found himself in the middle in yet another debate. It seemed that they always expected him to be the referee or the tie-breaker. Reimer's headache was starting to set in again. He didn't know where he stood on the matter. Currently, all he wanted was to get out of this ordeal. But behind that urge was his desire to serve his nation and help preserve what remained of mankind.

"How about both of you knock it the hell off," Reimer said.

"Is there a problem here?" Keegan said, marching over to them.

Bolden leaned against the tree, eavesdropping on the conversation. He pulled a Nutrigrain bar from his pocket and began to peel the plastic off. It was covered in mud from the bog. He ran his thumb over the grime, feeling a tar-like texture. What little remained of his appetite was gone and he tossed it away.

Bell slumped down against a tree, his lungs puffing deep breaths as he recovered from the shock and physical exhaustion. The former tank operator tried to maintain a straight face and positive attitude. After all, he was on a combat mission, and succumbing to fear would do nobody any good.

"You alright there, big guy?" Keegan asked him.

"Just getting it together, sir," Bell answered.

"Me too," Keegan muttered, more to himself than Bell. He raised his voice again to address the team. "Alright, we're taking ten here. Everyone keep an eye out. God only knows what else is waiting for us out here."

"Yeah, no shit," Dunn said. "First the birds, then the trees, then the fucking *Little Shop of Horrors*. What's next? Are the rocks gonna come alive?"

"Dunn, keep your shit together," Keegan said. "This is your last mission, remember? Help us get out of this alive, you get to be a civilian again." Dunn sucked in a few deep breaths through his nose, exhaling out his mouth.

"Yes, sir," he said.

"Now, go scout ahead and see what's along that ridge," Keegan ordered. Dunn inhaled another deep breath.

"Aye aye, Sir." At least they were out of the bog. He hustled up the hill, quickly disappearing behind the trees. The sun grew a bit brighter as he moved up the incline. After a hundred yards, he even came across a few golden streaks. Then finally, he found a break in the trees.

"Oh, shit," he muttered to himself. He dug his heels into the ground, stopping himself at the ledge of a fifty-foot rock cliff. He sucked in a breath of fresh air. The air was clearer up here than behind the tree line. The light was almost blinding after spending hours in that black forest. He gazed outward, looking at the forest that blanketed the landscape ahead of him. Like the forest they passed through, it was dead. Fog swirled above the canopy, the branches dripping a strange solution into the ground. The momentary sense of relief ended, and the PFC was filled with a new sense of dread. They would have to pass through that forest to get to the objective.

If that objective was even alive.

The silence was interrupted by the sound of cracking twigs, followed by a slimy growling. Dunn glanced over his right shoulder, seeing a stray ghoul lumbering toward him from behind a boulder. It was scrawny, its greenish skin hugging the ribcage. In a late stage of decay, the ghoul was visibly weak. There was hardly any muscle tissue in its arms for it to raise its hands at him. Its feet dragged, forcing the corpse to use momentum to take steps. Toe bones protruded from the split ends of tennis shoes on its feet, the ragged ends of khaki pants trailing threads.

Dunn stared at the flesh-eater as it stumbled toward him. His faced tensed with anger. His blood boiled inside him, turning his face a dark red. He let the thing draw near until it was only a few feet away. With a burst of energy, he set loose on it. He rammed an elbow into its forehead, knocking it down on its back. Mad with pent up rage, he kicked the ghoul repeatedly in the ribs. Splintered bones protruded from thin moldy skin tissue. The ghoul snapped its jaws at him, feeling nothing but a persistent hunger. Dunn kicked it in the chin, dislocating its jaw. Teeth sprinkled around its head and rolled away like stones.

Dunn kept kicking, keeping just enough control of his outburst to not yell out. He stomped on the arms, cracking the elbows, then repeated the motion with the legs and knees. Bones crushed into shards as he punished the corpse for all the sins of the apocalypse.

He staggered back, panting heavily as he recovered. He glared at the undead opponent, its brain still functional, though its body was now completely inoperable. It laid on the ground in a mangled position, its head twitching in an attempt to generate a biting motion.

The neurons in his brain lit up as he heard another snarling sound behind him. He turned, seeing another corpse staggering toward him. In his madness, he never heard it emerging from the woods. It was fresher, moving faster, already bearing down on him. As he reached for his gun, another figure burst from the tree line.

Reimer raised his knife high and hammered down, plunging the blade through the top of the ghoul's head. As it slumped into its permanent lifeless state, he withdrew the knife and kicked the body away with his boot.

"You trying to get yourself killed?" he said to Dunn. He looked past him, seeing the mangled corpse he had beaten. "A little recreation?" The PFC shook his head, his face still mad. In one final burst he lunged at the ghoul, grabbing it under the arms. Skin tore as he dragged it across the ground. With a twist of his hips, he hurled it over the edge of the cliff and watched as it splattered over the rocks below.

Dunn sucked in several more breaths before making eye contact with the Corporal.

"Just sick of seeing soldiers getting killed," he muttered.

"You're not the only one it wears on," Reimer said.

"Yeah, I know," Dunn said. "What are you doing up here, anyway?"

"Isn't it obvious? I'm checking on you, dumbass." They both grinned. "Turns out it was worth it. Seems you found the only clean patch of forest."

"I'm trying to enjoy it while I can," Dunn said. He pulled a pair of binoculars from his vest and started scanning the area. "Cable had the map. We have no satellite connection out here. At this point it's a guessing game."

"You see anything out there?" Reimer asked. Dunn didn't answer right away as he panned slowly. From what he could tell, there was nothing but forest ahead of them. The canopy rose and fell like an ocean current, with some lines of trees towering high above others, making Reimer believe that this wasn't the only drop-off in the area.

"There's a clearing to the north," Dunn said.

"A clearing?" Reimer took the binoculars and took a look. "That's gotta be the lake."

The two marines moved north along the cliff edge. Luckily for them, the slope seemed to increase as they went, giving them a higher vantage point. Dunn took the binoculars back and resumed looking over the area. He could see the water and some shore areas. The lake was flat and discolored, appearing as dead as everything surrounding it. It was easy to imagine that it was once a beautiful vacation spot with plenty of fishing that took place. Now, after everything they'd been through, he didn't even want to speculate what might be under that water.

"Could that be it?" he asked. He held the binoculars in place as he stepped aside for Reimer to look. A large structure towered over the trees across the lake. It was mechanical, almost resembled the Eiffel Tower from this distance.

"No, that's a radio tower," Reimer said. "Probably used by the park ranger station."

"Damn, I was hoping that was it," Dunn said. He took the glasses back and looked around. "Hang on a sec, didn't Cable say something about the bunker being three-quarters of a mile or so from a cove along the southside?"

"I believe so," Reimer said.

"Well, voila," Dunn said. He pointed out, seeing a small space between a group of trees. "That has to be the cove, which would put the bunker somewhere over..." he pointed his finger to the southeast... "there."

"Alright, then," Reimer checked the magazine of his Accuracy International, then slammed it back in place, "let's submit our report."

CHAPTER 15

The journey from the cliff to the bunker took over another hour. As Reimer had predicted, the landscape was rife with cliffs and rolling hills. Adding to their troubles were more wandering groups of undead. It was imperative for the team to not engage unless necessary, not only because of the low visibility and high numbers of ghouls, but also to preserve their limited ammo.

The area grew even darker as they came along a vast grouping of trees towering up to one-hundred-eighty feet. Dunn cursed the presence of these damned trees, as they were the reason they couldn't make their landing here, close to the bunker. But then again, would they have made it anyway? He thought about the bird attack and wondered if it would've happened here as well. The thought of the possibility began to stress him out further, provoking a worry that rescue might get caught in a similar ambush.

Though not in a bog, the trees did contain some type of outer growth similar to what they'd seen before. This time, the vines were dry. Disgusting little flowers bloomed along the stem, sporting dark yellow petals. Whatever they were, the team knew better to keep away from them.

The team moved down a hill, the ground full of numerous bumps and rock beds. The fog swirled around them like angry spirits guarding their domain. Keegan took the lead, holding up a closed fist to instruct the others to huddle down. He moved over the patch of rocks and army crawled to a small boulder that rested ten yards from the base of the hill. Pushing himself to a crouch, he took his binoculars and observed the small open area ahead.

Between the rows of trees and swirling fog was the bunker. The exterior was small, roughly the size of a trailer. A medium-sized radio antenna reached high into the sky, bent downward at the middle. He couldn't see the entrance from his position. What he could see were the corpses that roved around it. They seemed to be marching in circles, possibly following the drift that carried the fog. He carefully panned his glasses over the whole clearing, counting at least five undead. Five ghouls, five shots.

Keegan glanced back and pointed at Reimer, waving him over. With the rifle in his arms, the Corporal army crawled to Keegan's location. The Staff Sergeant reached out, silently instructing him to hand over the rifle. Reimer passed it over to him and spotted with his binoculars.

"We got five," Keegan whispered. "They're mine."

Reimer laid belly down on the opposite side of the boulder. Resting on his elbows, he watched the activity through the glasses.

"Got an ugly leaving the group," he said. Keegan panned left, seeing a tall ghoul starting to wander into the trees. In seconds, it would be too far into the brush for a clean shot. He followed it with his crosshairs, placing the point directly on the back of its head.

A squeeze of the trigger sent a .308 caliber round through its cranium. Reimer watched its body fall forward into the brush, its feet sticking out into the mud.

"One down." He watched as two other ghouls turned toward the sound generated by its fall. "We got one in a suit and tie and one with a cowboy hat. Looks like they'll be moving toward the body. They'll be wandering into the woods…"

Keegan fired a round at the fancy-dressed ghoul, taking the top of its head off. Its lower jaws flapped down to its neck, its tongue swinging about as it fell. Keegan aimed at the cowboy, following its path with the crosshairs. He grinned in satisfaction as he watched the next round explode its head into a spray of gooey matter.

He panned down and placed his sights on the fourth walker. It was looking in their direction, though it couldn't see them. Keegan placed the crosshair over its left eye. The eye socket expanded into a gaping hole. The fifth and final ghoul started lumbering toward its body, providing a convenient shot for Keegan. He fired the last bullet. Decayed flesh ripped from its jawline, splattering over its slain brethren.

"A little low," Reimer said.

"Eh, I was just letting off a little steam," Keegan said. Reimer looked through the glasses again. The head rolled completely off its shoulders. With no neurological system to control it, the body slumped to the ground next to its severed head. The Staff Sergeant handed the rifle back to Reimer, then gripped his AK-9. He waved to the others to follow him as he descended down the remainder of the hill.

The team formed a perimeter around the bunker as they secured the area. Though the immediate area was void of walkers, the soldiers could hear the spontaneous growling of wandering ghouls deep in the woods. However, it did not appear that they were aware of the soldiers' presence.

Keegan knew, however, that that luck could change on a dime. He moved around to the front of the bunker.

"Oh, shit," he muttered. The steel door had been caved in, as though hit with a battering ram. The door was detached, its center crumpled as it laid several feet into the mouth of the structure.

"What the hell could've done that?" Dunn asked.

"No idea," Keegan admitted.

"This forest has no shortage of weird shit going on, doesn't it?" Bolden said. Gordon stepped over to Reimer and Dunn.

"Back at the house, didn't you guys say something punched through the roof?" Reimer inhaled, his mind replaying the strange and terrifying events.

"Yes."

"At first it didn't make sense. But now…" Gordon looked back at the bunker. "Considering everything we've seen, it seems par for the course."

"Yeah, but that was wooden beams and roof tile," Dunn said. "This bunker is designed to withstand a blast."

"Perhaps we have a clue!" Bolden said. He pointed to another body laying in the mud. It was a male, lying face-down with his back torn open. The blood was fresh, forming red puddles around the body. "Looks like someone else was here."

"Who is it?" Dunn said.

"Looks like a local," Bolden said. "No gunshot wounds to the head. Whatever went down here, it happened recently."

"You think that guy broke down the door?" Dunn said. "He'd need a tank! Don't know about you, but I don't see any treads. I mean, just look at the ground! There's noth—" Dunn's words came to a complete stop as he gazed down at a strange indentation in the mud. The ground was covered in tracks, many of which were made by the undead. This one, however, stood out. The foot had the general shape of a human's except it was at least fifteen inches long. The toes appeared to be elongated, almost like reptile claws. Reimer and Bolden gathered over it with him.

"You okay, Marine?"

"The hell is that?" Dunn said.

"Probably a bear," Bolden said.

"Never seen no bear make a track like that," Dunn said.

"Alright, pull yourselves together," Keegan said. "Dunn, Bolden, Gordon, maintain a perimeter. Warn us if anything comes our way. Reimer and Bell, you're with me. We're checking inside. Let's do this fast."

As he spoke, the brush between two trees began to rustle. They heard the clunking of teeth as a short-framed ghoul stepped from the tree line. It staggered two steps into the mud then stopped to look at them. Recognizing food, it raised its arms and extended its jaw to snarl. Its breath barely passed between its teeth as Gordon lunged in and plunged a knife through the roof of its mouth. He twisted it, driving the tip through the top of its head. As he quietly lowered the dead ghoul to the ground, the team listened for any others. The forest was filled with many growls, most of them far back.

"Let's do this and be out of here before any more show up," Keegan remarked. He hugged the inner wall as he took the first steps inside. Bell and Reimer followed him into the front room. The bunker had an electric elevator dead ahead and a staircase to the left. Dried blood had coated the doorway and inner walls. A stale smell filled the air, mixing with the stench of the undead. It almost appeared that everything in this bunker was composed of rusty steel. There wasn't much equipment up on the ground level. More importantly, there wasn't any VIP.

Keegan stopped again to listen. They could hear growls coming from below. The Staff Sergeant hugged the corner and peeked down the stairway. The lights flickered below, making him wonder it the power generator had been damaged in the attack.

He led the group down the flight of steps, keeping each movement as quiet as possible. Luckily, there was no door at the end of the stairway. It was an open passage leading into the radio room. Keegan turned the corner, seeing three ghouls kneeling on the ground. They were feasting on a corpse in the middle of the carpet. Skin had been peeled back from the victim's trunk like an onion, making way for the ghouls to dig into the inner organs.

All three faces, completely painted in blood, looked up to the soldiers. There was no time to waste with close combat. Keegan put two of them down, their entire bodies quaking as the bullet pierced their brains. Bell took the third, placing a bullet through its right temple. The three soldiers infiltrated the room and immediately checked the kitchen and bathroom areas for any other flesh-eaters.

Keegan checked the body, kicking off one of the ghouls that had fallen over it. The facial skin had been entirely ripped off, the chest torn open completely. It was almost impossible to identify the individual.

"Shit," the Staff Sergeant said. "Reimer, check the pockets. Maybe, just maybe this fella has some ID." Reimer knelt down, finding nothing in the jeans pockets.

"Nothing, sir," he said.

"All this, for nothing," Bell remarked.

"We don't know that," Reimer said.

"Get on that computer and see if you can get a signal out to Border Command," Keegan ordered. The Corporal stepped over the bodies and approached the computer desk. The radio transmitter and microphone were nowhere to be found. The main monitor had been smashed as though struck with a hammer. Looking back to the ground, he found the bent mic, covered in blood just inches from the victim's hand. Near the wall a couple feet away was a Colt 1911, the slide locked back.

Reimer picked up the mic, seeing the stem completely bent out of proportion, the base tattered, and wires ripped.

"Our buddy here made a last stand," he said.

"Great," Bell said. "This just keeps getting better and better. How are we gonna get a radio call out?"

"We might be able to fix it," Reimer said. "Maybe." As he reached down to pick up the stray wires, he gazed at the victim's hand. Though the body was an average-sized individual, the fingers appeared fairly large, not like a woman of Dr. Hill's build. He recalled her photograph image. She appeared to be a fairly skinny individual with long golden strands of hair. He looked back at the victim's head and the surrounding carpet. Even though the scalp was ripped off, Reimer found it odd that there was no hair to be found.

"Sir?"

"What is it, Corporal?"

"I think our objective is still alive," Reimer said. "This isn't her. This body is male."

"Makes sense," Bell said. "He was probably with that other fella up top. Either they broke in, or Dr. Hill let them in. Either way, they were trying to seek refuge in here before the herd got them."

"But if Dr. Hill isn't here, then where is she now?" Keegan asked. He started looking around, digging through cabinets in search of layout plans.

"Whatcha looking for, Sarge?" Bell asked.

"A lot of times, they make these bunkers with a secret back passageway in case you can't escape through the front," Keegan said. He spilled papers over the floor, finding nothing but log notes from previous occupants. Nothing of use. Reimer started looking under the desk for any switches. Bell moved to the back wall for any features that could resemble a doorway.

"I think you're right, Sarge," he said. Keegan turned and approached the Army Ranger. He stood in front of a bookcase. It didn't appear to have any screws or bolts, yet, it would not budge as he tried to move it. It was tall and narrow, placed perfectly in the center of the wall. "If this is it, they really had haunted houses in mind when they made it."

"Sometimes they hold subjects here whom they don't want to get out," Keegan said. "However, it's possible they gave Dr. Hill instructions on how to escape should the infected breach the entry."

"Too bad we can't radio in and find out for ourselves," Reimer said.

"Quit your whining and find the damned switch. Most likely, it's something hiding in plain sight."

****

Dunn inched forward, knife in hand as he listened to the twigs crackling behind the fog. The steps were getting closer, the snarls more audible. Finally, another ghoul wandered out from the tree line. By the time it saw him, the marine had plunged his knife through its eye.

He gently lowered it to the ground then backstepped to the bunker. Bolden was on the other side, his knife embedded in the skull of another corpse. Dunn glanced back into the bunker entrance, growing more anxious with each passing minute.

"What the hell's the holdup?" he whispered to Gordon.

"Don't know, but I'm starting to get antsy myself," Gordon said. Another ghoul emerged through the fog. Gordon lunged at it, stabbing his knife upward behind its neckline.

"Guys!" Bolden spoke through their com. They looked his way, seeing four corpses wandering from the woods as he wrestled with another. All at once, they bellowed and quickened their pace.

"Shit," Dunn muttered. He and Gordon ran into the action, each firing several rounds into the ghouls. With new cavities drilled into their skulls, the corpses stumbled face-first into the mud. Bolden pushed his knife into the fifth ghoul's brain, killing it. As he pulled it free, another emerged from the trees. It was already lunging at him, aware of his presence even before reaching the clearing.

"Fuck!" Bolden yelled as he thrust a kick out, plowing it in the chest. It hit the ground, immediately reaching up. Its head opened up like an egg shell as a shot from Gordon ended its undead brain. The three soldiers looked back. Across the bunker, several ghouls were stumbling from the trees, now alerted to their presence.

"Just what we need," Dunn said. He lifted his mic to his lips. "Sarge! Get up here, sir. We've got multiple boogies in the area. We're gonna have to clear out!"

"*On our way*," Keegan responded. Dunn charged the incoming group. At least eight flesh-eaters were advancing, with several more snarling within the forest. Stingy flesh that previously formed lips peeled back, fully exposing yellow broken teeth.

"Come get some!" Dunn said. He squeezed the trigger, seeing the nearest ghoul jerk its head back and fall to the ground.

****

"Let's go," Keegan said. Bell looked back, having tried searching along the doorway.

"But sir, if we leave, we'll never find—"

"In two minutes, this entire facility will be compacted with corpses. Even if we make a stand, we'd be boxed in."

"Just give me a minute, sir," Bell said. "I have the heavy explosives. I can rig a charge and blast this thing off the wall."

Keegan paused, realizing the idea had merit. "You sure you can pull that off?"

"Hell, yes, sir," Bell said.

"Keegan," Reimer approached him, "Sir, what if there's no tunnel behind that door? What if it's like a saferoom or something? A blast could kill her if she's in there."

"I doubt that. Regardless, we don't have much choice. Besides, this beats running through the woods and the fog looking for her." Keegan looked to Bell. "Do it!"

As the Army Ranger tore into his demolitions bag, the two marines ran upstairs to join the fray. As they reached the surface, Dunn, Bolden, and Gordon were already gathered near the entrance, forming a firing line at the incoming ghouls.

"Make room!" Keegan yelled. The team spaced out, continuing suppressive fire. There were over twenty ghouls visible now, each coming in faster and more determined than the last.

"What's the plan, Sarge?!" Bolden asked.

"Hold em' off for another minute! There's a passageway, and Bell's gonna open it up with a concentrated explosive."

"Nice of the government to provide us with facility layout and plans," Dunn remarked.

"Focus on what you're doing, Marine," Keegan said. He stood at the center of the line and extended his gun, placing the muzzle onto the forehead of an approaching flesh-eater. With a squeeze of the trigger, its head split open down the middle.

He fired the rest of his magazine into the crowd, killing three or four more flesh-eaters before his final mag ran dry.

So much for stealth. Keegan dropped the gun and snatched his M4 Carbine, sending loud cracks through the air as 5.56 NATO rounds launched from the muzzle.

****

Bell looked up to the stairway, hearing the unsuppressed gunshots of the M4. It was a sign that they were running out of ammo for their silent weapons. Not just that, but if they were using M4's they were on the verge of being overrun. He placed the charge against the "bookcase" and inserted the triggering device. After snatching up his equipment, he hustled up the steps.

"Fire in the hole!" he yelled to the team as he darted out the entrance. The team quickly moved away from the entrance to avoid getting caught in any residual force of the blast. Bell triggered the explosive.

The earth shook beneath them as the blast echoed underground. Dust and smoke ripped up through the stairway and out of the entrance into the crowd of undead. The smoke was hot, near scalding to the touch.

"Hold tight," Keegan said. "Let it clear, or else you'll burn your lungs out!" He thrust his rifle out, bashing the butt over the head of a ghoul that was creeping toward a gagging Private Gordon. The marine turned around, shocked to see he was a heartbeat away from being bitten. "Pay attention, Marine!" Keegan said. He dug the heel of his boot into the biter's eye socket, crunching the skull inward.

Reimer moved to the left of the entrance to provide additional cover fire. He looked to the north, seeing the trees actually tilting ever so slightly as an unbelievably thick swarm marched their way.

"Holy fucking shit!" he yelled. The other soldiers followed his gaze, many muttering the same phrase. Keegan stepped into the bunker. The smoke and toxins had died down enough for them to have visibility and avoid burns. Stepping back into the mud, he pressed his back into the corner of the entryway and fired his M4 into the horde.

"Alright! Get your asses in there!" he yelled. "Bell, your explosive better have worked, or we're dead meat."

"So to speak," Bell remarked. He was the first to enter, followed by Reimer and Gordon.

"Go! Go! Go!" Keegan barked as Dunn and Bolden rushed past him. As they neared the stairway, Keegan stepped to the left to backstep into the bunker. A deep bellow pierced the air, infiltrating his eardrums. It was a roar from something from the Cretaceous Period.

Looking ahead, Keegan saw several corpses knocked aside as something rampaged through the crowd. It stepped out of the fog and set its eyes on the Staff Sergeant. It was human, yet it couldn't have been. It was at least nine feet tall, its skin a dark brown. Its arms were almost as long as his body, its fingers extended at least twelve inches, with razor sharp nails protruding from the tips. Its face was like a man's, though the skull was disproportionately shaped, resembling a melon rather than a skull. Pointed teeth protruded from gums, dripping pink saliva to its clawed toes.

"Christ," Keegan muttered. With his M4 set to full-auto, he fired into the abomination. With arms outstretched, it sprang at him with great speed, its entire path a blur. Keegan yelled as spear-like fingers punched through his ribcage. His feet dangled off the ground as the creature lifted him and drove him backward.

"Sarge!" Dunn and Bolden both yelled in astonishment as it pinned him against the back wall. Taking a bounding step to close the distance, Dunn pointed his M4 point blank to the creature's head and fired. Its head jerked to the right, the skin around the temple tearing and spilling a thick red blood. He staggered back as it turned its head and gazed at him, baring teeth. The bullet had skidded right off its skull.

Keegan yelled as it pulled one of its clawed hands out of him. The creature snarled and swiped, the tip of its nail grazing Dunn's Kevlar as he jumped out of reach.

"Dude! We've gotta go!" Bolden yelled. The view of the outside had disappeared behind the flood of corpses that spilled into the bunker. The two soldiers backtracked, quickly moving down the steps.

As the unintelligence legion spilled into the stairwell, the creature turned its eyes back toward the Staff Sergeant. Blood trickled from his mouth as he grabbed his Beretta. He yanked it from its holster and pressed the muzzle to its forehead."Chomp on this," he gurgled. He fired off a shot. The creature's head jolted back, then looked back at him. Through the perfect hole in its forehead was a thick intact skull. Gaping its jaws wide, the creature lunged, driving inch-long teeth into Keegan's neck. It ripped away, trailing blood and stringy flesh from his corpse.

CHAPTER 16

The air downstairs was still thick with smoke and dust. Bolden passed the last five steps in a single leap, joining the other soldiers along the corridor entrance. Reimer watched as Dunn followed. Numerous shadows stretched along the stairway wall as the army of corpses followed.

"Where's Keegan?!" Reimer yelled.

"It got him!" Bolden yelled out.

"What got him?" Gordon asked.

"I don't know," Dunn said. "It's a big one! Its freaking huge. We shot it, but its skull is thick! It's like a fucking mutant!"

"We need to go!" Bolden said. He tried rushing into the corridor, only to be stopped by Reimer and Gordon.

"In a minute!" the Corporal said. "There's another door down there. The opening mechanism was damaged in the blast, so Bell's gotta open it with a charge." He looked to the stairway. Bodies stumbled down the steps, many of them summersaulting forward. "Fuck!" Armed with his final AK-9 magazine, he began putting down walkers that followed. The stumblers pulled themselves to their feet, only to be shot in the head by Gordon, Dunn, and Bolden.

More and more came in a big flood, jampacking themselves into the doorway. Dunn and Bolden threw whatever they could at the doorway. Desks, chairs, and radio equipment, and furniture were packed against the doorway, while Reimer and Gordon hit the horde with suppressive fire.

Already, the blockade was bulging under the combined force of the undead.

"Hey, ARMY, you about done?!" Reimer yelled.

"On my way, Corporal!" Bell shouted from the corridor. The Ranger stepped back after securing the explosive to the doorframe. With the flick of a switch, the charge detonated, driving the door off the frame. Bell picked up the explosives pack and ran out through the smoke to meet the others. He gasped upon seeing the huge numbers of undead spilling into the radio room. "Holy mother of—this way!"

Nails scratched against metal as something scraped the walls of the stairway. The masses of undead were pushed aside as the hulking mutant raced between them, its jaws dripping Keegan's blood.

"Go!" Reimer shouted. As the soldiers descended into the hall, the beast sprang. Feeling it bearing down on him, Bolden turned on his heel and fired. Claws lanced his stomach, lifting him off the floor like a fish on a spear. It opened its jaws wide, revealing a dark red esophagus, reeking of flesh, both rotting and fresh. It bit down on Bolden's face, the upper row of teeth puncturing his forehead, the bottom ripping under his chin. With all its might, it clamped its jaws together, completely slicing off the front of Bolden's head. His body dangled, impaled on its claw, the faceless head exposing brain and fluid.

As it fed, the inferior horde flooded the corridor in pursuit of the four survivors.

The air grew hot as the tunnel filled with bodies. Reimer ran at the front of the group. The tunnel was narrow, only about four feet in width. The walls were made of a black steel. Lights flickered between pipes along the ceiling, flashing through the smoke and adding to the disorientation.

Gordon ran at the back of the group. They were putting space between themselves and the ghouls. However, that wouldn't last forever. They would eventually tire; the undead would not. He aimed his rifle and fired a few rounds, catching one of the ghouls in the face. It fell to its knees and slumped, causing others to trip over its body.

Reimer led the group through a left bend in the tunnel. In this segment, the lights were not functional, leaving them running in black air. With a twist of a knob, Reimer activated the flashlight on his M4. The light beamed into the tunnel, illuminating at least a dozen walking corpses that waited ahead of them.

As if this wasn't hard enough.

With the horde closing in from behind, there was no choice but to push through quickly. He and Dunn took the lead, each hugging opposite sides of the wall as they blasted the ghouls one-by-one.

Bell and Gordon dropped to firing positions as the horde came around the bend. Walking corpses, dripping flesh and hair with each step, grazed the walls as they marched in. The loud cracks of the M4s seemed to spur them on, forcing the most freshly dead to spring into a jogging pace.

Light brown blobs of blood spat from their heads as rounds punched through their skulls. But the horde just kept coming. It was like a freight train of undead.

Reimer and Dunn pushed forward, busting heads with carefully placed rounds. Reimer gritted his teeth, forcing the adrenaline to work in his favor instead of against him. These corpses were slow, making for relatively easy targets. Heads popped like balloons, spraying brain and decayed matter to the floor.

With one final shot, the path was clear. The marines shone their lights down the corridor. It came to a dead end roughly fifty feet down. A ladder ascended the wall, leading to a metal hatch.

"Let's go! We're almost out of here!" Reimer yelled. The group sprinted to the end. As they did, Bell continued to fire into the horde to slow it down. But their numbers seemed to be infinite. At the foot of the ladder, Reimer took firing position, assisting Bell with the suppressive effort. "Gordon! Dunn! Get your asses up there!"

Initially, they both wanted to urge Reimer to go first. But there was no time to argue. Gordon went first and ascended the eighteen-foot climb. The hatch was closed above him, with a steering-wheel shaped opening mechanism. At the top of the ladder, he grabbed the wheel and spun it to the left. The locking mechanism detached from its slot and the hatch yawned open, spilling a grim twilight into the dark tunnel.

Gordon pulled himself out onto a grassy area. Kneeling a meter away from the hatch, he panned his eyes over the surrounding area. Only a few stray corpses lumbered between some boulders in the distance. Nothing appeared to be coming out of the tree line.

Dunn was next. At the final ladder bar, he practically sprang like an insect up onto the grass. On his hands and knees, he poked his head back into the tunnel.

"Come on, guys!"

Reimer and Bell had already backed to the foot of the ladder.

"Get up there," Reimer ordered Bell.

"No dude! You first! I'm heavier and will take a little longer to haul my ass up. GO!"

Reimer grimaced as though in pain. But again, there was no time to argue. He strapped his weapon behind his back and hustled up the ladder. Bell fired off numerous shots until Reimer's boots were as high as his face. With his bag hung over his shoulder, he quickly ascended behind the Corporal. Reimer moved quick to give him space.

But the horde had closed in. Bell had climbed four feet off the floor when he felt teeth and nails tearing into his legs. Reimer whipped his head down at the sound of Bell's screams. Several arms were ahold of the former tank operator, their combined strength pulling him down. His feet came off the bars, his hands still gripping tight.

Reimer skidded down several bars and reached to grab him.

"Come on, soldier!" he yelled. Bell looked back up, tempted to accept the help. But with the infection having broken the skin barrier, Bell knew he was pretty much dead already. Holding tight to the ladder with one hand, he whipped the explosives pack up to the Corporal.

"Get out! It's gonna get hot in here in ten!" he yelled.

"BELL!"

The soldier released his grip, falling back into the river of corpses that filled the corridor beneath. As he landed on top of them, he pulled two grenades from his vest. Reimer hustled, accepting the extended hands of his fellow Marines. Together, they hauled him up onto the grass. Dunn shut the hatch door and sealed the lock.

Now encased in darkness, the ghouls tore at Bell, their teeth severing muscle tissue from his arms and shoulders. Finally, the two grenades went off, engulfing the flesh-eaters in a blast, amplified by the tight quarters.

The marines felt the concussion from above. It felt like a tiny earthquake, the blast itself sounding like a car crash taking place below. Reimer sat in the grass, staring at the few undead that approached them. Dunn took the pleasure of dispatching them, driving his knife into each one.

"At least he died on his own terms," Gordon muttered. Dunn yanked his blade from the last ghoul and shot Gordon a frustrated look.

"His terms? No. He died on someone else's terms!"

"Oh, Jesus, Dunn. Not now," Reimer said.

"Yes, now," Dunn said. "We're stuck here. We're all that's left. That scientist woman is nowhere to be found. What are we gonna do?"

"I don't see any tracks," Gordon said. "She definitely made it out of there alive. That's why those inner doors were locked. Those corpses we ran into in the tunnel must've followed her in. There was no body as far as I could see. She might still be alive."

"*That's* what you're thinking about?!" Dunn barked. "Bolden, Bell, and Keegan are dead, and you're all about saving this idiot who shouldn't have been here in the first place?"

"I get it, Dunn, but it's what we're here for. If we don't find her, then they all died for nothing!"

"Believe me, they have!" Dunn said.

Reimer sat, his mind in a haze. He heard every word spoken between his friends, knew he needed to intervene, yet couldn't seem to bring himself back to reality. It was as if his brain had powered down, rendering him inoperable.

"Corporal? CORPORAL?!"

As if awakening from a dream, Reimer shot to his feet. Dunn was now looking at him with questioning eyes.

"Did you guys get a signal out to Border Command?" Dunn asked.

Reimer hesitated. "Negative. The equipment had been destroyed in the previous attack."

"You've got to be kidding me," Dunn muttered. "Then we're screwed. We are absolutely screwed." He started looking around, appearing to be in a state of panic. "There's got to be a vehicle around here. Let's just get a vehicle and get the hell out of dodge. There were rumors that undead activity was low in northern Canada. We can go there."

"Dunn, I know we're friends, but holy shit man. You need a slap upside the head," Gordon said.

"Speak for yourself buddy," Dunn retorted. "We're alive now, but believe me, we are SCREWED! The government was always shitty, but now it's completely made to benefit the elites. You've probably noticed how they're forcing everyone to have jobs, and taxing them at, what? Fifty percent is it now? Now forced military service, laws forced by people who've never served. You really want to go back to that place?"

"That's enough, Dunn," Reimer finally spoke up. "We'll make for the radio tower. There's gotta be something there that can reach home base. We can get a ride out of here. Then you'll be a civilian again."

"Says you," Dunn said. "Keegan's dead. My luck has run out. If I get back, they'll just put me with another unit and use me till I'm too broken. Same with both of you."

"Well, until then, I'm the ranking officer," Reimer said, his voice assertive. Dunn stared at him, his face appearing angry and hopeless.

"You've got to be kidding me," he said.

"I don't have time to kid," Reimer said. "Too many guys have died. We need you to get your shit together."

"I'm the ONLY one with my shit together," Dunn barked. "Don't you see, I'm the only one who can see the strings around you puppets!"

"I'm pulling rank here, man!" Reimer said.

"Fuck your rank," Dunn said. "All the times you've froze up! All those hesitations…you're as dead as I am."

All three men jumped back as the hatch burst upward, the square segment launching several feet into the sky. They stood in unison, slowly backing away with their muzzles pointed toward the opening. Claws rose from the passageway, the nails tearing into the dirt. The disparate head of the mutant lifted into the twilight air, its yellow eyes quickly turning toward the marines. It bared teeth, almost appearing to smile. It hissed like a cat, gradually pulling its body out from the tunnel. Reimer held both arms out, goading both his men backward.

"Run."

CHAPTER 17

The marines ran, dodging trees and other obstacles as they retreated from the horrific mutant. The creature darted between the trees, its feet kicking gravel with each step.

It staggered, its head jolted by several rounds fired from Gordon and Reimer. Dunn didn't bother shooting, well aware that they couldn't penetrate the skull.

"I already told you, you idiots!"

"Yes…you did," Gordon muttered, amazed by the creature's resilience. Reimer aimed low, putting bullets into its torso and legs. The rounds broke the skin, possibly splintering bones within. But the creature clearly didn't feel any pain. Though the gunshots slowed it, it didn't detract from its goal.

Reimer lagged behind to attract its attention while the others ran ahead. The mutant came to a stop, watching both Reimer and the others as though deciding which to attack. Whatever this beast was, it was capable of basic thought and decision making. And it made its decision, choosing the nearest target. However, it lacked knowledge of weaponry beyond that it was aware its skull had evolved to withstand gunfire. Reimer knew this. Otherwise, it certainly would know to avoid the grenade he threw at it.

The creature marched at him with claws extended, taking no notice of the metal ball bouncing from its hip. The grenade hit the ground and detonated, the resulting concussion throwing the beast to the ground. It crashed against the trunk of a tree, covered in its own blood. Like the ghouls, its flesh was dead, yet, somehow functional. It pushed itself off the ground, its toothy face still fixed on its prey.

Reimer backed several steps, then turned and accelerated into a full sprint. Now he was terrified. Even a grenade explosion couldn't kill its brain.

The creature stood back up, its right leg mangled by the blast. Much of the muscle tissue had been severed, leaving exposed bone beneath a few strings of wet flesh. It leaned forward, putting some of its weight on its elongated arms like an ape.

Reimer could hear it starting to gallop as he cut through a patch of trees. Mud splashed under his boots as he zigzagged between obstacles. He dug his feet down to a full stop, hearing running feet approaching from ahead.

Dunn and Gordon emerged from a veil of fog, both shouting in surprise upon nearly colliding with Reimer.

"Not that way!" Gordon said. Looking past them, Reimer saw the silhouettes of several ghouls in the fog. Several heads moved above the brush, soulless eyes fixed on the fresh meat.

Reimer glanced back, unable to see the mutant. But he knew it was there, somewhere behind those trees. Going back was certainly suicide, as was going forward. He turned to the right and ran with his team mates. Their lungs burned and muscles ached as they traveled another hundred yards. They reached another clearing, their boots landing on solid rock.

"SHIT!" Dunn yelled. Laying several feet ahead of them was the edge of another cliff, leading to a steep fall of twenty feet or more. All three marines twisted in place, digging their boots down to stop themselves. Reimer, catching his breath, peeked over the edge. The bottom was composed of several rocks. The wall itself was jagged, with plenty of space to climb.

"Unpack your gear. We're going this way," he said.

"Corporal?" Dunn said. At first, Reimer suspected it was another protest. Then he noticed the marine pointing his M4 toward the woods. He followed the barrel, seeing its muzzle pointed toward the mutant. It limped from the trees, mouth agape. Its lips peeled back, fully revealing its bloodstained jaws. A strange slurping sound reverberated from its throat.

Its claws were still red with the blood of their comrades. Pieces of meat dangled from its teeth. Thick fluid oozed from the bullet wounds in its head, as well as the gash in its right leg. But it felt no pain. In its world, pain only existed in its prey. It was the same for fear.

The creature sprang forward, its injury slowing it down. With no time to rappel down the cliff, the team spread out. Gordon and Reimer ran to the right, putting several rounds through the creature's torso and neck. Dunn moved left, focusing his shots on its skull.

The creature started to go after the other two. But the numerous impacts on the back of its skull diverted its attention back to Dunn. The PFC fired another shot, hitting the beast square between the eyes. Skin and blood tore from the skull as the bullet ricocheted from its forehead. The creature bellowed, as though angry, and lunged. Dunn squeezed the trigger again, only to find that his mag was empty.

The creature closed the distance, drawing its arm back to swat him like a fly. The marine dove to his right, taking himself over the edge of the cliff. He rolled and reached out, his fingers finding a bump in the rock. He held tight, his chin and hands above the ledge. Everything else dangled twenty feet above the rocky floor. Dunn glanced down, seeing certain death below his boots. His eyes then went back up, as another certain death approached the ledge. In that moment, he debated which fate he'd prefer.

The creature stumbled, blood spraying as a round punched through some of its teeth. It whipped itself around to face Reimer, who struck it with another shot. The Corporal took steady breaths, focusing his aim. The creature leaned forward, ready to spring toward him. Its own blood seeped in thick globs from its mouth.

It launched itself, its head jolting back and forth from repeated hits. It turned its eyes back at him, shrieking as it drew down for the kill. Aiming carefully through the scope, Reimer fired one last shot.

The mutant's eye exploded. Its arms slumped at its sides, the forward momentum throwing its body several feet past the Marine. It hit the dirt, rolling twice before settling near the ledge.

Reimer reloaded, keeping the muzzle fixed on the beast. Gordon, panting heavily, inched toward it. Though it seemed dead, he had learned enough to never be too sure. It was laying face up, its remaining eye appearing glazed. Its jaw was slack, blood pooling into the back of its throat. The right eye was completely gone, strands of thin wet tissue hugging the sides of the socket. Deep down was minced tissue that was its brain.

"I think you got it..." Gordon looked at Reimer, "Sir."

Reimer hurried to Dunn and pulled him back up from the ledge. Dunn struck his hands over his uniform, still coming down from the fright. As he calmed, he glanced at the mutant's dead body. He then turned to Reimer, his mind remembering the things he had said moments ago. Things that were proven wrong. Before he could say the apology, he picked up his M4 and pointed to the woods. Reimer and Gordon turned, seeing several dozen ghouls stumbling from the tree line.

"Son of a dick!" Gordon shouted. He was teetering back and forth, his rifle aim swaying from exhaustion and frustration. "You'd think we'd get a break."

"It's a Z-level 10," Dunn said. "Nobody gets a break here."

"Can we still rope down?"

"These freaks don't care about the ledge," Reimer said. "Even if we got down, they'd be raining down on us before we could even set foot. We wouldn't make it in time."

"They'd probably miss," Gordon said.

"Tell that to Fisher," Dunn said. He watched the horde, counting at least twenty. "Want to take them on, Corporal?"

Reimer let his M4 rest on its sling, opting to use his two Berettas. He could already hear his arms trainer in his mind, *"Only an idiot would actually use a pistol in both hands."* Reimer allowed a small grin to form. He felt that adrenaline rushing through his veins, though this time, he was forcing himself to find a thrill in it.

As he prepared to charge, the air filled with shouts and hollers from behind the trees. Like ancient warriors attacking an enemy camp, five men dashed from the trees, wielding hatchets, baseball bats, and pistols.

The one in the lead, a man in his mid-thirties wearing blue jeans and a denim shirt, held a large serrated knife. The entire back of the herd turned toward the new assailants. The denim wearing man lifted his knee and thrust a hard kick into the nearest flesh-eater, driving it back into two others, creating a domino effect of falling bodies.

As they fell, he rotated to the left and plunged his knife into the skull of another ghoul. Baseball bats and tire irons creased the air, smashing into skulls. The strangers moved with precision, hitting one ghoul and moving right to the next one.

Two of the members, men of Japanese descent, moved at incredible speed. They zigzagged between the undead, driving pipes into their temples. The denim wearing man kept up his assault on the far right, rupturing bone and flesh with his knife and hatchet.

Suddenly, Dunn felt a sense of competition.

"Not sure who these guys are, but I'm not letting them have all the fun." With his rifle at his shoulder, the marine led the charge. He fired rounds into the nearest ghouls, opening their heads like broken ceramic pots. Several ghouls turned in place, now drawn to the cracks of the assault rifles. Reimer followed, firing both Berettas into the horde. Gordon took the right where the ghouls were more scattered. Unlike his friends, he opted for the use of knives, plowing the blades through eye sockets.

The Japanese duo took the advantage of the ghouls' distraction. Running up behind them, they plowed the sharpened edge of their pipes through their craniums. The fourth man, a black-haired individual with the frame of an NFL linebacker, swung an aluminum baseball bat.

A fifth man wore a tattered park ranger uniform and ball cap. He followed the burly man, swinging a machete into the neck of an attacking ghoul. The blade cut through skin with ease and snapped the bone. With repeated hacks, the head fell free and slumped in the soil, resembling one of the rocks scattered along the cliff.

The denim-wearing cowboy drew down with his hatchet, cleaving the skull of the last remaining ghoul. The blade sunk deep, separating both hemispheres of its head. Jaw slack, the corpse dropped to its knees and fell backward.

The clash was over in less than a minute. Bodies littered the ground, their rotted flesh permeating the soil. Dunn and Gordon panted heavily, the former now so exhausted he was on the verge of collapse. Reimer holstered his pistols, checking some of the nearby corpses to make sure they were really dead. Like his friends, he was so exhausted he felt he could sleep for a month. His uniform was now soaked in his own sweat, his pants covered in grime. But behind the exhaustion and physical ache was a feeling of gratitude. He looked to the man in denim, believing him to be the leader.

"Thanks for your help, Mr...?"

"Where's Dr. Hill?" the man said. He sheathed the knife and hatchet into his belt before clutching the handle of his revolver. Reimer stopped, cautiously grabbing his Carbine.

"Whoa, whoa, whoa!" Gordon and Dunn both aimed their rifles, spurring the park ranger into drawing his Glock. The two groups stood at a standstill, the two Japanese men standing off to the side. Their hands reached behind their backs, clutching the handles of snug-nose revolvers, ready to draw should the situation escalate further.

Reimer kept his eyes on the cowboy, his fingertips resting over the frame of his Carbine.

"You know Dr. Hill?"

"Where the hell is she?"

"*We're* looking for her," Reimer said. "The bunker's been overrun. Did you have people looking for her there?" The burly man with the baseball bat lowered his bat and looked wide-eyed at them.

"Oh, no...TWO men?"

"Yes," Reimer said. "The corpses got them before we got there. Dr. Hill wasn't there." The big man looked to park ranger, who already had his Glock lowered. Both men then turned their glance toward the cowboy.

"Ford, they're here to help. Put it away," the big man said.

"Bullshit," Ford snarled, his gun still pointed at them. "You think I'm gonna trust her with THESE guys."

"In case it's not obvious enough, we're with the military," Gordon said.

"Three of you?" Ford said, chuckling. "What is your plan exactly? Take the Doc through the black forest and extract? Looks to me like you barely survived the first trip. So, it'll be a cold day in hell before she goes with you."

"How do you know how we came?" Reimer asked. Dunn, on the other hand, didn't care to know. He was growing impatient in addition to being enraged.

"How 'bout we just shoot you and go on about our day?" he shouted. Ford smiled, as though wanting to accept the challenge. The burly man noticed the revolver slowly turning toward the nervous marine.

"Ford, DON'T!"

"Shut up, Tanner," Ford said.

"We could use their help," Tanner said.

"The hell with that," Ford said. "They'd be dead right now if not for us. Probably should've let it be that way."

"They're good, man. Fuck, man! They killed a mutant!" the park ranger said.

"Yeah? So have I," Ford muttered. "I'm not leaving the doc in these guy's hands. They'll get her killed."

"Get her killed?" Reimer said. "You consider yourself Dr. Hill's caretaker or something?"

"Kept her alive so far," Ford said.

"Not convincing me, considering you can't find her," Reimer said. Ford narrowed his gaze, fixing his eyes on the Corporal. Reimer carefully watched him, specifically his eyes. He held his own hand steady, ready to grab his M4 if necessary.

The revolver lowered as Ford looked high to the sky a mile behind the marines. Everyone turned to look at what he saw. A fizzling streak of light had launched through the air like a rocket.

"Flare!" Tanner said.

"That's her!" Ford said. "Probably heard the gunfire and knew we were close by."

"Wait," Dunn said. "How do you know that's her?!"

"I gave her that flare gun," Ford said. He holstered his pistol and ran past them, moving along the edge of the cliff before disappearing behind the trees. The other four followed. As they passed by, the burly man, Tanner, waved to the marines, gesturing for them to come along.

Reimer and Gordon didn't hesitate to join the group. Dunn paused for a moment to take a breath. He felt uneasy about these people. However, they led to the objective. With Reimer and Gordon accompanying their group, what choice did he have?

Wiping the sweat from his forehead onto his sleeve, he took off after them.

CHAPTER 18

The mouth of the cliff started to bend to the right, forming a near perfect semi-circle. Running clear of the trees, the group could see the cliff wall ahead around the bend. At the mouth of the cliff was a giant horde of the undead.

Ford ran at the front of the group, gauging the numbers as he went. There were at least two hundred of them down there. Corporal Reimer caught up with him and pointed his finger down at the foot of the cliff.

"I see them just fine. You don't need to…"

"No! Look above them. On the wall!" Reimer yelled. Ford squinted and leaned forward. There she was. He could see Dr. Hill clinging on a rock shelf about twelve feet above the horde. She kept her back pressed to the cliff, the toes of her boots protruding over the rounding bump she balanced on.

"Holy crap!" Tanner said. "How are we gonna get her off of that?"

"We got rope," Reimer said. "One of us will have to go down and get her."

"Let's get our asses over there first," Ford said.

The group hustled around the bend. As they neared Dr. Hill, the combined groans of the undead grew louder and louder. Several of them bunched at the mouth of the cliff, compressing those unlucky enough to be in the front. Arms with sagging skin reached up at her.

Dr. Hill took each breath slow and deep, keeping her nerves as calm as possible. She hugged her athletic figure against the wall to keep as still as possible. Even the slightest of movements caused pebbles to break from the tiny ledge. She had dropped her pickaxe during the climb down. By then, there were only three ghouls. But with the twelve-foot drop, she couldn't risk landing without injury, which would leave her susceptible to the ghouls.

She had one flare left and debated how long she should wait before using it. One thing she did know was that she had no plans to die. She didn't believe in offing herself. She believed that a good life awaited, and she needed to overcome great turmoil in order to get to it.

Above her, the team assembled at the edge of the cliff.

"DOC!" Ford called down. Hill looked up, seeing her friends along with men in military gear standing over her.

"Hey!" she called back. "Kinda in a pickle here."

"I'm Corporal Reimer with the U.M.S.C! Just keep still. We'll pick you up," Reimer called down.

"OH! Well, okay! I thought I'd take a stroll, but if you say so..." she joked. Reimer didn't offer a return comment. The day had been long and much had been lost. He unpacked his harness and strung it over his waist and shoulders. Gordon secured the rope to a nearby tree, pulling tight to make sure the loop was secure.

"Give me the rope. I'll go down," Ford said. Reimer chuckled.

"Cowboy, I've known you for about two minutes," he said. "You even know how to do this?"

"How do you think we've survived up here this long?" Ford said.

"Good point," Reimer said. "But the answer's still no. This is my job."

"Fine." Ford leaned close. "But don't think this means I'm letting you take her out of here. You hear me?" Reimer knew his answer wouldn't be well received, so instead he opted to give none.

He slung himself over the ledge and pressed his feet to the wall. He bounced away, descending several feet at a time. He looked down below him, seeing nothing but writhing corpses crowding the ground. The stink rose with the air, thickening with each step down.

The group huddled at the ledge. Dunn inched to the side, still wary of these new companions. It wasn't clear they were to be trusted. Already, he was growing anxious of a future clash. It was clear they would resist Dr. Hill leaving with them, should they ever find a way out of the area.

At the moment, he chose to focus on the task at hand. Reimer was about halfway down now. The undead were growing increasingly flamboyant, likely excited at the sight of fresh meat coming their way.

"Almost there," Reimer called out to Hill. She didn't venture any sarcastic response this time. Instead, she was breathing nervously. She felt the ledge shift under her feet. Gravel rolled down the slope. The shelf, which was practically a bolder wedged into the side of the cliff, was starting to give way. Reimer could see the slight wobbling taking place. He only had seconds to go.

Kicking hard against the wall, he freefell the next fifteen feet, re-securing the grip on the rope and landing right beside Hill. He reached his arm out and she threw herself on him, wrapping both arms under his shoulders. The shelf dipped, not coming out of the wall, but sloping at an angle impossible to stand on.

"Okay, hang tight," Reimer said. He looked back up to the group. "I got her! Mind pulling us up?"

"Yes!" Tanner cheered, high-fiving with the two Japanese men. He and Gordon teamed up around the rope and started pulling up. Ford hurried behind them and grabbed a fistful of the rope to help. All three of them pulled at once, hauling Reimer and Hill up the cliff.

The park ranger looked down over the ledge, informing the other how far they had yet to pull. They pulled together, coiling the slack behind them. After the third pull, Dunn decided to grab the rope behind Ford and help. As they tugged in unison, he watched the cowboy. Ford took no notice of him, as he was focused on the task. Dunn glanced to the Japanese men. They had moved several yards to the side as a couple of corpses roved out from the trees. They bashed their heads with their metal pipes, eventually impaling them with the tips. With them busy and everyone distracted, Dunn watched Ford. It was clear that he was the leader of the group. His mind raced through several scenarios, his anxiety causing him to fixate on the worst cases. Each of them involved a deadly altercation with this group.

Perhaps, once Reimer and Hill are up...

The presence of his sidearm somehow became more evident on his thigh. He was a fast draw. The cowboy's attention would be off of him. The big man didn't appear to carry a gun, he'd be easy to neutralize. If he acted quick enough, he could get them and then the ranger.

A rustling in the brush brought the silent planning to an end. He dropped the rope and whipped around, securing his Carbine and aiming it into the trees.

Feeling the added tension to the line, Ford and Tanner looked back.

"What is it?" Ford asked.

"Don't know," Dunn said. Now the park ranger was looking back, his hand clasping the grip of his Glock. The Japanese duo both reached again for their revolvers.

The snapping of twigs drew their attention to the left, where a small group of undead stepped from the same spot as the recent two. The park ranger rushed in to assist. He jumped into the action, bringing his machete over the forehead of a heavyset ghoul. Dunn watched the melee as it took place. It appeared that the corpses were few enough in number for the survivors to handle. At this moment, he started to question himself over his recent thoughts.

Was I really thinking of going that far?

His mind went back and forth on the topic, as though he had an angel on one shoulder and a devil on the other. His breathing grew heavy and a new sweat accumulated at his brow. He began to wonder if he had lost his nerve. All he truly knew was that he didn't want his remaining friends to die, or any other soldiers for that matter. The memory of Cable screaming under the ground carried in his brain as though it was presently happening. A flood of anxiety struck him.

He looked back to the woods, hearing a high-pitched shriek. It almost sounded like a person in pain.

Next came the sound of fast paced footsteps. Another shriek filled the air.

It came lumbering from the trees. It was a scrawny figure, only about five-foot-six. Its skin was as pasty white as drywall. Its head was perfectly round, the eyes bulging from the sockets, displaying catlike pupils. Its jaw had mutated, the cheeks almost completely gone, exposing pointed sharp teeth where the crowns had previously been.

Its hands were gone, the flesh around the wrists peeled back, revealing a dark red flesh as spear-tipped bones protruded from the forearms.

"Holy..." Tanner muttered. Dunn aimed his rifle and initiated pressure on the trigger.

At that moment, it darted into the group with the speed of a cheetah. Dunn fired off a shot, the bullet going wide as it closed.

"JESUS!" He panicked, dashing to the side. The group split apart, everyone but Gordon letting go of the rope. Suddenly, all two-hundred-and-seventy pounds were resting on him, causing him to stumble to the edge of the cliff.

Dangling twelve feet below, Reimer and Hill tensed, hearing the horrid sounds above.

Ford drew his revolver and fired, striking the ghoul in the neck as it sprinted. Like all its brethren, it felt no pain. It cocked both arms back at shoulder height and closed in on the park ranger. Two shots from his Glock punched through its chest as it lunged. It tackled him to the ground, the pistol bouncing from his hand. The park ranger yelled out as it repeatedly stuck him in the gut with both arms. Blood sprayed in large gushes, smothering its white skin.

Ford fired again, the .357 caliber bullet skidding off the back of its head. The mutant slammed its face down into the ranger's mashed torso, its shark-like teeth ripping chunks of entrails free. It looked at the others, face stained bright red. It jumped off of the ranger as though weightless as a bird. It let out a horrifying shriek as it ran at them again. The group scattered, bullets whizzing in a frenzy.

The ghoul jumped like a grasshopper, landing on top of Tanner. Teeth immediately came down on his face, tearing his cheeks and lips as the spear bones stabbed into his belly. The burly man stumbled back, dropping his baseball bat in fright. He pressed both palms into its belly and pushed, but it held on like a cat. It yanked its head back, teeth tearing away scraps of cheek, then clamped its jaws onto his hand. Tanner screamed as flesh and bone tore away. The creature shook its head, severing the index, middle, and ring finger from his right hand.

Consumed by pain, shock, and confusion, Tanner fell on his back, the creature still on top of him. A series of grunts left his lungs as the mutant punched its forearms through his ribcage, showering the cliffside with blood.

Gordon watched in helplessness as the creature ravaged the man just ten feet from where he held the rope. Below him, Reimer tried pulling himself up. They could see glimpses of the creature as it tore into Tanner. Behind it, Ford and Dunn rushed in.

The creature jumped to its feet, ready to attack. Dunn fired an automatic at full blast into the creature's chest and face. Like the other mutant, its skull had evolved to withstand gunfire. However, it wasn't hardened to the same extent. The final few rounds cracked the forehead, causing the creature to stumble back toward the ledge. The formerly round skull was now disproportioned, the bone having been broken. However, the brain was still intact.

Ford threw himself at the beast, knocking it back with a kick to the chest. The mutant staggered backward and tipped over the ledge.

"Adios, motherfucker," Ford said.

In its fall, the creature threw its arms out wildly, the tip of the bones splintering against the earth that made up the cliff. In that same moment, it found itself hugging the wall, its right arm lodged in a crack between two rocks.

Reimer and Hill looked down. At the same time, the creature gazed up at them. One eye bulged completely from its socket as the broken portions of skull shifted. Blood, both human and its own, trickled from its mouth. It dug its arms and feet into the cliff and began its climb.

"Get us up!" Reimer yelled.

The survivors assembled behind Gordon and helped him tug back. Reimer pulled one of his Berettas and aimed down. The creature was ascending rapidly, its head now appearing as soft as membrane. With the constant jolting and swinging, he couldn't fix his aim. He fired off a shot, the bullet missing it by a yard. Subsequent shots produced the same result.

"Get us up!" a terrified Dr. Hill called out. They were just a few feet from the ledge. The Japanese duo reached down and grabbed Dr. Hill by the wrists. As they hauled her up, Dunn and Ford reached for Reimer. They grabbed him by the vest and yanked back. He cleared the ledge, just as the creature had lashed out at them. It missed, almost losing its hold of the cliff in the process.

Ford drew the hatchet from his belt and rushed toward the cliff edge. The mutant was only two feet below the shelf. It looked up at him, smiling with prickly teeth.

He swung his axe down on top of its skull, splitting bone and brain matter as it carved down to the base of the neck. The head peeled apart in two folds, and the mutant fell freely into the horde below.

Dr. Hill rested on her hands and knees, brushing strands of blond hair from her eyes. Sounds of labored breathing turned her gaze over her left shoulder. Tanner was still alive, his entire torso appearing as if he had fallen over a buzz-saw. She put her hand over her mouth and looked away...only to see the park ranger's corpse.

"Ohhh...my god," she was nearly sobbing.

Ford stood over Tanner, barely recognizing his face. The flesh around the mouth and eyes had been chewed. Muscle and bone tissue were exposed on the right side of his face, including the edge of his eye socket. He shook in pain, unable to speak.

"Sorry, man," Ford said. He pressed the muzzle of his revolver to his friend's temple and squeezed the trigger.

CHAPTER 19

The journey from the cliffside was long and quiet. Hardly a word was spoken within the group as the marines followed the survivors along a hidden path downhill. They had walked the edge of the cliff to an incline that led down a large hill. On their way, they passed several ghouls, many caught in barbed wire fence. There were several rows of this fencing strung up in the forest as they approached the lake. With struggling bodies entangled and dead ones lying about, it resembled a World War 1 battlefield.

Even Dunn didn't ask questions about their destination. At the moment, with no pickup available, they didn't have much choice other than to put their faith into this band of survivors. The leader, Ford, took the lead, with Dr. Hill at the center of the group. The group formed a tight circle around her. There were no qualms that she had to be protected.

Only a few stray ghouls walked the path, all easily eliminated by Ford and his tomahawk. A chill began to overtake the air. The fog had thickened, moistening each person.

"Don't swallow it. Try not to let it in your eyes," Hill whispered back to the marines. Reimer nodded, wiping some of the condensation off his forehead with his sleeve.

"What if we breathe it in?" Dunn whispered.

"Don't," Hill said. She had already put a medical mask over her face, as did the others. Realizing the marines didn't have any, she handed out a few spares. The supply balanced out, as these were intended for the other members of her group.

The ground grew moist as they approached the lakeshore. Grey fog danced into unfathomable shapes as it slowly moved over the water. The surface was completely still, resembling a sheet of glass. The trees around it were barren. Even the pines were void of life, their needles all turned to brown and broken away. The branches were dried out, many having broken off and scattered onto the earth. The cattails stood at the edge of the shore, though discolored and cracked.

"Hold here," Ford whispered. He and the two men walked behind the trees, while Hill and the marines waited at the shoreline. The water was discolored, almost like a soup broth. Reimer wasn't sure if it was the mist or lack of sunlight, or something in the molecular structure. Whatever it was, the last thing he wanted was to take a sip of it.

Gordon looked down, growing nervous at the sight of mud beneath his feet. Dunn was looking back into the woods. His hand never left his Carbine. Through the trees were the whispers of a thousand undead corpses, all in the distance. The whole forest sounded alive, but instead of bugs, birds, and deer, it was the gnarling sounds of decaying bodies. Some were louder, close to resembling yells. Dunn shook as a high-pitched scream echoed from the west. It was distant, sounding like a female's voice.

"The hell?" Gordon said. With his rifle raised, he began to step away from the shore. Dunn's bodily expression came alert, his eyebrows lifted high into his forehead.

"Don't even begin to suggest we go out and—"

"Shh, ignore it," Hill said. All three marines looked at her. "Believe me, you'll get used to it. Consider it the replacement for the loons." They looked to the right of the mud trail as they heard the grating sound of metal. Ford and the two Japanese men stepped out from between the trees, dragging two twelve-foot aluminum boats.

"What? We going fishing?" Dunn said. Ford gave him a glare, then looked at Hill. They could see the reluctance in his eyes. Without saying anything, he and the other two pushed the boat two-thirds into the water. The group gathered into the boats. Reimer, Hill, Dunn, and Ford gathered in the right, while Gordon went with the others. He took the center seat to row, only for one of the others to gesture for him to move.

"I'm more than happy to…"

"Best to just let him do it," Ford said. "Keep quiet and trust us." He sat at the center seat of his boat, while Reimer gave them a shove-off before jumping in. The boat glided several feet out, fishtailing slowly into the weeds until Ford steadied it with the oars. Moments later, the second boat was right behind them.

Ford rowed in silence, moving the boat around the cattails. Each thrust was slow, with minimal disturbance to the water. They punched through a thick fogbank, traveling blind for several yards. Reimer held his breath. Even with the facemask on, he didn't want to risk inhaling any of that moisture. After a minute, the cloud passed away.

"Whoa," Dunn muttered, ducking his head as they passed under a low-hanging branch. He looked back, then at Ford with disdain, then looked down into the water. They were traveling in shallow water. He could see the weeds bunched in groups under the surface. They clung to the oars like octopus arms. Ford shook them off, then proceeded several meters, then repeated the same motion. The pace remained extremely slow, causing Dunn to grow impatient. "Hey, *Billy Jack*." Ford turned to look at him. "If you're too afraid to hustle it up, I'll be more than happy to give it a go."

The cowboy shook his head.

"You obviously have no clue what's happened here."

"I understand things are different," Reimer said.

"It's beyond different," Hill said. "It's worse."

"Shh!" Ford hissed. The group sat in silence as he continued to steer their boat east along the shore. Ghouls walked the shoreline, several of them having fallen and bunched in the weeds. Looking left, they could see bloated bodies floating further out in the lake like rafts.

Twenty more minutes passed in silence before Ford steered them into a thin cove. A low hanging tree leaned over the water, casting shade as though it were an umbrella. Beneath that tree was a large fifty-foot Gibson boat, anchored twenty feet off shore.

The formerly white hull was discolored from residue from the tree as well as the water, now appearing clay-colored in places. The cabin was a little under seven feet tall, with sliding glass doors providing access on both sides. A sundeck stretched over the cabin and living quarters, divided into two sections by a small set of stairs in the middle. A walkway surrounded the cabin, leading to a forward and aft deck.

Looking through the mist, Reimer could see figures leaning on the port guardrail on the aft deck. He counted three of them, two males and a female. After spotting the group, they began assembling at the stern deck edge. One of them, a muscular man with a thick bushy beard, extended his hand to Dr. Hill after Ford brought the boat along the Gibson.

The other two looked at the boats in surprise. The woman's mouth gaped with alarm after realizing numerous members of their group weren't there.

"Wait...who are these people?" she cried out.

"Where's Tanner and Nick?" the second man said.

Ford shook his head and tossed him a rope to secure the boat.

"There was another mutant," he said.

"You're shitting me!"

"I'm sorry. Rick got a few rounds off, but it was fast," Dunn said. He glanced over at Reimer. "Nick was the park ranger you met back there."

"I'm sorry I didn't get to know him better," Reimer said. The two men climbed aboard, followed by Dunn as the other boat brushed along the hull. The bearded man helped Gordon and the others secure their boat. Reimer and Ford stepped to the starboard rail to make space while Gordon climbed aboard. The second male survivor, a black man around the age of forty, approached Ford.

"What about Jacques? Or Shoemaker? What happened to them?"

"They checked out the bunker and got overrun. Joe and Kevin bit the dust in the woods near the place. Got confused in the fog, I guess," Ford said. The man took a step back, his face a riptide of shock. The brunette woman ran off the deck, overwhelmed with shock and disbelief.

"Damn idiots wouldn't listen to me. Told them not to split off," Ford said.

"Probably Shoemaker's idea. Always wanting to be the boss. I always told him his ego would get him killed."

Ford glanced at the marine. "Corporal Reimer, this is 57. 57, meet Corporal Reimer of the U.S. Marines."

Reimer struggled to hide his puzzled look as he shook hands.

"He says I look like Wesley Snipes," 57 said, answering the Corporal's unspoken question.

"Oh, I get it now," Reimer said. He pointed to his fellow marines. "That's PFC Dunn and Private Gordon."

"Unless the marines are crazy enough to only send a three-man team, I'm assuming you guys are what's left of your unit," 57 said.

"Started with ten…" Reimer said.

"Twelve, if you count the pilots," Dunn said. His eyes were fixed on Dr. Hill as he spoke, his voice like a radio announcer. He wanted to be sure she knew.

"Now it's just us," Reimer continued.

"We lost six people. You lost nine. Sounds like we've both had a rough day," the bearded man said. He shook his hands with each of the marines. "Name's McCartney. These fellas there, just call them Han and Jones."

The two Japanese men looked up and nodded, then proceeded to get back to work. McCartney forced a smile.

"Japanese interns. Came for the school, stayed for the apocalypse."

"They speak English?" Dunn said.

"They call it English. Not sure I'd agree," McCartney joked.

"Go jerk yourself, McCartney!" the one nicknamed Han called out.

McCartney smiled. "Okay, maybe better than I let on. Though, I can't even begin to pronounce their real names correctly. You can thank Ford for their nicknames."

Gordon thought about it for a minute. Suddenly, it all came to mind. Jones, Han…Ford? Suddenly it made sense. He chuckled. "Very clever."

"What can I say, he's my favorite actor…was. And we share the same last name," Ford said. Gordon smiled then glanced at 57.

"Shocked he doesn't call you *Lando*."

"He told me he would have, but then Disney butchered the character," 57 said.

"Bastard movie was the last thing I saw before the world went to shit. Probably what stirred the dead from their graves," Ford muttered. The stern look had shed from his face, replaced by a surprisingly warm smile. It lasted a few seconds, only to disappear as he stared across the deck. The missing presence of six people couldn't go unnoticed. "I need a beer."

"You have beer?" Dunn said. Ford grimaced, regretting speaking his thoughts out loud. He sighed and waved them on.

"Come on," he said.

He led them through the starboard walkway and opened the sliding door. They entered the cabin, hearing the brunette's cries through the closed doors of the master bedroom below. Ford opened the fridge and tossed beer bottles to the marines and the other survivors. McCartney declined, opting to check on the brunette.

"Michele, it's me. Open up."

Dr. Hill took a seat on the sofa near the helm. As she sipped her beer, she noticed a piercing stare from the cowboy as he twisted the cap off his bottle. Reimer noticed it too. He had seen the same look in Dunn's eyes.

"You and I are gonna talk," Ford said to her.

"I told you, it HAD to be done," she said.

"Bullshit," he said. "You manipulated those two to escort you. I told you we'd discuss going to that bunker. You deliberately waited until I was out on a supply run."

Hill sighed and downed half of her bottle. She inhaled deeply and ran her sleeve over her mouth. "Can we do this another time?"

Gordon pressed the cold bottle to his face, the cool sensation helping him relax. The realization came to him that the refrigerator was working. The lights were on, meaning the boat had power.

"How long have you guys been here?"

"I don't know," Ford said. "What's the date?"

"Since it began," 57 said.

"Weren't there transports?" Gordon asked. Ford's angry expression seemed to deepen.

"Transports?" he faked a chuckle. "You know? They said there'd be transports. It was all over the radio. The TV. They gave designated locations. I went there. My fiancé was with me. So were, like, a thousand other people. But it never came. At least, not to ours."

"What do you mean?" Reimer asked.

"My fiancé and I," he paused briefly as he reminisced, "we both knew something wasn't right. Word was starting to get around, something about settlements to the west. That was when New Mexico went dark. Idaho had become a warzone. We waited for days, but the pickup never happened. So, we tried for it ourselves. Got in a truck and went west, hoping we could get to those settlements we'd been hearing about. We made it maybe a hundred miles when we saw a chopper. Big military kind with the drop doors, forgive me if I don't know the name. But we saw it coming down over a patch of trees near the Castle Hills. Of course, none of the broadcasts said to group there, but hell, we didn't care. We went. Truck broke down. Undead began gathering around us. But we got through. We saw the chopper in the grass. Its ramp door was open. Soldiers were escorting several suits inside. Wasn't no regular citizen, I can tell you that. We ran, waving our arms to flag them."

"Maybe they didn't see you," Gordon said. A fist caught him on the jaw, knocking him to the floor. Beer splattered over the wood floor. Reimer and Dunn jumped to their feet, their hands ready to go for their weapons. Ford unbuttoned his denim shirt and pulled down the collar of his undershirt. Gordon looked up, hand rubbing his jaw as he saw what Ford was showing. It was a rounded scar near his shoulder. He had seen many like it. Judging by its greyish-red color and jumbled skin around it, it was about eighteen-months old.

"What?" he said.

"They *saw* us, alright," Ford said. "Like I said, you guys don't know what's going on. You think, with a remaining area composed of two-and-a-half states, that they'll want the whole country swarming there? Eating up resources? Hell no."

Reimer sat down. Suddenly, it made sense why Ford was quick to draw on them back at the cliff. Dunn helped Gordon get up to his feet. He then turned to the doctor. She was tapping her fingers against her beer bottle, looking somewhat disconnected from the conversation. Dunn stared at the boat, then glared out the window into the surrounding area. He downed the rest of the beer. It did little to calm his nerves. He couldn't stop dwelling on the fact that they had no extraction. The thought of living on this boat for years to come made him as uneasy as walking through the forest. He looked back at the doctor.

"So, this data you have? Is it on a disk, or a—"

"It's a flash-drive," she said. Dunn looked around. He didn't see any lab equipment inside the boat. Everything pertained to survival.

"How'd you develop…"

"I had a laboratory," she said. "Ten miles across the river. I was given coordinates of the old bunker. Managed to make it to the lake, almost got overrun. These guys found me. Told them the mission, and here I am."

"You guys GOTTA get her to the Border," 57 said. "I'm sure they've got labs there. She says they can make an anti-virus that can inoculate people against this disease."

"We're well aware," Reimer said. "Problem is, we have no extraction."

"What?" Hill said, wide-eyed.

"Chopper went down. Flock of...birds...came and attacked the cockpit," Reimer said. He narrowed his gaze at Hill. "You care to explain that to us?"

"Freaking undead birds," Dunn remarked.

"They're not undead," Hill explained. "They are diseased but not undead. They're just one example of the phenomenon that's taken place. We've noticed effects in the animal life that feeds off the ghouls. The birds and insects will pick the dead skin off the corpses, just like they used to do with roadkill. But in this case, they're ingesting infectious meat. They're still technically alive, but they suffer extreme cognitive defects...and a heightened sense of aggression."

"A heightened sense of aggression. Explains why they went after us."

"It's happened with insect life. Birds, as you saw. Some mammals. Hell, even the fish. Bodies float in the lake, fish pick at them, you can figure out the rest."

"What about everything else that's going on?" Gordon said. "The plants? The mist? The *mutants*?"

Hill glanced at him, then looked at Reimer. "When you said things are different, and I said they're worse, well...it gets worse."

"What's going on here?" Reimer said.

"You see, the effects on the environment: the plant-life, the undead, the soil, water... it's all part of the progressing evolution of this disease. Even though the ghouls have a partially functioning brain, they're still decaying. They've been lumbering around, flaking off skin cells onto the ground. Each cell filled with disease, is consumed by the earth just like everything else. If one is killed and its body left on the ground, everything is eventually consumed by the soil just like every other creature in life."

"So, you're saying that the environment is...mutating, so to speak?" Gordon said.

"That's one word," Hill said. "Another is *evolving*. It's adapting to survive this outbreak. This forest was one of the first areas to have widespread outbreaks, thus, the environment has had more time to adapt and evolve. We're seeing whole new species turning up all around this forest."

"Like a giant Venus Fly Trap?" Gordon said. All eyes turned to him with interest.

"Haven't seen one of those," Hill said. "But I've seen other species. Saw one that looks like a big pod, with acid in its center. It pulls in prey with vines, and…"

"I get it, that's enough," Reimer said. "How exactly does this allow the plant life to survive? Is it a cellular thing?"

"Partially. But evolving into carnivorous beings allows the plants to feed off the dead as well. This process is probably why the animals are surviving as well, except their process is far more gradual. It might take a few generations for them to adapt."

"What about us?" Dunn asked. Hill shrugged her shoulders.

"I'm sorry to say, humanity gets the shit end of the stick," she said. "Those ghouls, life after death, *that* is our so-called evolution. And it doesn't stop there."

"The mutants," Reimer said.

"That's right. As the disease has progressed, it's allowed several of the hosts to adapt. Some of them generated increased calcium levels in their bones, notably their skulls to provide greater protection for the brain. Takes more than a shot to the head to put them down. There's the one we saw at the cliff. More agile, able to move with bursts of speed. The disease in these hosts doesn't alter the flesh the same way as normal corpses. Others have evolved to slow their decay in certain environments. Some live in the water. Others burrow under the ground."

"We saw them," Gordon said.

"Doctor, you said this disease has been affecting the environment, and that this area has had the longest exposure," Reimer said. "What about the rest of the country? Hell, the world? You mean to say that what's happened here will happen everywhere?"

Hill took a final slug of her beer then nodded.

"No," Dunn said. "It can't be. It'd be impossible to survive outside of the Border."

"It's inevitable, Corporal. Rest assured, this disease is adapting to every terrain and every climate. There's nowhere to go. What you've seen here is just the beginning. This is how the world survives." She tossed her empty bottle into a nearby bin, shattering it along the bottom.

CHAPTER 20

Reimer woke up from his snooze in a fury. The dreams were like lightning strikes in his brain. Once again, he had seen every man and woman he had lost. This time, the dreams focused heavily on Lowry. Even as he sat awake on the sofa, Reimer could see the young man's terrified face as the chopper pitched. His screams still rang in his ears. Reimer found himself going over the normal routine to silence the imaginary sounds and images. He closed his eyes, which resulted in nothing but clearer mental images. He sat silently and faced the truth: there was no shutter for the mind's eye.

Looking out the window, he could see it was still daytime, though it looked like dusk. He pulled his sleeve back and checked his watch, realizing he had only slept for an hour. Across the room, Dunn way laying back on the other couch. Reimer recognized the subtle twitches in his face. He was having the same nightmares. Reimer looked around the room, unsure where Gordon was. Through the window, he could see McCartney and 57 moving through the pathway toward the forward bow.

From the stairway which led to the sleeping quarters, the brunette woman approached. Her eyes were still red from her previous weeping. Otherwise, she looked like an entirely different person from who he saw when he arrived on the boat. She stood straight with her hair hanging out through a ballcap. Her shirt was buttoned down, tucked into cargo pants. A Sig Saur was holstered on her left hip.

"Hi," she said. "Sorry I didn't take time to introduce myself before. I'm Michele."

Reimer reached out to shake her hand. "No need to apologize."

"I saw all you in the boat, I thought most of our people made it back. When I saw all your faces, I realized we lost more than we thought. I guess it hit me a little hard."

"If it didn't, I would think less of you," Reimer said. He glanced at her weapon. "How much ammo do you people have?"

"Not a lot," she said. "We've salvaged. I got this from my brother, who was a gun guy. He didn't make it. When we go on supply runs, we try to focus on moving quietly and using knives and blunt weapons. The undead are attracted to the sound of gunshots anyway."

"Yeah, but you're in the heart of undead territory," Reimer said. "Getting around unseen is near impossible."

"It is," Michele said. "Believe me. Our group was even bigger before. Seems like every time we go out, someone doesn't come back."

She stared out the window into the fog, as though wondering when it would be her turn. There was an underlying anxiety that she clearly lived with day-to-day. Reimer couldn't blame her. He'd only been here for a day. He couldn't imagine living here for over a year. Michele turned from the window and looked back at him, her eyes filled with hope.

"Are you gonna get us all out of here?"

Even though he expected the question, he was still taken off guard. He didn't know what to say. He hadn't planned on rescuing anyone other than the VIP. He gazed back at her. The attempt at a tough look didn't hide the pain that was in her eyes.

"Of course," he said. "We just need to get in contact with Headquarters." Michele's face seemed to brighten. A small smile cracked over her lips.

"Oh, thank God," she whispered. She even let out a small laugh. "If you do, you're my fucking hero."

Reimer smiled back. "It's my job."

Now, his mind was focused on extraction. He had found the VIP and her cure, now he had to get her the hell out of this area. At that moment, his brain exploded into action as he tried to work out a plan. The burst of energy suddenly triggered the discomfort in his bladder.

He stood up and went to the bathroom. While relieving his bladder, he noticed conversation coming from the master bedroom. There were two voices, one male, one female. Right off the bat, he could tell the conversation was not a pleasant one. His mind flashed to the gathering in the cabin, when Ford confronted Hill about going out on her own. At that moment, he recognized the voices as theirs.

"No, don't give me that shit about timing. I told you to wait until I got back. You didn't listen. You got two people killed taking you out there, and we lost FOUR more trying to get you back. All for what?"

"I'm sorry, Ford, but you don't understand."

"I think I understand just fine."

"No. If you think you can get me out of here yourself, you clearly don't understand. We have no vehicle. Even if we did, the roads are blocked. The only way out of here is through airlift."

"If you think I'm gonna put my faith in them, you're mistaken. You're lucky I even let them aboard this boat."

"My research isn't doing any good here on this boat, Ford. What happened to you is tragic, but believe me, it's not gonna happen with them. I won't let it."

Reimer stepped away, not caring to listen to any more. It was more evidence he would have to deal with Ford at some point. He stepped out of the bathroom, surprised to see Dunn standing there.

"Jesus, Dunn," Reimer said, keeping his voice down. "If I hadn't just went, you'd have made me piss myself." Dunn didn't smile at his joke.

"Are you hearing this?" He pointed at the door. Reimer glanced back, making sure nobody else was around. Michele had stepped outside and he could see Han and Jones through one of the windows.

"Not now," he said.

"If not now, when?" Dunn whispered, his face mad with anticipation. They walked away from the door toward the helm. "If we manage to get a pickup over here, this guy might initiate a mutiny against us. I'm telling you, he's paranoid."

"*He's* paranoid," Riemer said, failing to conceal a small laugh.

"All I can say is that he's not gonna let you bring someone in," Dunn said. "He's gonna compromise the mission. I don't know about you, man, but I just wanna get back home."

"Wait...you want to go back? Weren't you the one suggesting we desert and go north?"

"Look, after everything I've seen, I have to assume that the doc is right. The environment is changing. If it happens everywhere, there won't be anywhere to hide. I hate to say it, but I'm better off behind the Border."

"What would you suggest then?" Reimer said. Dunn glanced around again, double checking for anyone in listening distance, then leaned in close.

"We can't trust them. They're loyal to that Ford guy. I say, let's just take them all out now. We have superior weapons and the advantage of surprise."

"Dunn, I actually thought you were turning sane for a moment," Reimer muttered. "You can't be serious."

"I'm dead serious, Reimer."

"Motherfucker, I thought I knew you!"

"Reimer, we need to think of the facts here—"

"The fact is, you need to get a damn grip!" Reimer muttered harshly. "I have a plan, and these guys are a part of it. We're rescuing them all. They've taken us in. They kept the doctor alive up till now. Have some faith, for the love of God. Hell, have some humanity. We're marines, not murderers."

"Is it humanity you have? Or are you just unwilling to make the tough decisions?" Dunn said. Reimer glared at him in complete disbelief. He had served with this man for years. And for years, he watched him degrade, though the downward spiral really accelerated with the fall of mankind. But never did Reimer think he'd hear these suggestions coming from his friend's mouth.

"Whoa! There he is! Get 'em!" 57 shouted from outside. Next was the sound of a loud grunt followed by a splash. Dunn and Reimer grabbed their rifles and dashed outside. They saw the water rippling from the aft deck. 57 and McCartney stood at the starboard railing, the former holding a sharp metal pipe.

"What's going on?"

"A swimmer," 57 said.

"A swimmer?" Dunn asked.

"Yeah. Remember how the doc mentioned their evolving? Well, some are adapting to water," McCartney said, brushing the moisture from his beard.

"Well shit," Dunn said. "Why the hell are we anchored in the shallows?"

"The weeds are thicker here," 57 said. "They usually get stuck in them or avoid them in general. They're more prone to attacking in the deeper waters."

"Perhaps they're getting more of an appetite," McCartney said. He moved across the deck to the port side. The marines followed, seeing another swimmer reaching up from the water. The stench radiated from its flesh as it fought against the weed bed. Whatever humanity was in its face had disappeared under its soggy looking skin. Its eyes were glassy and black, the skin having taken the murky green color of the water. Its skin peeled back, revealing purple veins. Its hand slapped the side of the deck, webbed fingers clawing at the helm.

57 reached up with his pipe and thrust it through the swimmer's eye. It twitched and spasmed before falling back into the weeds. 57 dabbed the tip of the pipe into the water to rid it of the syrupy goo that accumulated, then stepped away from the railing.

"This is what we call "swimmer patrol,"" McCartney said. "Like we said, normally, we don't get many over here." Another splash echoed from near the forward deck. The two survivors moved toward the port walkway.

"Han! Jones! What's up?"

"Another one," Jones called back.

"He speaks English okay," Reimer said.

"Maybe it's just their names that's hard to pronounce," McCartney joked. "But those guys are good at supply runs. You can rely on them for anything."

"Because we're short and quick. Not big and clumsy like you, white boy," Hans called from the forward deck.

"Charming," Reimer said. "What were they studying?" 57 chuckled and glanced at him.

"International Political Science," he said. "They wanted to be ambassadors."

"Sounds like they would've been great at it." Reimer moved around to the steps, seeing Gordon standing on the sundeck. He was sitting on one of the chairs, clearly distraught. Even from the deck, Reimer could see the defeat in his eyes. After hearing Ford's story, his world view had been shattered. He always took refuge in believing they were making a difference with their missions. Now, he was questioning every operation he had ever been a part of since the outbreak. He was never so naïve to think that his government was without sin. However, he didn't think they were so far gone. Each thought was plain on his face.

Reimer stepped up to accompany him.

"How are you doing, Private?" he asked. Gordon let out a sigh and crossed his arms.

"World's changed I guess, sir," he said.

"It isn't the first time, and it won't be the last," Reimer said. He glanced back, making sure to keep an eye on Dunn. He was standing halfway on the steps, his face maintaining the same grimacing stare. Reimer looked back to Gordon. "But you're still the same guy."

"What's that worth, sir?" Gordon said.

"It's worth everything," Reimer said. "These people are counting on us to help them. And that's what we're gonna do." He spoke loud enough to make sure he could be heard from everyone on the ship. The ploy worked, as he heard the sliding doors open up. Ford marched around the walkway and came around the steps to the sundeck. Reimer watched him in his peripheral vision, while keeping his main focus on the Private. "Most importantly, we're gonna get the VIP and the data back. Even if your leaders failed you, at least you're playing a big part in saving mankind. If we get her back and get everyone inoculated against this virus, then everything we've been through wasn't for nothing."

"What's the plan, then?" Dunn said.

"We use this boat and get to the radio tower," Reimer said. "There's gotta be functioning equipment there. We can get a signal out to Headquarters and get evac sent over. They can pick us up right from this boat. We won't even have to be fighting off the undead during the meantime."

"What about the birds?" Gordon asked.

Dr. Hill stepped up the stairway. "We haven't seen any birds in this area. I think they avoid the mist. They seem to keep beyond the black forest."

"That sounds about right. That's where we were attacked," Reimer said.

"How high were you at the time?"

"Our altitude was low. We were looking for a place to set down," Reimer said.

"The birds seem to keep to the trees. I would advise any aircraft to travel at as high an altitude as possible until arriving at the lake. Once they're here, they should be okay."

"Too bad we didn't know this before," Dunn muttered.

"I...I lost contact before I could give specific instructions," Hill said.

"Never mind that," Ford said. "Corporal, say you succeed; what's gonna happen to the rest of us once you get Stacy out of here?"

"Ford, I'm planning on getting you all out of here," Reimer said. Ford's expression was blank. Reimer saw his head slowly shaking back and forth.

"Why don't I believe you?"

Reimer noticed Dunn glaring at him, mouthing the words "*We can take 'em.*" The Corporal tensed as he started growing nervous. He shook his head slightly, hoping nobody was catching on to their silent conversation.

"I will tell Border Command about the whole group," Reimer said. "You all will come back with us." The whole group of survivors were now assembling on the aft deck behind Ford.

"Ford, listen to him," Michele said. "He's our only ticket out of here."

"I get you have trust issues man, but she's right," 57 said. "I don't know about you, but I'm tired of living like this."

"I for one, never thought I'd be sick of a vacation boat," McCartney quipped.

"That's because you're supposed to be fishing for FISH off this thing," 57 said. "Not swimming corpses!" Ford turned around, his face red with anger.

"You idiots don't get it," he said. "Even if the Corporal's intentions are pure, those commanding him do not see this the same way. They will see that we don't make it over the Border alive. We've all been left behind already. They don't see us fit to be a part of their new 'civilization'."

Reimer watched Dunn's facial tics. The marine was growing increasingly unhinged hearing Ford speaking. His hand was tightening around the grip of his M4. With the survivors all assembled, it would be a clean shoot. Reimer stepped toward them, inconspicuously putting himself between Dunn and the group.

"It doesn't make sense," 57 said. "I think you're wrong, man."

"I'm not," Ford said. "I've already seen it happen. I barely survived the first time. I'm not going through it again, nor am I gonna let you all stumble into this trap."

"It's not a trap!" Reimer yelled.

"We can do this," Dunn muttered.

"Shut up, man," Reimer snapped at him. "Ford, listen! I'm the commanding officer of this mission! The evac team will have to do as I say. I will inform them that you are all part of Dr. Hill's security team and staff."

"Bullshit," Ford said. "Even if you're telling the truth, your superiors will see right through that lie."

"Not quite," Reimer said. "A lot of the CDC's records were lost when the outbreaks went widespread. It's possible that many of the staff profiles were lost. Dr. Hill, what do you say?"

"It's a strong possibility," she said. Ford glanced at her, then at each of the survivors behind him. It was clear they wanted to put their faith in the marines. Ford's hand moved away from his revolver.

"Why should I trust you, Corporal?"

A few moments of silence passed between them. Reimer felt the presence of all the people he had failed to save. He pictured Lowry's face on the Super Stallion.

"I give you my word," he said. "I have your back." He pictured the poor boy falling to his death, then shook his head to rid the image from his mind. He was going to succeed this time.

Ford slowly ascended the steps until he stood in front of Reimer. His hands were clenched into fists, the doubt in his heart overwhelming. The inner conflict was overwhelming, the doubt evident in his eyes.

His right fist opened up as he extended his hand. A rush of relief swept through the Corporal as they shook hands.

"I'm holding you to it, Marine," Ford said.

"I expect nothing less," Reimer said. The tension subsided, allowing everyone to rest at ease. Dunn stepped back, his finger now away from the trigger. He was still apprehensive, but at the moment, he was outvoted.

Reimer walked with Ford down the steps and around to the cabin. "We need to get cracking. The longer we wait, the worse it'll get. By the looks of it, these swimmers are getting hungrier."

"If they're coming into the shallows, they are," Ford said. "What do you need me to do?"

"Get everyone geared up with whatever you got," Reimer said. "We need to take this boat across the lake and find the shore nearest to that radio tower. Any idea how far it is from the lake?"

"Just under a mile," Ford said. "If we move fast, it won't take long to get there by foot."

"That's assuming you don't meet any of the infected," Dr. Hill said.

"That's why we need to take almost everybody," Ford said. "We need to get these marines safely to that station for the plan to work. None of us know the frequency." Ford nudged the Corporal. "Congratulations. You get to be the VIP this time."

Reimer smiled. "Feels good to be special." He glanced back to the doctor, who was standing in the doorway. "Dr. Hill, you'll be waiting here on the boat. We didn't come all this way for you to be torn apart out there. Ford, I suggest at least one person stay with her in case the swimmers show up."

"McCartney will stay. He's big and strong, but he's not a fast runner. I'd feel better he wait with Hill."

"Then we have a plan," Reimer declared, knocking on a wood plank.

"Excuse me, Doctor," Ford said as he moved through the doorway. "Han! Jones! Clear up the propellers! We're moving out in three!"

The interns grabbed up some paddles and poles from the forward deck and sprinted to action. They gathered on the deck edge and stirred the water, pulling the weeds away from the rear of the boat. As they worked, 57 and Michele patrolled the walkways for swimmers.

"Okay!" Hans yelled. "Give it a try."

Ford turned the ignition, firing up the engine. The boat vibrated hard as it came to life after being stationary for months. He applied light pressure on the throttle, moving the boat forward."

"Wait! Stop!" Jones yelled out. Ford eased back, killing the accelerator. He glanced back through the doorway, seeing the interns on their hands and knees pulling away more weeds. He stepped back to the helm, seeing a concerned look from Reimer.

"Believe me, it wasn't our first idea to be in the shallows. But we've tried being anchored out there. It doesn't work."

"Man, I just hope they don't evolve to fly," Reimer said. Ford bit his lip and nodded in agreement.

"Okay, try again," Han called out. Ford throttled slowly and again the boat moved forward. He kept it slow until they cleared the weeds. He accelerated, racing the boat across the large lake in search of a place to dock.

CHAPTER 21

The fog was thickest at the center of the lake. The fifty-foot boat broke the glass surface, sending twelve-inch swells rolling out toward the shore. Every so often, the group would hear a *thump* echo through the boat as it struck swimmers floating on the surface.

The fog began to disperse as Ford brought the boat along the other side of the lake. He studied the shoreline to determine the location nearest to the radio tower. But much of the shore was impossible to dock. One area had weeds so thick, they bunched up into mounds as he steered close. Had he continued, the propellers would have certainly got hung up in them. The shore in other areas was too shallow to bring the boat close, and others too high. There had been much growth since the state park had ceased to function.

Ford steered the boat into a cove on the north. Directly ahead was a relatively open shoreline. A broken dock protruded, the legs rotted out from under it. Past the mushy sand was a grass area and abandoned grilling equipment scattered throughout. A few ghouls lingered in the grass. One laid in the sand in a mangled state, its one functioning arm clawing at the water's edge. He recognized the area and knew the route from there to the radio tower.

He could hear the hull scraping against the bottom as he steered the boat into the shallows. He noticed the Corporal nervously watching the sediment stirring around the vessel. Finally, the boat pitched as it hit solid ground. Ford throttled back, feeling the engine reverberate as the vessel struggled to free itself. The stern swung like a bat, the bow teetering on the soil bank they had wedged themselves into. Finally, the boat broke free, the keel scraping against the lake floor as the propellers reversed it further back into the cove.

"Okay, tie up the anchor," Ford called out. The interns hauled the anchor over the stern and pulled away at the slack until the line was taut. Ford shut the engine down and stepped out to the starboard walkway. The mist collected on his face like a cold sweat as he walked to the forward bow. He watched the ghouls roaming about on shore, several of them now roaming toward them. "We're gonna have to take the rowboats the rest of the way in…exactly what I was trying to avoid."

"Hope you're not afraid to get your feet wet," Reimer said.

"Likewise, Corporal," Ford said. "Alright, everyone get your stuff together! We're moving out! 57, get the shotguns out of the trunk.

McCartney, you'll be staying here with the doc. Anything happens to her, it's your ass."

"You got it, Ford," McCartney said.

57 hustled into the cabin and moved downstairs to the trunk. He removed the lock and pulled out the three Remington shotguns that were inside of it and the box of shells. Ford clipped a speed-loader pouch to his belt and checked the cylinder of his revolver. He held his hand out and accepted the shotgun from 57. Michele arrived and accepted the second one.

"Only got about ten shots each," 57 said.

"Not much to work with," Reimer said.

"Yeah, hence we don't normally take them," Ford said. "However, with a little luck, this will be our last run." He chambered a shell and looked to the shore, then at the three marines. "Looks like we're storming the beaches of Normandy."

"Let's get to it," Dunn said.

They assembled at the aft deck and boarded the two rowboats. Dr. Hill and McCartney handed down the supplies. McCartney stopped and held up the demolition bag.

"You guys need this?"

"Yeah, never know when we might need it," Reimer said. McCartney tossed it to him, the boat rocking back and forth as it landed in his arms. As he sat down in the center seat, Dr. Hill extended a two-way radio to Ford.

"I tried fixing the receiver on yours. Hopefully it'll work this time," she said.

"You know anything about electronics?" Ford said.

"Not that kind," she said. "Had to wing it."

"Guess it'll have to do," Ford said. He sat down at the center of the second boat and took the oars. "Let's do this."

McCartney untied the lines and tossed them back to the boats. Oars smacked the water as Reimer and Ford rowed back with all their might. Gordon, Dunn, Michele, and 57 watched the shore as their boats neared the sandbank. Water rippled as they moved in, while a stringy saliva-like substance clung to the oars. After several yards, the hull began to brush the bottom. Ghouls waded in toward them, their feet sinking in the loose sand.

Michele stood up, wielding the park ranger's machete in her right hand. She drew down, embedding the blade in the skull of the nearest corpse. On the other boat, Dunn leapt from the bow. Water splashed as he landed ankle-deep. It splashed again as he bludgeoned a ghoul with his rifle, its open head leaking decayed contents into the shore.

57 and Gordon immediately jumped out next and joined the fray, followed immediately by Han and Jones. With the boats wedged sufficiently into the sandbank, Reimer and Ford splashed down and stormed the shoreline, striking ghouls as they ran into the grass area. Knives, hatchets, and machetes swung wildly, splitting skulls as they found their marks.

Ford thrust his knife upward through the jaw of a corpse. It shook and clawed at him until the tip of the blade finally reached its brain. As it slumped against him, another one sprang at him. Saliva, peppered with decayed cells, dripped from black teeth as it lunged for a bite. Ford twisted his body, putting the recently deceased ghoul between him and the new attacker. Teeth ravaged the shrunken neckline of the corpse shield. Ford stepped back to give himself space. The ghoul abandoned the attack on the body and lunged for him once again. He pivoted on his left boot, thrusting a high kick out. The heel of his boot crunched the ghoul's jaw, knocking it on its back. Its arms flailed, still attempting to grab at him as he closed the distance and plunged his knife through its eye.

Several feet away, Reimer and Gordon stood side-by-side, plunging knives into approaching ghouls. The Corporal twisted his blade as it entered the eye socket of a bloated corpse, killing it. Pulling it free, he looked to the trees. A few more were stumbling out from the forest to greet them with snapping jaws.

Ford and 57 rushed the incoming collection of ghouls. 57 swung his heavy pipe like a baseball bat, indenting the side of a skull. Ford struck another with his hatchet, thick blood squishing from the fleshy crevice atop its head. Han and Jones dashed past him, crowbars raised high over their heads. Metal struck bone, rupturing the ghoul's one truly functioning organ.

Back on the shoreline, Dunn approached the ghoul stuck in mud. He walked calmly and silently, watching as it reached at him with its broken limbs. Its face hardly had any flesh on it. Whatever was there had been eaten away by the sand and water. Yet, it was looking at him, somehow able to see him despite no eyes being present. He clutched a pickax he had taken from the Gibson boat and held it high over his head and brought it down. The metal spike ran through the skull before penetrating six inches into the earth.

Dunn yanked the tool free then watched the clash taking place near the trees. He stared blankly, seeing his friends fighting alongside the three survivors. Bone and guts trickled from the scrimmage like salt and pepper. A series of hopes filled his head. They were all different, some contradictory. He hoped, while he watched, that some of the undead would overtake these new 'allies' who he wasn't convinced were allies. On the other hand, he hoped there would be enough room on the chopper for everyone. If that were the case, then everyone would win. It would prevent any need for escalated conflict between the two halves of the group. Similarly, he hoped that Reimer was right: that this group did not present any threat.

Most importantly, he hoped to see no more soldiers be killed uselessly in infected zones such as this. Even Reimer and Gordon, despite their disagreements. After all, they were friends. But sooner or later, they would be among those whose death he'd have to witness. He still had doubts about Dr. Hill's importance. After all, it seemed odd that she didn't have any lab samples with her. Then again, he didn't understand the digital era of science. If she did have the cure, then hopefully these missions would have to end.

In this moment, he'd settle for never returning to this place. Even if he couldn't get himself discharged from the Marine Corps, he would see to it that he would never return here. In his mind, he vowed never to come here again.

The fray came to an end, with numerous bodies embedded into the mushy ground. The group formed a circle, carefully watching their surroundings. The air was filled with the heavy panting as everyone caught their breath. Reimer noticed Dunn standing at the water line, his expression blank. He let go of the pickax, letting it drop into the sand.

"You okay there?" he asked. Dunn faked a smile and started walking toward them.

"Yep. All good." He realized Reimer was staring down at the pickax. "Too heavy to take along," Dunn said. He strolled past the group toward paved pathway between two enormous pines, then glanced back at Ford. "This way?"

"Yes," Ford said. He led the group past the picnic area to the asphalt trail. The path was long and narrow, the farthest points almost appearing black as night due to the canopy. "Let's get this done quick." He held his shotgun to his shoulder and took point. Gordon raised his M4 and walked the opposite edge of the trail.

Dunn stood to the side, allowing the rest of the group to go in ahead of him. As he walked off, he noticed Reimer was waiting as well. He glared at Dunn, his eyes heavy with suspicion and concern.

"I'm fine, Corporal," Dunn said.

"Are you?" Reimer asked.

"Yes. I just want to get out of here," Dunn said. Reimer continued his stare, trying to gauge what was going on in Dunn's thoughts. Whatever was going on, the one sure thing was that he was being honest about wanting to leave. He felt uneasy about trusting him. However, given the circumstance, he had little choice.

"Alright then," he said. The two marines hustled to catch up with the others. The group walked in unison as the path zig-zagged further into the forest.

CHAPTER 22

The path rose and fell with the hills, winding further into the forest like a slithering python. Moving past discolored tree trunks, the team came to the top of a large hill. From there, they could hear the distant growling from multiple ghouls behind the trees. Ford led the team off the path. After hustling fifty yards through the trees, they ducked at the ledge of a small drop off overlooking the radio tower.

"There it is," he said. Less than a thousand feet away was the base of the radio mast. Stretching two-hundred feet high, the structure was intact, held up by four supports embedded deep into the ground. Between the tower's four 'legs' was a cubed shaped building with wires leading up through the mast. The metal was discolored from the constant exposure to the mist and the diseased elements of the forest. It appeared much of the metal was starting to rust.

However, the group was barely paying attention to the condition of the tower. Instead, they were focused more heavily on what surrounded it. Like a herd of wildebeest in the African plains, thousands of undead had gathered around the tower.

"Oh, you've got to be kidding me," Gordon whispered. The group ducked as low as they could, staying hidden behind clumps of rock and soil at the cliff edge. The horde were jam packed into the small clearing like sheep, some snapping jaws at others that mindlessly bumped into them. The combined smell of their rotting flesh stretched high into the trees. It was proving too much for Michele, who had to back away and cover her mouth. Han and Jones moved aside, letting her pass between them. She spat and dry heaved until she regained control. Even the marines struggled to not succumb to the nausea.

"We'll, we're fucked," 57 said.

"No, we're not," Ford muttered.

"Dude, are you blind?" 57 pointed down at the horde. "There's no way we can fight through that."

"…and live," Han added.

"We NEED to get to that tower," Reimer said.

"He's right," Dunn said. "If we don't do it, we're as good as dead." 57 stared down at the horde. Bodies stumbled back and forth, packed so tightly together that the group couldn't even see the ground they walked on.

"If we go *down there*, we're as good as dead," he said.

"Don't panic. And for chrissake, keep your voice down," Ford whispered. 57 held his breath, his shotgun shaking with his hand. He took his finger off the trigger-guard to avoid an accident.

Ford glanced at Reimer. "What do you think?" Reimer watched the horde in silence, pondering ideas in his mind.

"We're gonna have to draw them off somehow," he said. Gordon snickered.

"What are we gonna do? Ring a dinner bell?"

"Something like that," Reimer said.

"I got the bell right here," Dunn said, tapping the bag of explosives. Gordon glanced at the bag, then back at the horde.

"You gonna blow them up?"

"No, stupid. We're gonna set off a blast to lure them off," Dunn said. He pushed himself up on his elbows and scanned the surrounding forest with his eyes. "Ford, you know this place best. Where can we set off a charge that'll lure these freaks away?"

Ford propped himself up and gazed over to the left.

"There's small canyon over that way. There used to be a stream there. The land just dips into a small crevice. If we lure them to it, not only will they be out of the way, but most of them will fall in and get trapped."

"It's worth a try," Reimer said. "Let's go." He started to get up, only for Ford to stop him with a hand to the shoulder.

"I'd rather only a couple of us go," he said. "We need to be as quiet as possible. Plus, we'll only need a few charges, not the whole damn bag, so there's no point in everyone going. Also, I want someone to keep a lookout here. If they start to wander our way, I want one of you to let me know."

Reimer nodded. "Understandable. Who's going?"

"I'm not planning on staying here," Dunn muttered. "I'll go." Ford watched as Reimer shot Dunn a look. He saw something in the Corporal's eyes he didn't like, though he wasn't sure what it was.

"We need to move now. Is there a problem with him going?" Ford asked. Reimer heard a hint of suspicion in his voice. Reimer's mind raced as he thought of an answer. He didn't trust Dunn. Yet, he couldn't admit it. Given Ford's past and the knowledge that he was still wary of trusting the marines, he didn't want to risk their fragile alliance. Making it known, even hinting his suspicions about Dunn, would possibly cause Ford to turn against him again. Yet, he was nervous about letting Dunn go off alone with Ford.

There was no time. He had to answer.

"No…it's good," he stuttered. "I, uh, was about to volunteer, was all." He opened the explosive bag and handed three blocks of C-4 to Dunn.

Shit, what am I doing? he thought.

Dunn took the explosives and the triggers and stuffed them into his vest. He and Ford shared a nod, signaling that they were ready to go.

"Don't attract attention," Gordon said.

"No shit," Dunn remarked. He and Ford crouched low and moved away from the ledge down a narrow space between some trees. Reimer watched as they hustled away, stopping every few yards to make sure they weren't seen by the horde.

"You okay there, Corporal?" Michele asked. Reimer whipped his head around to look at her, sending beads of sweat zipping off his brow. He faked a chuckle and gestured toward the huge horde below.

"Just a bit anxious to get down there and call our ride," he said. Michele smiled back.

"We'll owe you big time if you can get us out of here," she said. She stared down at the horde. "I'm serious. Sooner or later, we'd be dead. But thanks to you, we have a chance. Ford will see that."

"Shh," 57 hissed at them. Reimer held a hand up, mouthing "sorry" to him. He took in a deep breath, the smell almost causing him to gag. It seemed no matter what he did, he could not calm his nerves. The only thing he could do was sit and wait in silence, and hope his concerns were not warranted.

****

Ford and Dunn kept their pace at a minimum as they moved from the foot of the hill. They were on even ground with the horde. Any wrong movement would easily attract their attention.

Dunn kept looking over his shoulder at them, fighting the urge to quicken his pace. Ford walked in front, his stance low. They moved out further, stopping every few feet to make sure they weren't seen. Surprisingly, there didn't seem to be many undead walking ahead of them. For whatever reason, they had all gathered around the tower and stayed. Ford wasn't complaining, as anything more than a few stray ghouls in their path would spell certain doom for them.

They moved another few yards and stopped. After waiting, they repeated the process, gradually putting more trees between them and the horde. After traveling a couple of acres, the duo quickened their pace.

"It's over this way," Ford whispered. They stepped over some exposed tree roots and ran over a gravely area. But it wasn't made of rock. Much of the soil had dried up like mud after a rainstorm. Dunn paused, worrying it was another form of environmental mutation. However, everything seemed normal.

Up ahead, Ford drew his tomahawk and plowed the blade through the forehead of a stray ghoul. Dunn sprinted to catch up, while Ford engaged a second one. Black droplets pooled over the ground from the corpse's open head as he ripped it open. He looked around, seeing nothing in the immediate area.

"Here it is," he told Dunn. They approached the small crevice. It was an empty creek, the bottom full of pebbles and dried plants. It was a short and easy climb, only descending about six feet.

"I'll be best to set the charges on the opposite side," Dunn said. "I'm gonna set the charges to detonate separately. The first will be loud enough to attract the bastards from the tower. The second will keep them coming. Then the third should continue drawing them over once they get near. Those in the back will end up pushing the ones in front into the pit."

Ford turned on his heel at the sound of another snarling corpse. It strutted between two trees, the stained white t-shirt tearing as it brushed against the bark. Goatee hairs protruded from its chin like syringe needles as he lunged for the cowboy. A kick to its chest knocked it to the ground. Ford knelt to the left, finding a large chunk of rock from the edge of the creek. He lifted it high over his head, then slammed it down with all his might, flattening the ghoul's head to the earth. As he backed away, another one strutted out from the maze of trees.

"Might wanna get to it before more of these things show up," Ford said. Dunn lowered himself over the edge of the creek. With several edges to grab ahold, it was an easy climb down. He crossed the ten-foot gap in only two strides and jumped onto the opposite wall.

As he lifted himself up onto the other side, Ford rushed the approaching ghoul. He raked the tomahawk across its face, scraping its nose and other tissue from the bone. The ghoul staggered back from the blow, then turned its face back toward him. Cracked teeth dangled, their roots barely held in by the decomposed gums. They fell off completely, shaken loose by the force of the tomahawk smiting down the face.

Ford ripped the weapon free and watched Dunn rush several yards away from the creek. He placed one charge over the root of a tree and armed it. After he completed the task, he ran several yards out to set the second one. Ford spun to turn around, alerted by the snarls of another walker. This one was disfigured, its body disproportioned like a hunchback. Ford sucked in a breath, feeling his lungs beginning to burn. He waited for the corpse to draw close enough to lunge. It did, dragging tissue and fabric behind its feet. As the hands lashed, he sidestepped and shoved the blade of his knife through its left temple. The ghoul let out a horrid call, as though it were actually in pain. Then, like unplugging a computer, it ceased to function. Ford stepped away from it, panting heavily. Twigs cracked in the distance, bringing his attention back to the deep woods.

Across the crevice, Dunn set the final explosive atop a fallen tree. He inserted the triggering device and armed it. All three explosives were now placed. He stood up and ran to the edge of the creek.

Ford's back was turned, his weapons raised. Ahead of him, Dunn noticed at least three of the undead bearing down on him at once. Dunn dropped to a firing stance. He raised the muzzle of his M4. He put his eye to the scope and hesitated, the red dot accidentally set on Ford himself. The world suddenly seemed to slow as he pondered previous thoughts. For what seemed like forever, he stared through the scope as the ghouls closed in on the group leader.

He was already engaging the nearest one, blades indenting the top of its forehead. Ford followed the actions with the barrel of his rifle, hesitant to make an action. The two others closed in. Ford ripped the blades free of the dead one and started swinging at them.

Dunn gritted his teeth and squeezed the trigger.

****

"Corporal, you have to wait," Michele said. "We can't go running off into the woods."

Reimer was antsy. Several minutes had passed since the single gunshot echoed through the woods. It wasn't loud enough to attract more than a few of the ghouls below, but it was enough to make him concerned, though he didn't want to express why.

One gunshot? Only one? He knew it was an M4. The sound was embedded in his brain. He grew restless as he waited, hunched down with the others. Every fiber in his being wanted to run out after Ford and Dunn to find out what happened.

"I do hope they get back soon," 57 said. "I'm about ready to piss my pants."

"That's because you're sissy," Jones remarked.

"You know? I liked you better back when I thought you didn't speak English," 57 said.

Reimer kept his eyes on the woods, desperately trying to spot any movement. He felt Gordon nudge him on the shoulder.

"Corporal, what's up with you?" he asked.

"N-nothing," Reimer said. "Just hoping they didn't run into another horde of these things."

Minutes passed with no sign of Dunn and Ford. Reimer's heart battered the inside of his chest. He felt his hand beginning to quiver against the grip of his weapon. Waiting was driving him insane.

"I think I need to go out there," he muttered.

"You do that, you'll screw up the plan," 57 said. "Corporal, this was all your idea, remember?"

"Yes, I know. But—"

"But what?"

"I'm not sure if they made it," Reimer said. It was a partial truth he told; he wasn't sure what had happened. But something else bothered him. His mind raced through all the possibilities in an attempt to convince him the worst hadn't happened. Yet, all it did was make him more impatient. He propped himself up to his knees, slowly giving in to the urge to go after them.

"Wait," 57 said. He pointed out to the left. "Look." All eyes followed the tip of his finger and spotted the two men as they moved between trees, pausing every so often to avoid being seen by the horde.

It took a couple of minutes for them to reach the top of the crest. When they did, they were met with enthusiastic smiles and pats on the back. Reimer felt ten pounds lighter, relieved from the weight of concern as Dunn hunched down near him and Gordon.

"What happened? I thought we heard a gunshot," Reimer asked.

"Yeah," 57 chuckled. "Nervous Nelly was two seconds away from running after you."

"Which would've been ridiculous," Ford said. "Anyways, we were met with some, resistance, let's call it that. I had some of the freaks trying to get at me, and he was across the creek. He's a good shot, I'll tell you that."

Reimer nodded then glanced at Dunn. "He is." The PFC didn't offer any response as he dug the trigger from his vest. With a press of a button, the detonated the first charge. A loud echo rang through the forest, generating a shockwave that shook the ground.

All eyes went down to the horde. The collection of bodies turned to the direction of the echo. Groaning with curiosity, the horde started lumbering into the woods.

"It's working," Michele said. Ford raised a finger to his lips.

"Shh."

Several bodies bumped against trees as they mindlessly lumbered into the woods. It took several minutes of patience for the whole group to clear the radio area.

"Okay, hit the second one," Ford whispered to Dunn. The marine punched the button on the detonating device, triggering the second blast.

The groaning from the horde grew more intense as their curiosity spiked. For them, it was the first unnatural sound they had heard in months. Their speed increased as they moved like a flood toward the creek.

Ford watched as the last of the group disappeared from sight. They waited several more minutes, while he and Dunn estimated the speed and distance. After waiting sufficient time, Dunn detonated the third charge.

Beyond the trees, the explosion burst out, stirring grit and smoke throughout the creek area. The horde moved with greater intensity, rushing toward the edge of the crevice. A waterfall of bodies rained into the small ravine as they mindlessly stumbled into the trap. Those in the back pushed against the undead in front, unknowingly adding to the spill. In minutes, a mountain of bodies filled the section of the creek, serving as a bridge to the others as they stumbled across into the wall of smoke.

The remainder of the horde branched out as each ghoul marched through the forest in search of food.

CHAPTER 23

The group of eight lowered themselves down to the foot of the ledge. The ground below was flat, composed of dried mud. The surface was littered with the remnants of dead flesh that had fallen off the bodies that walked this area for months. Ears, toes, fingers, and teeth littered the surface, the earth beneath it discolored from the effects of decomposition.

"Will this thing even work?" 57 asked. He stared up at the wires connecting to the conductors high along the mast. "There's been no power to this area...or anywhere, for over a year."

"There's a generator hooked up to keep it working," Reimer said. "It's a high voltage generator. I just hope it has enough juice."

"The gage is half-full," Gordon said. He pulled the lever, roaring the generator to life like a truck engine. "Feel better?" 57 answered with a grin. The interior of the building began to power up. Computer screens flashed to life while static crackled through the receivers.

Reimer opened the door. Two ghouls roamed inside. They wore military outfits. Headphones dangled from their necks as they stumbled toward the door. Gordon and Reimer stepped back outside, luring the ghouls out of the building. Han and Jones waited outside the doorway, ambushing the ghouls with crowbars. With the threat neutralized, the marines reentered and began looking the equipment over.

The interns looked the bodies over. Both ghouls had a sidearm holstered to their hip. Han pulled one out along with the spare magazine. Content with the revolver he carried, he handed it off to 57, while Jones was happy to keep the other for himself.

"Take a look at this," Michele said. She went to the far corner of the square-shaped room. Two M16s leaned against the wall near a few fully loaded mags. "At least this trip wasn't for nothing."

"Hells yes," Han muttered. He picked one up and shouldered it as if he was a commando.

"You even know how to use that?" Reimer asked.

"I can show him," Ford said. "I've shot these things a couple times."

"Might want to test it now!" 57 called out. Ford, Michele, and Han rushed out the door. 57 rose his bat high over his shoulder as three ghouls stumbled out.

"No guns! You'll bring the herd back down on us!" Ford hissed. Looking into the trees past the corpses, he could see a few marching bodies straying back toward the radio station. He glanced back to Reimer. "We'll hold them off. You guys get to it!"

"Make it quick, why don't ya!" Michele added. She rushed the corpses ahead of the others, striking one with her machete. Han and Jones ran past her and engaged the other two, while 57 and Ford awaited the strays that approached within the woods.

The three marines dipped back into the station. Gordon threw himself into the seat and started working with the knobs.

"I'm no radio tech, but this shouldn't be too difficult," he said. "What's Border Command's frequency?"

"Bravo-Two-Five-Charlie-Five," Reimer answered. Gordon adjusted the frequency and connected the wires on the transmitters.

"Alpha-Four-Eight calling Border Command. This is an emergency transmission. We have the package. I repeat: this is Alpha-Four-Eight. We have located Dr. Stacy Hill. Our chopper is down and our team has multiple casualties. Request IMMEDIATE extraction." Nothing but static returned through the receiver, sparking nervous anxiety in the Private. "Oh, no, no, no, no." He started adjusting the frequency.

"Something wrong with the transmitter?" Reimer asked.

"I don't think so," Gordon said. "I'm not sure what it is. It might have something to do with the equipment."

"Just what we fucking needed," Dunn remarked.

"Calm down. Try again," Reimer ordered. Gordon leaned into the transmitter and repeated the message. As he did, the Corporal glanced out the window. Several of the undead had wandered back. The five survivors worked diligently to fend them off. Blood and skin rained down on the already polluted soil as their decayed heads burst from various impacts. "Damn, we can't drag this out much longer."

Gordon was getting increasingly frustrated. He adjusted the knobs and made another call. "Border Command! This is Alpha-Four-Eight! Please respond! This is a Priority One assignment, and we need extraction!"

"*This is Charlie-Five, responding to emergency transmission.*"

Gordon threw his hands high, ecstatic to have gotten a response.

"That's a chopper unit," Dunn said.

"Good to hear from you, Charlie-Five. We're in a highly contaminated zone in Montana and could really use your help."

"*Montana? What you doing there?*"

"We're on an extraction mission to get a government scientist," Gordon said. "Might have the key to curing this virus. You might have heard of it."

"*No, never heard of such a thing. Where exactly are you?*"

"The coordinates are Latitude forty-six degrees north, Longitude one-eleven west. Look for a big lake called Lake Cavern. You'll find us in a houseboat on the northside. We'll need to be picked up by long-line."

Reimer moved in beside him to speak into the transmitter.

"Charlie-Five be advised, the infection here has escalated differently than the rest of the country. What is the maximum altitude of your chopper?"

"With present weight, about twenty-thousand feet."

"Proceed at that altitude. Do not descend until you're above the lake. I know it sounds weird, but I'll explain when you pick us up."

"Roger that. Listen Marines, we're coming up from another rescue mission and have very limited capacity available. How many are left in your unit?"

"Three marines," Reimer said.

"And one VIP, correct?"

"One VIP, and six other survivors," Reimer said. A few moments of silence followed. "Charlie-Five, how much capacity do you have available?"

"Only four seats," the ensign responded. *"I can try to alert Border Command, but as you found out, they're having technical issues on their end. AGAIN! I can proceed to your destination, but I can't get everybody on board."*

"Shit!" Reimer muttered. "No choice. We need to get the VIP out of here. She's the priority."

"Understood. We're not too far out, so we should arrive at that destination in over an hour. Be ready."

"Copy that. Thanks Charlie-Five. Alpha-Four-Eight, out." Reimer stepped away from the radio and ran a hand over his face. He cursed under his breath as he looked out at the group.

Behind him, Dunn was as nervous as he had ever been. He was already pacing across the room, his face alive with several expressions.

"This isn't good man," he whispered. "I'm telling you, this is NOT good."

"Dunn, I get it!" Reimer snapped.

"No, man, you don't," Dunn said. "That guy, Ford, he's gonna think we're bailing on him."

"No, he won't," Reimer said.

"Yes, he will," Dunn said.

"No...HE WON'T!" Reimer's voice nearly rang into a shout. He took a breath and paced. "I just need to figure this out."

"Figure *what* out?" Dunn said. "You heard the guy. They only have room for four people. I'm not staying here, I'm telling you that much."

"Guys, relax," Gordon said. "Let's get back to the boat and discuss it with them. We'll get Dr. Hill back then we can come back and pick them up. If they stay on the boat in the meantime, they should be fine until a unit can get over here."

"You think that guy will go for that?" Reimer said.

"I think so," Gordon said. Dunn shook his head and stepped in Reimer's face.

"Corporal, I'm telling you, he's gonna think we've betrayed him. It won't matter what we tell him. This will escalate, I assure you."

"What would you suggest, then?" Gordon said.

"Maybe we can keep it to ourselves," Dunn said. "Let's say nothing. Wait for the chopper. Maybe we can get on board, make the other's think they'll get pulled up next, then fly off. No struggle, nothing."

"I'm not abandoning these guys like that," Reimer said. "They've helped us. They deserve our honesty. I'm with Gordon on this one. I'm gonna arrange with Command to get a rescue team out to get these guys."

"Oh really? And who do you think they'll send?" Dunn said.

"Oh, for chrissake…"

"They will send us, Reimer. By then, who knows what surprises this place will have waiting for us. I'm not keen on making a return."

"You're not keen on much," Reimer said. "I'm not writing these people off. I gave these guys my word."

"You give a lot of people your word," Dunn muttered. Reimer lunged at him, grabbing ahold of him with both hands.

"The fuck you just say to me?!"

Dunn held both hands out, surprised by the Corporal's reaction.

"Dude, nothing. I misspoke!"

"You implying I get people killed?" Reimer continued.

"No," Dunn said. He kept his stance peaceful, not wanting to get in a physical fight with his friend. "It's not what I meant. I mean, you gave your word to us too, and we want to get out of here alive."

Reimer held tight for several more seconds and let him go with a small push. Dunn backed away, rubbing his hand over his chest where Reimer grabbed him.

"I'll see to it they discharge you from service when we get back," Reimer said.

"They won't listen to you," Dunn said. "Nor will these guys. At least, not Ford. He'll think you're betraying him. He won't respond well. Whatever he does, the others will support him."

"No, man, we're here to save people," Gordon said.

"At what cost?" Dunn asked. "Six of them? We already lost seven people." The opening of the door made all three of them jump. Ford entered the shack, his breathing heavy from all the fighting.

"You guys cozy in here?" he said, panting with each word.

"We got the transmission through," Reimer said. "Chopper is en-route now."

"Thank God," Ford said. "Then let's get the hell out of here, because we've got a whole circus out here." He moved back outside and started calling for the other survivors, rounding them up to leave.

Gordon and Dunn both looked to the Corporal, both wondering what he was planning on doing.

"Let's get to the boat, first," he said. "I'll have a talk with Ford alone once we're there." He looked at both his men, both of them standing quietly. Gordon clearly agreed with the decision, while Dunn's concern was obvious. With no more time to waste, they exited through the door.

Dunn was the last to step out. He watched the survivors' interaction as Reimer and Ford started to lead them back up the asphalt trail. As he walked, he watched the mindless bodies swaying deep within the woods. Despite being on the brink of rescue, he felt more fretful than he had ever felt. He looked at the guns in the hands of the survivors as they trotted up a hill. His concerns generated a squeezing sensation in his chest. His heart was fluttering, adding to the sensation of doom.

He trailed at the back of the group, his eyes now watching each of them with caution.

CHAPTER 24

"How far is it?" Michele asked.

"You're like a kid in the back seat," 57 whispered.

"I wish! At least I'd be in a damn car," Michele retorted.

"Keep it quiet," Ford hissed at them. He kept his shotgun ready at his shoulder. He felt himself growing edgy along with the others. The path seemed darker than before. It was late afternoon thus the sun had lowered into the horizon, its rays lost in the trees and fog.

They had been walking back for over thirty minutes. What would normally be a fifteen-minute walk was consistently slowed down as they stopped to study movements within the forest. It seemed their diversion had backfired on them. The horde had branched out far, with many ghouls migrating toward the lake instead of steadily moving west.

It shouldn't be long now. Ford recognized the bend in the path. They were getting close to the cookout area near the shore. Even he was feeling the urge to chance a mad dash for the boats. His foot rolled as he stepped on a narrow object, nearly causing him to trip.

"Fuck," he muttered. He looked down at the walkway. Rope-like vines stretched out from the woods, intersecting over the asphalt like highway lanes. They were over an inch thick, their exterior like bark. Tiny little stubs protruded from the side like broken tree branches.

"Were these here before?" Reimer asked.

"Don't know. Don't care," Dunn said. "Let's just get out of here." Ford looked ahead, seeing several more rows of these strange vines. He carefully stepped between each one. They were stationary and stiff as tree roots. Whatever they were, they didn't seem to be a threat.

The group stepped over the vines as they continued along the trail. They moved around the bend, listening to the growls of distant ghouls. Movement could be heard from feet scraping against the asphalt. Reimer lifted a fist, alerting everyone to halt.

"Crouch low," he instructed. Everyone moved to the side of the sidewalk and hunched down. They could see several corpses stumbling across the path ahead. There were at least a half dozen or so in the open, with no way to tell how many were among the trees.

"Shit," Ford muttered. "What do you suggest we do?"

"Let's wait a sec, maybe they'll pass," Reimer said.

"We can take 'em," 57 said.

"There's probably more than we can see," Reimer said. "We don't want to go toe-to-toe against a blockade of those things."

"We'll wait," Ford said. "Give it a few minutes. If no more show up, then maybe we can chance it. Everyone monitor your surroundings in the meantime."

The group spaced out, while those in front kept their eyes on the corpses. Reimer looked over his shoulder at Dunn and reached a hand out.

"Pass me the binoculars, will ya?" he asked. Keeping low, Dunn moved up to the front past Han, Jones, and Michele and handed the binoculars to the Corporal.

Gordon, now at the back of the group, inched back to keep from bunching up against 57. He tapped his finger against his Carbine, eagerly awaiting the order to move. In a place like this, nothing felt worse than sitting still. A minute of empty silence passed.

Gordon's knees felt like they were about to cramp, adding to his restlessness. He looked to the forest, drawn to a strange scraping sound in the brush. Whatever it was, it sounded like something was being dragged along the ground. Yet, there didn't appear to be any corpses nearby.

He felt a tightening around his ankle. He whipped his gaze down to his left foot. Like a python, the vine had come to life. Fibers protruded from the stubs, wrapping around his ankle.

"Corporal!" he yelled. The vine slid back into the woods like a fishing line, yanking his foot from under him. The marine yelled as his back hit the asphalt, the yells echoing into the woods as the vine dragged him away.

The group jumped in surprise, seeing Gordon disappear behind the trees.

"What the—" 57 gasped.

"Get after him!" Reimer yelled. All seven of them dashed after him, following his screams and the sound of dragging.

"Hang on, kid!" Reimer yelled.

Dirt, twigs, and pine cones bunched under his back like tire treads as the vine pulled him further into the woods. He leaned his head up, trying to see where it led. He threw his hands over his face as the vine scraped him against the trunk of a tree.

Looking back, he could see the others running to catch up with him. He lunged for the vine, his fingers attempting to untangle its grasp. But the fibers were too tight.

Looking ahead, he saw a dip in the ground. He could see the vine spiraling, leading down into a strange formation that almost looked like a firepit. In a last, ditch effort, Gordon threw his hands out. He needed to grab ahold of something, ANYTHING to keep from getting reeled into whatever destination this was.

His hands found the trunk of a small tree. Both hands clasped as he hugged the bark. He let out a painful cry as his body went taut. The vine tugged, stretching his leg to the max.

"Gordon, hang on!" Reimer yelled to him. Their footsteps grew louder as they neared. Han and Jones broke from the group, smashing their crowbars into a nearby corpse that approached.

Reimer and Dunn pulled at the vine. It was as tight as rebar. The coil tightened its hold, causing Gordon to yell again.

"The hell is this?" 57 said. His eyes followed the vine to the strange circular formation in the ground. It was like a rounding pit that spiraled into the ground, the center covered by some type of barrier. The vine, along with many others, protruded from a pore in this barrier. It rippled like a tarp in the wind. Triangular slits began to widen as the pit came to life. Like a blooming flower, the barrier folded outward into four flaps.

"Jesus, Mary!" 57 shouted.

The flaps waved freely above the ugly pit they covered, as if each had a mind of its own. Beneath them was an abyss of yellow digestive liquid. Swirling within it were the bones of other creatures unlucky enough to have stumbled into the trap of its vines.

Gordon was losing his grip as the plant tugged harder. Reimer cursed as he tried to untangle its grip, but the vine wouldn't give way.

"Look out!" Michele yelled. She swung her machete into the face of another corpse. Looking about, the group could see several figures converging on their location, attracted by the commotion.

"Holy shit, they're everywhere!" 57 said. He started moving ahead, only for another ghoul to lash out as it emerged from behind a tree. 57 pointed his shotgun and fired, exploding the ghoul's head into unrecognizable bits of meat.

There was no use for stealth at this point. The horde knew where they were. Han and Michele picked up their M16s and started shooting into the crowd. Bodies jolted as bullets pierced their targets. Brains exploded into muck and bodies collapsed onto the dirt.

Dunn aimed to the right, seeing several more ghouls moving in from the opposite direction. He turned, succumbing to the temptation to run back to the trail. He stopped, only to realize several more coming from the direction they came.

"Figure something out! They've got us surrounded!" he yelled.

Jones grabbed ahold of Gordon's vest as he began to lose his grip. The Marine's hands peeled apart from each other as the vine overpowered him. He clawed at the ground, grabbing at anything.

Reimer and Ford ran after him, the former jumping down on his fellow marine and pulled back as though in a tug-o-war.

Gordon's feet were now inches from the edge of the pit. Fumes radiated upward from the digestive fluids like breath. Mounds of dirt scraped from under his boots as the vine inched him closer.

Ford ran to Gordon's feet, his hatchet raised high above his head. He hammered the blade down hard, splintering the skin of the vine. Repeatedly, he hacked the limb.

Reimer positioned himself behind Gordon, his arms now wrapped under the Private's armpits. He watched the blade gradually cut the vine, spewing a sap-like fluid from tiny veins under the skin.

The view between the trees was now gone, hidden behind a horde of the undead. They closed in, dripping saliva and other fluids as they approached.

"Look out!" Reimer shouted. Ford leaned up and spun to the right, just in time to avoid the reach of a skeletal corpse. Its jaws extended and a horrid retching sound vibrated from its throat. Ford struck it in the face with the hatchet. As he did, another one stumbled from around the pit. He pulled the hatchet, but the blade was lodged in the forehead of the other ghoul. Cursing, Ford abandoned the hatchet and faced the threat. He thrust a hard kick into its abdomen, the force driving the ghoul backward. It stumbled back, snarling at Ford as it unwittingly slipped down into the pit. The flaps closed, the gnarling sounds still reverberating from underneath.

Putting his boot down against the dead body, Ford yanked on the hatchet with all of his might, freeing the blade from its head.

"Shit! We've gotta go!" 57 yelled. Ford whipped around, seeing dozens of ghouls bearing down on them like an invading army. Summoning every ounce of strength in his body, he brought the hatchet down on the vine. The blade broke through, the handle snapping as the vine whipped back through the pore.

Gordon sprung to his feet, his eyes wide with shock. Reimer and Jones stumbled backward, gathering their weapons as several corpses closed in on them. The group scattered. It was every person for themselves. Through the chaos, Reimer and Ford yelled directions, directing everybody to a certain point.

Whatever that point was, Dunn couldn't figure it out. He ran to the right, unable to see the others or where they went. Dodging trees and other obstacles, the marine fired off random shots. Some struck their mark, killing the brain function of their targets. Others struck chest tissue, providing nothing other than a momentary jolt before the undead continued its chase. Some shots missed completely.

Dunn passed several trees, yelling as he came to a dead stop, just beyond the grasp of a wall of undead. He twisted to the right and continued running uphill. He slowed to fire at a group ahead of him, this time keeping enough control to place each bullet carefully. Matter exploded from their heads, bringing them to a permanent end. With the path ahead somewhat clear, Dunn sprinted as fast as he could. His eyes swept through the forest in search of the others. But there was nothing to be seen but trees and an ever-increasing swarm of rotting bodies, all eager to take a bite out of him.

Cracks of gunfire streaked the air ahead of him, prompting Dunn to alter his direction slightly further to the right. Dirt and pines kicked from under his boots as he weaved around corpses. They were slower than he, but their numbers were gradually boxing him in. He had to find the group member. Whatever gun that was, it was a military style weapon. He wondered if it was Reimer or Gordon discharging their M4s.

He continued along the hill, rolling down the next slope as he moved over the top. Thirty yards away, he saw one of the group running through the horde. It was Jones. Like Dunn, he had been driven apart from the others, now alone. He squeezed the trigger of his M16, placing shots into the horde, mostly striking low.

"Dunn!" he yelled. "This way!" Jones was pointing out behind him. Dunn looked ahead, seeing a break in the trees past the insane number of ghouls. Beyond that point was the trail. The marine started another dash, spit and dirt spewing between his teeth. He shot another ghoul, kicking it in the groin as he ran over it.

Now fifteen yards away, Jones struggled to reload the M16. The exhaustion and adrenaline proved too much for him to execute a fast reload. The full mag slipped from his fingers, forcing him to drop to his knees.

Dunn aimed his M4 and fired repeatedly, killing numerous ghouls between him and Jones. As their bodies collapsed, he aimed his scope further up, focusing on several corpses that approached Jones. The intern successfully reloaded the rifle. Firing from his crouched position, he put down the closest ghouls. He stood and swung his body to the left, firing into a few other ghouls that stood between him and the trail. His knees were bent, his weight on the balls of his feet, ready to take off in a sprint.

Dunn watched through the scope, firing a bullet passed Jones through the eye socket of another corpse. Dunn's breathing intensified. Sweat accumulated on his forehead. His vision felt blurry from the rush of anxiety. Suddenly, everything he feared was back at the forefront of his mind.

He aimed lower. His fingers twitched as he contemplated every possible outcome for the near future.

With teeth bared, he squeezed the trigger.

Jones staggered forward, hit with an invisible force that ripped out his abdomen. He looked down at his waistline. His shirt and pants were soaked in his own blood, which spilled freely from his body. With the blood loss came sudden weakness and shock.

He fell to his knees unable to hold the M16. Mouth agape from pain and astonishment, he looked back over his shoulder. Dunn still had his gun aimed on him, the muzzle rising and falling with his breathing. The marine watched as several ghouls closed in on Jones, spurred further by the sight and smell of fresh blood. With the little energy he had left, he punched his fists into the horde, only for hands and teeth to come down on his arms.

Dunn rocked back on his feet, his mind spinning like a tornado. Jones' screams pierced his eardrums as the horde tore entrails from his belly. With several approaching his location, the marine ran for the trail. The ghouls pursued for several yards, only to divert their attention to the feeding frenzy taking place nearby.

Multiple gunshots echoed behind the obstruction of trees. As Dunn continued on, he could hear indistinct shouting from numerous voices. His feet hit the asphalt. Numerous ghouls turned to look at the Marine, immediately lashing out as they recognized him as food.

Dunn thrust his rifle out, knocking several of them backward. With the camp area in sight, he took off running. Countless ghouls emerged from the trees. They moved at a sluggish pace, which then turned into a slow run as they spotted Dunn. He ignored each one and focused all energy on his retreat. After ten long seconds, he ran past the edge of the trail.

Another gunshot rang out from the shore. The others had run out from the tree line to the boats. Reimer and Gordon provided suppressive fire, dropping one ghoul after the other while Ford and the others pushed the boats out.

"DUNN!" Reimer yelled. He rotated his stance and fired again. Dunn flinched, throwing his arms over his face in pure instinct. He felt the whistle of the bullet speed past his ear. In that same second, brain residue from a ghoul splatted on the back of his pantleg. He glanced back, seeing the body collapsing a mere twelve inches from him.

"You staying or what?!" Reimer yelled at him. His voice was muffled by the thoughts and feelings that swirled in Dunn's mind. He felt in a daze as he ran across the campground. Reimer ran out to get him, emptying his magazine into numerous other corpses. No matter how many he put down, they just kept coming. He grabbed Dunn by the shoulders and dragged him several feet into the water. Both men climbed into the boat, while Ford, Han, 57, and Michele got in the other.

"Kunihiko-san!" Han called out. He stood at the bow of the boat as Ford rowed it out.

"Jones!" 57 called out. "Where's Jones?" Everyone looked around, realizing they were one-short.

"Dunn!" Reimer shouted. "Did you see Jones?"

"We... we got—" Dunn gagged, suppressing the urge to vomit. "We got separated. They were all over him. I kept shooting but my mag ran dry."

"We need to go back!" Michele cried out.

"I saw him go down," Dunn said.

"No!" Michele yelled.

"57, take the oars, will ya?" Ford said. He watched the shore as an army of ghouls lumbered into the water after them. He moved from the center seat and grabbed his radio. "McCartney! Hill! This is Ford, you read?!"

"*We're looking right at you!*" Hill answered. Ford looked to the Gibson's bow rail, where McCartney and Hill stood.

"Good! Start the fucking engine right now!" he said. He watched McCartney turn back and hurry through the sliding doors. The engine came to life, the water shaking along the hull.

"Swimmers!" Gordon yelled. He stood up and discharged his rifle into the forehead of a wrinkly corpse that reached up from the weeds. He crouched down, the rocking of the boat nearly tossing him into the water. Reimer thrust the oars through the surface, rippling thick strands of weeds.

Webbed hands reached over the bow of their boat, tilting it forward as a spongy swimmer began pulling itself aboard.

"Son of a...BITCH!" Reimer shouted. He yanked one of his Berettas from his holster and fired. The bullet entered the bridge of the nose, the hollow point expanding the back of its head like a balloon. The swimmer slipped beneath the hull, its feet thumping against the metal. Reimer holstered his pistol and rowed as fast as he could, following the other boat around to the stern of the Gibson.

McCartney ran to greet them. He reached down, first helping Michele, then Han. As he pulled 57 up, he saw the other boat coming about, and that they were missing Jones.

"Where the hell is..."

"They got him," Ford said. He climbed aboard and reached down to help the marines. The water splashed behind the aluminum boats as several swimmers congregated. "Holy damn shit," he muttered. He pulled his revolver and fired. 38. Caliber rounds punched through bone, reducing the infected hosts to lifeless floaters.

With all three marines aboard, Ford sprinted for the cabin.

"What about the boats?" McCartney yelled.

"Forget 'em! No time!" Ford answered. He grabbed the helm and throttled in reverse. The propellers twisted in place, backing the large boat away from the shore. The horde was a little over chest deep, now only a few meters from the bow.

Thumps echoed through the hull as the aluminum boats bounced off the stern. He accelerated at full speed, crunching swimmers as he went. He adjusted the rudders to turn the boat to starboard. Like the trailer of a semi-truck on an icy highway, it began to fishtail.

Ford throttled forward at full speed, turning the bow out to the center of the lake.

"Oh, SHIT!" he said. He saw the strands of weeds accumulating directly ahead. He turned further to starboard. But it was too late. The boat passed over the weed bed, tangling up the propellers. Cursing repeatedly, Ford throttled down. Metal groaned behind him as the gears became stuffed with weeds.

57 and McCartney got on their stomachs and looked beneath the guardrail to assess the damage.

"There's no way we can get at this," he yelled.

"Damn it!" Ford stuck his fists against the helm.

"Ford, it's okay," Hill said.

"Okay?" Dunn asked.

"We're in at least seven feet of water," Hill said. "The undead won't be able to get onboard."

"Those weeds are freaking huge down there," Ford said. "I don't know if they're mutating too, but the point is, those ghouls aren't simply walking on the lake floor. The bunching of weeds gives them higher elevation."

"It's still too deep," Hill said. "Besides, they'll get tangled up. Just like the swimmers."

"Son of a bitch," Ford muttered. He stepped outside and gazed out at the shore. Looking further back to the campsite, he could see more bodies continuing to emerge from the tree line. Out in the water, the undead at the front of the horde were now face deep, still several meters out. By the time they would reach the boat, they would be completely submerged. Perhaps the doctor was right.

"Everyone, keep an eye out for swimmers," he said. He walked away, taking a few moments to ease the tension. Reimer took a seat in the cabin, pondering how to inform Ford of the chopper.

As he thought, he noticed Dunn's eyes burning into him. The PFC knew what he was thinking, and he didn't like it. But there was something else going on. Dunn seemed more tense than usual. He was hunched as he sat, his hand quivering ever so slightly. He was swaying back and forth in place.

Probably an overload of adrenaline, Reimer thought. He was a bit shaky himself.

"Hey man, you're alright," Reimer said. Dunn's eyes were locked on him, his face as flushed as the ghouls.

"Am I?" he said. "How long until the chopper gets here?"

"Half hour or more," Reimer said. Dunn continued his labored breathing. He stood up and walked out onto the walkway, dry heaving over the railing. Gordon began to check on him, only for Dunn to walk off.

"Let him be," Reimer said. Gordon's eyes followed Dunn as he walked to the aft deck.

"You sure he's alright?" he asked.

"It's been a busy day, Gordon," Reimer asked. "I'm sure he'll be fine. I have other things I have to focus on right now." He leaned back in the seat and rested. He felt his heart rate gradually decrease to a relaxed pace. He hoped Ford was doing the same.

In a few minutes, he would speak with him.

CHAPTER 25

Reimer closed his eyes and listened to the splashing of water. The army of undead had filled the whole side of the lake. Many had marched under the bow, their fingertips scratching the bottom of the hull. He opened his eyes and looked out the cabin's rear window. Several heads stuck out from the water as they waded out, disappearing beneath the surface roughly a hundred or so feet out. Luckily, the bastards couldn't climb, with the exception of the swimmers. From what Reimer had seen, the swimmers weren't large in numbers, and the survivors were more than capable of handling them. After his careful study of the situation, Reimer felt absolutely confident that they would survive long enough for a secondary rescue unit to fly in.

The guest bedroom door opened up. Michele stepped out. She held a grocery bag in her hand. Reimer could tell from the way it was bulging that it was packed with belongings. The corner of a picture frame had peeked from the top. Reimer was deep in thought, considering whether to tell her. He noticed her smile at the moment it faded behind a look of concern.

"Everything good?" she asked.

"Oh…yeah, everything's good," he said. The smile returned as Michele lifted the bag.

"It's amazing how much shit I actually acquired during the apocalypse," she said. "You'd think I was packing for a trip to the Bahamas. Who knows? Maybe it's still paradise over there."

"One can only hope," Reimer said. It was the only response he could think of.

"You know, we really owe you one," Michele said. "Hopefully, we can keep in touch after we get out of here."

"That sounds great," Reimer said. He forced a smile. It was a prospect he wanted to see come true. Michele nearly blushed before stepping back into the room.

"Gotta collect a couple more things, you know?" she said with a chuckle. She dipped back out of sight behind the doorway. Reimer's smile disappeared as quickly as she did. He wished he said something. He hesitated, considering it once more. No, he'd better tell Ford first.

There wasn't much more time to waste. Reimer opened the sliding starboard door and stepped out, stopping in surprise as he saw Dunn leaning against the guardrail. The marine turned to face him, his eyes glancing off to the sides to make sure they wouldn't be heard.

"Dude, I'm telling you one last time, this won't go over well," he whispered.

"Dunn, we've been over this," Reimer whispered.

"Please, man. Reconsider. We can trick them into letting us up on the chopper first. We can take off and not worry about it—"

"Dude, stop it," Reimer said. Dunn bit his lip and hit his hand against the metal rail. He shook his head and looked out to the water. With a sigh, he turned back to face Reimer. "It's your call."

"We're doing this," Reimer answered. His voice was direct. Dunn understood once and for all that he would not be persuaded.

"Okay," he muttered, raising his hands out as though saying 'whatever.'

"Where's Ford?" Reimer asked. Dunn almost didn't want to answer. His eyes looked over Reimer's head.

"Up on the sundeck," he reluctantly answered. Reimer nodded in silent thanks and started walking to the aft deck. Dunn followed him with his eyes until he turned the corner.

Dunn wrestled with the thoughts in his head, trying to concede to the possibility that Reimer was correct. But the feelings wouldn't go away. Telling Ford that they wouldn't be extracted with them was a foolish mistake, and Reimer couldn't, or wouldn't understand that. In Dunn's mind, the consequence was clear as day. His mind flashed back to Jones. It was a reminder to the choice he had committed to. His stomach was in a knot as he mentally goaded himself to follow through.

He peeked around the forward deck. 57 and Han were waiting idly, the intern still in a state of shock from losing his brother. A shadow stretched across the deck from the port rail. Studying the black figure, he recognized the shape of McCartney's beard. He stood just out of sight, but the lack of motion in his shadow indicated he was leaning against the rail. All he cared about was that their attention wasn't on him.

Dunn hurried into the cabin. He glanced down the small stairway to the guest bedroom's open door. He waited to make sure Michele wouldn't step out and see him. After a few quick moments, he hunched down to the explosives pack, which way laying near the edge of the sofa. He pulled the zipper back slowly, keeping his eyes on the open door.

With the bag partly open, he dug inside and pulled out several blocks of C-4. He stared at the explosives for a moment, his conscience questioning him once more. That inner conflict was stopped short with the sound of footsteps on the sundeck. He looked up as he listened to Reimer converse with Ford.

****

Ford had both arms crossed over his chest as he leaned against the sundeck's forward rail. The sound of footsteps turned his attention behind him.

"Hey man," Reimer said.

"Howdy," Ford said. "Need something?"

"Yeah, I'd like to have a private word with you in the cabin," Reimer said. Ford nodded and stepped away from the rail.

"Something wrong?" he asked.

"Yes and no. It's a little complicated," Reimer said. "I want to discuss it with you first."

* * * * * * * *

Their footsteps echoed against the ceiling as they started walking aft. Dunn hurried and stuffed the C-4 blocks under his uniform. He only needed two or three. With time dwindling, he settled for two and grabbed the triggering mechanisms. He zipped the bag and pushed it back where he found it. He stood up and hurried out the door.

"Whoa!" 57 called out, staggering back as the two nearly collided. Dunn opened his mouth, unsure of what to say. 57 stood aside, looking the marine over. Dunn felt his blood beginning to race. He wondered if the C-4 blocks were evident beneath his shirt.

"Uh, my bad," he said.

"Almost had an accident there," 57 chuckled.

"Yeah, almost!" Dunn said. He glanced down the walkway. Reimer and Ford had just turned the corner and were coming his way.

"Everything good?" 57 asked. Dunn whipped his head at him. 57 was looking down to Dunn's hand, which was instinctively placed over his sidearm.

"Oh..." Dunn moved his hand away, "I'm just...you know! What did you call it? Swimmer patrol!"

"Ha! Won't have to worry about that for much longer," 57 said.

"Amen to that," Dunn said. He glanced back as Reimer and Ford approached. "Well, I'd better get to it. See ya later." Dunn walked aft, hugging the guardrail as he passed Reimer. He gave them a nod, attempting to look inconspicuous. They passed by, following 57 into the cabin.

He arrived at the aft deck and looked around. Dr. Hill was seated on the bench under the sundeck awning.

Shit.

She looked up at him as he glared at her.

"Need something?" she asked. Dunn wasn't sure what to say. He could not afford to fake small talk. Time was not on his side. Reimer and

157

Ford would be starting their conversation within the next minute. He didn't want to wait for whatever happened next.

"Us? Need something?" he remarked in a gruff voice. "Lady, I'm impressed you even had the courtesy to ask."

"Beg your pardon?"

"Oh, gee? Let's see…only nine soldiers died trying to get you. God only knows how many of these guys you got killed. Considering you're worth so much, I should be bowing down to you asking what your bitch-ass needs." Dr. Hill's face lit with disgust. "Oh! Did I hit a nerve? Lady, I don't need anything from you. That is, unless you're willing to blow me."

Dr. Hill stood up violently, her eyes burning with fury.

"Jesus Christ, you're a fucking pig," she muttered as she walked to the port walkway. Dunn seethed as she disappeared from sight. At least it was an easy show to put on, as he genuinely felt much of what he said. He glanced up to the sunroof and down the other deck. The coast was clear.

He got down on his knees at the deck edge and dug the C-4 from under his shirt. While continuously checking over his shoulder, he applied a sticky substance to the plastic explosives. He inserted the triggering mechanism and reached his hand down into the water. He pressed the block to the hull just above the waterline. He watched as the water rippled with the reaching fingertips of countless flesh-eaters. He fought against the nervous strain and grabbed the second block.

****

Reimer and Ford waited as Michele and 57 collected their things. Ford's impatience was beginning to show through taps of his foot against the flooring.

"Hey guys. You mind giving us a minute?" he asked. Both 57 and Michele glanced at them with inquisitive looks. A dozen jokes rolled through 57's mind, each competing to expose itself through his lips. But the stern expression on Ford's face made it clear they would not be received well.

"Okay," he simply said. "Uh, everything alright?"

"It's good," Reimer said. "You'll know in a minute. I just want to speak with Ford first."

"Okay," 57 said. He opened the portside door and stepped out, only to swiftly step aside with a rambunctious "Whoa!" Dr. Hill marched in past him and fixed her fiery eyes on Ford.

"You have a problem with me too?"

"I beg your pardon?" Reimer asked.

"Listen, I get you guys lost a few folks, but you need to get a handle on the ones who are still alive!" Hill's voice was just under a yelling volume, each word filled with resentment. Reimer's jaw opened with astonishment.

"What are you talking about?"

"That asshole back there, whatever the hell his name is, telling me to go suck cock! Who does he think he is?!"

Reimer and Ford both glanced at each other, both uncomfortable by the confrontation. The Corporal could see Gordon standing out on the forward deck with McCartney, meaning it had to be Dunn she was talking about.

Of course, he would start something now of all times.

"Ma'am, I'll handle it. Right now, I need to—"

"Oh, you'll *handle it.* Is this how they run things in the military? You realize who I am, right? What I have?" She pulled out the flash drive, as though showboating her significance.

Even Michele felt awkward. In the time she knew Dr. Hill, she did notice a sense of self-importance, but this was near over-the-top. Even if what she said was true, anyone with a hint of empathy would know that Dunn had more than a typical rough day. Uninterested in walking past the standoff, she decided to slip back into the guest room and shut the door.

Ford was shaking his head. His patience had run dry, eliminating any tolerance for ridiculousness.

"Doc, get a grip. So, the guy insulted you. Get over it." Dr. Hill's eyes and jaw opened wide in disgust. A hundred arguments came to mind, and she wanted to spout every one of them. But Ford was already guiding her out the door. "Go. Now. We need the space. Bye."

The door slammed shut inches from her nose. Seething with contempt, Hill marched to the forward deck, her anger increasing as she noticed the amused grins forming on the face of everyone on deck.

57 placed a hand over his mouth to suppress a laugh. It was a shame: he needed a good laugh, and hell, he had no qualms about having it at her expense. She didn't even offer condolences to Han. Even Gordon was smiling. The smile escalated into a small giggle, which was moments away from becoming a full-blown laugh. As casually as he could, he walked the length of the boat to the aft deck.

His eyes found Dunn hunched by the deck edge.

"Looking for swimmers?" he asked. Dunn whipped around at the sound of his voice. He had the look of somebody caught doing something they weren't supposed to be. In his hand was a black block-shaped object with a tiny electric rod protruding from its center. Gordon marched forward, as if confirming what he saw was real. "Dunn! What are you doing?"

"Shh! Be quiet!" Dunn hissed. He grabbed Gordon and hunched him down. Gordon looked over the edge of the deck, seeing the other explosive sticking to the hull.

"What the hell? You've completely lost it, you know that?" he said, his voice sounding panicked.

"I'm telling you this is the right thing to do. Reimer's about to tell Ford, and when he does, it'll be chaos," Dunn argued in a sharp whisper. "You can help. Lure the others over here. Once they're here, I'll detonate the charge. It'll be painless. The bow should remain afloat. We'll be fine until the bird arrives."

"Dude, you've COMPLETELY lost your mind," Gordon said. "No way, man! I'm not gonna let you blow up the ship!" His attempt to grab the explosive was suppressed as Dunn grabbed him by the wrist.

"Gordon, you need to listen!"

"I'm not listening to shit. You're unhinged." Gordon yanked his hand away and reached back down.

Their voices elevated above a whisper and carried throughout the deck, drawing the attention of a curious 57. Though he couldn't hear what they were saying, he could sense the harshness in their tones. His ears caught a few curse words, though he couldn't pinpoint the context. Whatever it was, he thought it was best to make sure nothing hostile was occurring. He walked down the pathway to the aft deck, where he saw the two marines hunched at the deck edge.

He noticed Gordon reaching down over the edge of the boat. Dunn was right beside him, holding a block in his hand. He noticed the tiny wires protruding from the triggering device. He froze as both men spun to look at him.

Their gazes locked in a tense moment. 57 stood, his amusement now turned to shock. The shotgun hung from his right arm, the muzzle nearly touching the deck.

Gordon raised his hand and began to speak. "57, wait—"

As the muzzle began to lift, Dunn drew his Beretta and fired from the hip. 57 spun around, blood spraying from his face. The man stumbled back toward the walkway, dropping the shotgun as he pressed both hands to his face. Dunn jumped to his feet and took several steps toward him. 57 bumped hard against the cabin. Blood formed a tiny river under his feet from the gaping hole in his right cheekbone. His right hand lowered to his pants pocket in search of his pistol. His body jerked repeatedly as Dunn punched three more rounds through his back.

****

"The fuck?" At the sound of the first shot, Ford turned and yanked the portside door open. By the time he poked his head, he witnessed streams of red ripping from exit wounds in 57's chest. The man fell forward, his lifeless body sprawled onto the deck.

McCartney and Han ran to the perimeter, seeing Dunn standing behind 57's corpse with the pistol in hand. Dunn saw them as soon as they saw him. Without hesitation, he raised his pistol and fired.

Ford and Reimer darted back into the cabin, while McCartney fired several return shots from his pistol as he ducked around the corner on the forward deck.

Ford turned, his face tensed as his eyes burned into Reimer's. The Corporal's heart pounded in his chest. He recognized that look and knew exactly what was going through his mind.

"Ford...DON'T!"

Ford grabbed his revolver and yanked it from its holster. Reimer sprang at him, grabbing his wrist with both hands and redirecting the muzzle toward the ceiling. His ears rang as the gun went off, punching a bullet through the sundeck. Reimer struggled, wrenching Ford's arm back and forth to rid him of the gun.

"Ford, stop!" the Corporal pleaded.

"You son of a bitch! I knew it!" Ford snarled. With his other hand, he threw a punch into Reimer's ribs, then thrust his body weight forward, pressing the marine against the console.

****

Dunn dipped around the back corner of the aft cabin structure as McCartney returned fire. Bullets whizzed by, one splintering the corner inches from Dunn's face.

"Please stop!" Gordon yelled. He ran around to the starboard walkway, only to duck back when Han emerged with the M16. Automatic gunfire splintered the deck and cabin side. "Guys! Listen!" Gordon's calls went unheard as the survivors worked their way down the walkway. Han had switched the weapon to semi-auto, peppering the aft corner with bullets. Gordon jolted as the shots began to punch through, emerging just inches from his left shoulder.

On the portside, Dunn attempted to fire another round, only to jump back to the inner deck. McCartney had a shotgun pointed, the buckshot narrowly missing his target. He pumped the weapon, sending the empty shell into the crazed horde splashing below.

"Listen, this is not—" Gordon flinched as another round passed by. He spun to the left as Dunn grabbed him by the collar.

"This way, man!"

"No, don't!" Gordon yelled. Dunn ignored his calls and dragged him up the steps to the sundeck. As they cleared the first set of stairs, the two survivors closed in on the aft deck. Dunn pushed Gordon down and pulled the detonator device from his vest.

****

"Goddamnit Ford!" Reimer shouted, his body jolting from another blow from Ford's fist. Ford pressed his arm down, trying desperately to position the gun barrel toward his face. Reimer leaned back, fighting against Ford's weight and strength. As the muzzle slowly lowered, he could see the rifling inside the barrel.

With no choice left, Reimer launched his arm out, his open palm plowing Ford's face. In that same moment, the Corporal twisted his other arm, redirecting the revolver as Ford squeezed off a shot. The .38 caliber round punched through the windshield, a second going into the ceiling as Reimer forced his hand up.

Reimer kicked down on Ford's right knee, weakening his stance before twisting his gun arm and locking it behind his back. With Ford locked up behind him, he stomped on the back of his leg, putting him down on his knees. He yanked up high on his locked-up arm, weakening Ford's hold on the revolver.

His eyes went to the back of the cabin as Michele stumbled out of the guest room. She flinched as further gunshots rang out from outside. Her eyes watered, representing a woman feeling betrayal and a desire for reprisal. Reimer watched as her hand inched for her Sig Saur.

"Michele…"

"You son of a bitch…he was right…"

"Michele…MICHELE!! DON'T!"

Michele yanked her Sig Saur free and pointed it. The gun twitched as she applied light pressure on the trigger.

In that same moment, Ford reacted in a new attempt to get free. Reimer struck him with an elbow to the back of the head, and whipped his body around, turning the revolver toward Michele.

The gun discharged. Blood gushed from Michele's lower abdomen, the shot throwing her against the closed door of the master bedroom. The gun fell from her hand as she fell to her knees. Both hands pressed beneath her stomach, blood running in streams down her legs.

Reimer froze in complete shock. His body felt cold as he watched the poor woman slide down against the door. Her mouth was gaped open, her paling face staring at him unblinkingly.

Ford let out a roaring yell and pushed back on his feet. He twisted from Reimer's grip and pistol whipped him across the face with the revolver. Reimer's head jerked back as he fell hard against the console. He looked up, seeing the blurry image of Ford aiming the muzzle to his forehead.

The hammer clicked back. Reimer tensed.

All three fell to the floor as a tremendous explosion pitched the boat forward. Ford twisted and spun, the gun discharging off to the side.

The bow plunged into the water, driven by the fiery force from the aft deck.

****

Both Han and McCartney hit the deck hard as the boat settled back. Water splashed down from the bow and ran back in little rivers down the port and starboard walkways. Behind the smoke, the water swirled, carrying debris and carnage from the ghouls caught in the blast.

Water surged into the gaping hole in the boat, pulling the stern six feet down into the water. In seconds, what remained of the aft deck was flooded, forcing McCartney to scurry to his feet.

The path was now an upward slope, with the bow being the only part above water. He grabbed the guardrail and hauled himself up.

The stern settled down on the lakebed, serving as a ramp for the horde of ghouls congregating beneath the surface. McCartney looked back, watching as dozens of them lumbered up the slope, dripping water and sopping strands of meat.

McCartney turned to face forward, ready to sprint the rest of the way up. As he did, he saw Dunn extending his pistol down over the sundeck rail. Before he could react, three shots punched into his chest, snapping ribs and deflating his lungs.

The breath blew out of him like air from a balloon, forcing the stunned McCartney against the deck. He tried to lift the shotgun to shoot back, but Dunn had already jumped down on to the lower deck. He launched himself at the wounded man, ripping the shotgun from his grasp and striking it against the bridge of his nose. McCartney stumbled back and fell, rolling down to the feet of the herd.

His scream was nothing more than a gurgling moan as they came down on him. Fingers entered his gunshot wounds like bowling ball grips and pulled outward, tearing them wider until internal flesh was exposed. Teeth embedded into skin as they ripped skin and muscle tissue from his arms. He shook violently as several of them bit down on his face, catching nothing more than gulps of hair. Their clenched jaws pulled back, pulling segments of beard out from the follicles, tearing the facial skin like tissue paper.

Dunn raced around to the forward deck, where Dr. Hill screamed, her hands pressed against her ears.

"What are you doing?!" she screamed.

"Oh, shut up," Dunn muttered. He struck her with the shotgun. As she fell to the deck unconscious, he worked his way around to the starboard walkway to take care of Han.

The intern was waiting, already in a kneeling stance. Rifle shots cracked the air as he ducked back, one round catching him hard on the upper left arm.

"Agh! Damn it!" He yelled out. He attempted to fire back, only to duck back as more M16 shots rang out.

"You killed him!" Han yelled. "You want to kill us all! Ford was right!"

"No!" Gordon yelled from above. He held himself over the starboard guardrail, waving a hand at Han. "Han! PLEASE! Listen!" His voice was lost behind numerous pops of the rifle. Bullets ripped by his face, missing him by centimeters.

Gordon screamed and fired wildly with his Carbine. The M16 shots stopped and the rifle hit the deck. Han stared up at Gordon, eyes bulging as he pressed his hand to his stomach. Blood surged from his gut and through the exit wounds out his back.

Han leaned back against the guardrail, unwittingly teetering over the top. Gordon reached out, "NO!" He was long out of reach. He watched helplessly as Han splashed into the lake. His body floated, arms and legs twitching with the last remnants of life.

As he began to sink, swimmers gathered around him like bluegills attacking discarded bait. The lake turned red as they pulled away at him, exposing entrails. Arms detached from the shoulders as they tugged at him several feet under, his body disappearing under a blanket of blood and the bits of flesh that floated along the surface.

Gordon was numb with shock. Dunn's calls for him were nothing more than faint echoes as he watched the man he shot be torn apart. Reality was gone, replaced by a drunken sensation.

"GORDON!" Dunn's voice finally broke through the haze. Gordon saw Dunn firing his gun aft. Corpses collapsed down on the walkway, their heads ruptured by Dunn's shots.

Gordon looked to the right, seeing the mass of corpses walking up onto the sundeck. He frantically looked left and right in search for a way out. With little option, he hauled himself under the rail and descended the short distance to the starboard walkway.

He landed outside the open cabin door, seeing Reimer and Ford locked in a fierce embrace. They were on their feet, fighting over the revolver. Reimer, gritting teeth as he struggled to keep Ford locked up, saw the marine standing dumbfounded in the doorway.

"Get the doc!" he yelled.

Ford seized the opportunity of Reimer's distraction. He threw his elbow upward, striking Reimer in the chin and breaking his hold. Ford followed with a kick to his chest, sending Reimer barreling into the wall.

"Ford!" Gordon yelled. He held both hands out, trying to display goodwill. Ford never saw them. He spun at the sound of his voice and fired the last remaining round. Gordon fell back, immediately feeling the hot pressure in his ribs. He slumped against the rail, blood pouring into his hand as he clenched the wound.

Dunn yelled with fury as he fired one last shot into the horde. He ran to Gordon then redirected his aim at Ford. Ford, his revolver already aimed, squeezed his trigger, only to hear the click of an empty gun. In a fit of rage, he threw the gun. It struck Dunn in the face, throwing his aim off.

Ford drew his knife, ready to move in for the finish.

"NO!" Reimer yelled out. Ford ignored his pleas and continued marching toward the other marines. He raised his knife like a slasher villain. The sound of a pistol filled the air, the round piercing Ford's lower back. Ford hit the edge of the doorframe, blood coating the glass. He felt the blood pouring over his jeans and denim. He turned and looked back, seeing Reimer breathing heavy with his Beretta extending from his hand.

Moans of approaching corpses loomed over as the horde advanced on both sides. Dunn grabbed up Gordon and dragged him up to the forward deck. Dr. Hill began to stir as they gathered near her. A droning sound reverberated from above, followed by a heavy downward draft. They looked up, seeing the Sikorsky descending from the heavens.

Ford staggered, his knife still raised. Reimer shook his head, his face seemingly expressing as much pain as Ford's. He wanted to tell him to stop, but it was too late. He was too far gone.

Reimer squeezed the trigger and watched as a red hole exploded in Ford's chest, knocking him down onto the floor. His chest rose and fell rapidly with labored breathing. He was still alive, though immobilized. Reimer looked to the windows on both sides, seeing the horde advancing toward the doors.

He jumped down the stairs to Michele. She laid against the closed bedroom entrance atop a pool of her own blood. Her face was pale, her strength almost completely gone. Her droopy eyes opened and she gazed at Reimer.

"You're going to Hell," she muttered.

Reimer shook, not knowing what to say or do. Shock began to overtake him. The whole event was so abrupt. His brain hardly had time to process it. Part of him wanted to try and rescue Michele, while another part of him knew she couldn't be saved and he should end her suffering. By the time the critical thinking had started, the ghouls were starting to fill the cabin.

Reimer turned, seeing the corpses staggering through the doors. He drew both pistols and fired numerous shots. Heads cracked and bodies fell, only to be stepped on by other ghouls. Reimer turned his head for a way out. The doorways were blocked and there was no sunroof. He pointed both pistols dead ahead and emptied both mags into the windshield. Bullets punched through the glass, which then shattered completely as he launched himself through it. Shards bounced over the deck around him while he rolled onto his feet, blood trickling from numerous cuts.

Immediately, he felt the downdraft from the chopper. Its belly was only about ten feet above them. A line and harness extended downward.

A scream drew his attention back to the cabin. The dead had converged inside and had begun feasting on Ford and Michele. The nearly dead woman let out another scream as chunks of muscle and fiber were ripped from her bones. There were a few pained moans from Ford. However, his were cut short as one of the ghouls bit down directly over his throat, severing his vocals.

"Corporal!" Dunn yelled. He was grabbing the harness and was beginning to put it on. Reimer lunged at him and yanked it from his grip.

"Her, first!" he yelled. Dunn tensed with brief hesitation, then grabbed Hill and yanked her to her feet. She was still in a daze from the blow, and barely seemed to understand what was going on. Reimer gave the hand signal to the chopper crew to begin hoist. The rope lifted, hauling Hill high overhead. As she disappeared into the hatch, Reimer grabbed Dunn.

"You know what you've done?!"

"I did what needed to be done!"

"You're insane! YOU'RE ABSOLUTELY INSANE!" Reimer was screaming, his voice drowned out by the rotating blades. The undead began to converge from the walkways. Reimer reloaded both pistols and started firing into both crowds. The harness came back down. "Get Gordon secured!"

Dunn propped the young marine up against him and slipped his arms through the harness. He clipped it shut and signaled the chopper crew. Blood trickled onto the deck as Gordon was lifted high into the air.

Dunn reloaded his Beretta as he and Reimer backed into the forward rail. Heads cracked with each gunshot. Bodies, many with hardly any meat on their faces, marched toward the two marines. Fallen corpses littered the deck, only to be crushed by those behind it.

Reimer fired rapidly until the horde was almost point blank.

The harness came down between them. Without a second's hesitation, both men reached out and grabbed it.

"GO! GO!" Dunn yelled.

The chopper pulled up, lifting the line and the two marines.

Dunn jolted, feeling the toes of his boots caught up under the guardrail. Dunn screamed as the sudden lurch tore his grasp from the harness. He twisted and fell, both arms snapping as they hit the rail bar. He rolled off of it and slumped into the deck. His eyes opened. The sky was obscured by the sight of countless hands reaching down on him.

Reimer couldn't help but watch.

Dunn screamed, unable to fight them off. Hands pulled away at his uniform, exposing bare flesh. Ghouls tugged away at his arms, the flesh giving way to the unending force. Strands of meat stretched as both arms separated from his body. He wiggled in placed, another stuck its fingers into his belly like knives. Several other hands entered along with it, pulling the ribs outward. The ghoul, its teeth exposed through rotted lips, sunk its entire head into his body.

Dunn convulsed as it bit at his insides, his screams suppressed by the hands of another ghoul tearing at his throat.

The event looked like a blur of grey rot as the chopper lifted high overhead. The view disappeared behind a wall of steel. Reimer emerged through the hatch and slumped on the floor. The chopper crew gathered around him.

"Sir, are you okay?"

Reimer gave a slight nod, while staring blankly at the wall. Yet, it wasn't steel he was seeing. In his mind, he saw one huge, distorted image off all the things that had just occurred. In the center of that image was Michele's dying gaze and her expression of hatred toward him. Though he no longer held his gun, he felt the pressure of the trigger. In the midst of it all was the question of the price of this loss in humanity.

With glazed eyes, he looked into the cabin. Medics were tending to Gordon, attaching IV lines and applying dressings to his injury. The young marine was in a state of similar shock, thinking repeatedly about shooting Han.

Beside him, another crewman had knelt by Dr. Hill. She was still in a daze, unable to answer their questions. She didn't even notice them extracting her ID from her pants pocket. They pressed a cloth to her bruised forehead and lifted her into a seat.

"Corporal?" Reimer looked up and saw the crewman standing over him. "Sir, do you need medical attention?"

"No…no thank you," Reimer said. "Uh…contact Border Command. Tell them Alpha-Four-Eight has the package."

"Will do," the crewman said. He moved off into the cockpit and began speaking to the pilots. Reimer stood up from the floor and watched the medics tend to Gordon. He glanced to the interior of the aircraft, seeing numerous computer hard drives taking up much of the space. He was surprised, as he assumed the reason they had limited space was because of other passengers. These weren't just ordinary computers, but super high-tech ones. There was some medical equipment, including MRI machines. No passengers.

Clearly, the government didn't want to wait for a new manufacturing facility to be constructed.

"Medic?"

"Yes, Corporal," one of the medics said.

"If I may ask…did you lose anyone while acquiring this stuff?" Reimer asked. The medic's jaw tightened, as though he didn't want to answer.

"Two," he muttered.

Reimer stepped aside and took a seat. One of the medics approached Dr. Hill once more to check on her.

"I'm good," she said, waving her hand at him. "Just get me out of here."

"Already on our way," the soldier said.

"Good," she said. She held the cloth to her head, glaring at Reimer as the chopper carried them off.

CHAPTER 26

Evening stretches of sunset never looked so good as Reimer watched the window. The chopper had cleared the wall and was descending down to the helipad. Long shadows stretched over the dirt as ground crew waited below.

"We're home now, bud," Reimer said to Gordon. The young marine breathed through a facemask, resting comfortably on a stretcher. Hill said nothing, though she was eager to get off the bird. The landing strips had barely touched down when the fuselage door came open.

Two security men in black suits greeted her off the chopper and guided her away. There was no thank you or farewell to Reimer as she walked off into the distance. He was okay with it.

Reimer helped the crew as they lowered Gordon down on his stretcher. Ground crew assessed his injuries and started wheeling him away. Several federal vehicles pulled up where the guards were leading Hill.

Reimer stepped away from the chopper, seeing General Spears approaching. He looked down at Gordon and then at the Corporal, returning his salute.

"Nobody else?"

"No, General," Reimer said. Spears nodded.

"Congratulations, son. You did well. I'm proud of you."

"Thank you, sir."

A man in black trotted back toward the chopper.

"Excuse me. But the lady says she left some belongings in the chopper," he said. Reimer glanced back, seeing that the chopper crew were busy unloading.

"I'll get it," Reimer said. He stepped back to the chopper and entered the cockpit. Luckily, Hill's wallet and flash drive were in plain sight. As he snatched them up, the wallet unfolded, spilling the tattered picture ID. Reimer picked it up to put it back in its place. He paused as his eyes noticed the written name.

Rebecca Stacy Clair.

Reimer glared at the photo. It was definitely her picture. Yet, it wasn't her name. A sick feeling entered his gut as he glanced at the flash drive. Curiosity was getting the better of him. He tucked it into his pocket and hurried out.

Spears was on his phone, in conversation with another authority. Reimer walked to the guard and handed him the wallet.

"Does she need her data?" he asked. The guard glared at him with mild bewilderment.

"Data?"

It was the answer Reimer feared.

"Never mind."

The guard turned and walked toward the big limo-style car. Reimer watched as the man approached, taking a few steps to get a better look. With no care in the world, he observed as the man opened the side door.

There she was, Rebecca Stacy Clair and the president in a passioned embrace, lips pressed together. They broke away as she snatched the wallet. The president waved his hand, ordering the man to shut the door.

No, Reimer thought. His blood began to boil. It couldn't be. His breathing was rapid. The numbness had come back. He doubted his eyes, praying that what he was told had some truth to it. His team had died, his humanity gone in a firefight with civilians. For what? A mistress?

"No," he muttered. He marched away to the barracks. As he went, he saw Gordon's stretcher as they wheeled him to a vehicle to take him to the infirmary. He couldn't ignore his hand as he waved at him.

Reimer jogged to his side.

"You'll be alright, bud," Reimer said. He could see the distraught in Gordon's eyes. The physical pain wasn't the problem. It was the overbearing feeling of guilt spawned from what they had done.

"We did it," he said, then looked at Reimer, "right? We got her back. Everything…it was all worth it in the end?"

"Yes," Reimer comforted him. "Go take it easy. The docs will take care of you." He stepped aside as the crew got him into an ambulance vehicle and took him away.

Reimer walked as fast as he could into the barracks. Luckily, there were computers available in this facility. Still, he looked around, certain he shouldn't be seen doing what he was about to do.

He inserted the flash drive and opened the existing file. His heart grew heavy. He slumped back in his chair, looking at the blank file. There was no data on the flash drive.

He ripped the flash drive from the computer and tossed it to the floor. He stood up from the chair and marched outside. The world was like one big blur. He watched as choppers descended, while others took off to various destinations. With each one, he questioned the truth of their objectives.

"You see? They don't see us as marines. They see us as personal assistants, which can also be cannon fodder. We're their personal slaves. Hence everyone's being forced to remain in service after their term has expired."

Dunn's voice almost seemed to be right beside him as his words echoed through Reimer's mind. He stood, his expression as blank as the walking corpses outside the Border.

In the corner of his eye, he saw General Spears approach him.

"Just wanted to say again: good work son. Now, get some rest. Won't be long before we'll need you again."

THE END

CHECK OUT OTHER GREAT ZOMBIE NOVELS

Z BURBIA
by **Jake Bible**

Whispering Pines is a classic, quiet, private American subdivision on the edge of Asheville, NC, set in the pristine Blue Ridge Mountains. Which is good since the zombie apocalypse has come to Western North Carolina and really put suburban living to the test!

Surrounded by a sea of the undead, the residents of Whispering Pines have adapted their bucolic life of block parties to scavenging parties, common area groundskeeping to immediate area warfare, neighborhood beautification to neighborhood fortification.

But, even in the best of times, suburban living has its ups and downs what with nosy neighbors, a strict Home Owners' Association, and a property management company that believes the words "strict interpretation" are holy words when applied to the HOA covenants. Now with the zombie apocalypse upon them even those innocuous, daily irritations quickly become dramatic struggles for personal identity, family security, and straight up survival.

ZOMBIE RULES
by **David Achord**

Zach Gunderson's life sucked and then the zombie apocalypse began.

Rick, an aging Vietnam veteran, alcoholic, and prepper, convinces Zach that the apocalypse is on the horizon. The two of them take refuge at a remote farm. As the zombie plague rages, they face a terrifying fight for survival.

They soon learn however that the walking dead are not the only monsters.

CHECK OUT OTHER GREAT ZOMBIE NOVELS

RUN
by Rich Restucci

The dead have risen, and they are hungry.

Slow and plodding, they are Legion. The undead hunt the living. Stop and they will catch you. Hide and they will find you. If you have a heartbeat you do the only thing you can: You run.

Survivors escape to an island stronghold: A cop and his daughter, a computer nerd, a garbage man with a piece of rebar, and an escapee from a mental hospital with a life-saving secret. After reaching Alcatraz, the ever expanding group of survivors realize that the infected are not the only threat.

Caught between the viciousness of the undead, and the heartlessness of the living, what choice is there? Run.

THE DEAD WALK THE EARTH
by Luke Duffy

As the flames of war threaten to engulf the globe, a new threat emerges.

A 'deadly flu', the like of which no one has ever seen or imagined, relentlessly spreads, gripping the world by the throat and slowly squeezing the life from humanity.

Eight soldiers, accustomed to operating below the radar, carrying out the dirty work of a modern democracy, become trapped within the carnage of a new and terrifying world.

Deniable and completely expendable. That is how their government considers them, and as the dead begin to walk, Stan and his men must fight to survive.

CHECK OUT OTHER GREAT ZOMBIE NOVELS

VACCINATION
by Phillip Tomasso

What if the H7N9 vaccination wasn't just a preventative measure against swine flu?

It seemed like the flu came out of nowhere and yet, in no time at all the government manufactured a vaccination. Were lab workers diligent, or could the virus itself have been man-made? Chase McKinney works as a dispatcher at 9-1-1. Taking emergency calls, it becomes immediately obvious that the entire city is infected with the walking dead. His first goal is to reach and save his two children.

Could the walls built by the U.S.A. to keep out illegal aliens, and the fact the Mexican government could not afford to vaccinate their citizens against the flu, make the southern border the only plausible destination for safety?

ZOMBIE, INC
by Chris Dougherty

"WELCOME! To Zombie, Inc. The United Five State Republic's leading manufacturer of zombie defense systems! In business since 2027, Zombie, Inc. puts YOU first. YOUR safety is our MAIN GOAL! Our many home defense options - from Ze Fence® to Ze Popper® to Ze Shed® - fit every need and every budget. Use Scan Code "TELL ME MORE!" for your FREE, in-home*, no obligation consultation! *Schedule your appointment with the confidence that you will NEVER HAVE TO LEAVE YOUR HOME! It isn't safe out there and we know it better than most! Our sales staff is FULLY TRAINED to handle any and all adversarial encounters with the living and the undead". Twenty-five years after the deadly plague, the United Five State Republic's most successful company, Zombie, Inc., is in trouble. Will a simple case of dwindling supply and lessening demand be the end of them or will Zombie, Inc. find a way, however unpalatable, to survive?

www.ingramcontent.com/pod-product-compliance
Lightning Source LLC
Chambersburg PA
CBHW032210170626
46808CB00006B/2410